SS SHADOW EMPIRE

Canon I
Passo Romano

Palais Cêlesta

author Tycoon SAITO
translator Yoshie HIYAMA
publisher Yasushi ITO
ISBN978-4-7876-0108-7
English Edition Dec.2019

SS SHADOW EMPIRE

Author Tycoon SAITO

Those worthy of reading this works
Les Centuries the hundred psalms 2-78、

1行目　バブル経済の崩壊で海底に沈む景気の海神（＝アメリカ）。
2行目　アフリカの遺伝子にフランス系の混血者が為政者に
3行目　救援の遅れで（カリブ海？の）島々の住民は流血のままに放置されるだろう。
4行目　この事実のほうが下手に隠されたスキャンダルよりも失脚の原因となる

英語訳

　　The grand Neptune: USA, under collapsed bubble economy
　　African gene mixed French blood to act statesman's role
　　Way too late to rescue so people of (Caribbean?) Islands shall be left in blood shed
　　This fact will damage him more than the badly hidden scandal will

Middle French

　　Le grand Neptune du profond de la mer
　　De gent Punique & sang Gauloys mesle

Les Isles a sang, pour le tardif ramer

Plus luy nuira que l'occult mal cele

The first line can be translated as a great Neptune sank deep in the bottom of the sea, but this literal translation would sound nonsensical so the writer paraphrased it as America in the depression after the fall of bubble economy.

The second line would mean a dual heritage of African and French genes and is telling such person will appear in America. The first statesman that satisfies this condition is President Obama.

The word Isles on the third line means islands. In the middle ages, this word Isles was often used to call the islands in the Caribbean Sea. If the relationship of this word with the first half of this statement is taken into consideration, England and Japan are also called as islands, however, the writer deems it more reasonable to decipher this word isles as islands in the Caribbean Sea. In this assumption, this line is taken as expressing the chaos caused by natural desasters and civil wars and so on.

Then, the forth line can be taken as that, the fact that he left the problems on the Caribbean Islands unattended later led to drive his political life into a corner.

The above translation is of that part of the psalms written by Michel Nostradamvs in 1555. This psalm exactly means the end of the Obama Administration! Whoever understands the writer's writing so far in this way, this book would become worthwhile for him to read. The ancient Latin spells present U as V so the writer is following this way here.

What the writer wishes to state here is to tell you the readers that in the contents of Les Centuries matters that cannot be taken as what already happened in the past are the ones that are for sure to happen in the future. Nostradamvs who penetrated the future was an issuer of cryptograph so he must have naturally seen through that cryptograph breakers would appear in the later times. Cryptograph does come to have its meaning only when breakers of the cryptograph exist. Most of the cryptograph breakers come to realize the true meaning of the cryptograph after the reactor event comes to be apparent. Therefore, to those who lack ability of deciphering the cryptograph, it remains for ever to be totally meaningless. To show an actual example of reaction of those people who do not have any such ability, the writer's acquaintance took this cryptanalysis to one major publishing company, he was questioned if he could clearly state what had not happened was going to happen in coming days for sure. The writer is talking about one completed work which was taken to this publishing company in early October, 2008.

As an overall flow of this work, what the writer is intending to aim at is to pile up the fictional stories without losing the direction to have the work help leading the readers to follow the basis of the writer's deciphering of the flow of the story so that this work is not a simple fiction but an implication of natural disasters and damages of wars that will arise in the future. His prime intention is to present a clue to the readers to survive the coming future offering his readers to read his work in this understanding. To those readers that come to realize such writer's intention this work should be able to offer them a significantly great value.

■ Introduction

The Human race experienced worldwide wars as many as twice in the 20th century. Despite this fact and the disastrous results caused by the two wars, war is repeated under the name of Justice. This can be called the destiny that humans who are unable to learn from the past are to face. Now, countries are showing the limit of being the countries in the frame of definition of the term of country and losing the original meaning of the word, country and have totally deviated from peoples' happiness. Victims of former WW are now no longer victims. They underwent a transfiguration at the point they themselves came to obtain the power of the state.

For the purpose of benefiting one's own happiness, to sacrifice other's happiness with no argument is an unforgiven deed in front of the supreme existence of what we call God. Now that countries cannot guarantee their people's happiness, it is no wonder if such group that handles countries at its will beyond the border of what countries ought to be.

Is what this group aims at creation of the tide of time securing the power which supersede the power of countries and which could never be achieved in the previous century? We tend to believe what cannot be seen by the human eyes does not exist. This is wrong. What cannot be seen can only be seen by those who try to see as God does.

Now, the gate of Hell is open. For wide is the gate and broad is the way that leads to destruction. When power arbitrarily start dashing to get another power, people must know what will be waiting for them. This work is to show where an organization which exceeds a country which is not a country is to end up. This country does not own its terriory but own all the territories. Such organization will not easily show its existence. All what we can see is to see it in its shadow and just to feel its being there.

Provided truth exists in this world, uncontrollable desire will lead the world to ruin and destraction.

There exists no victory.

CONTENTS

TABLE OF CONTENTS

SS SHADOW EMPIRE

Those who are qualified to read this book

Introduction ···6

CANON Ⅰ. Passo Romano ······································ 11

1. While Listening to jazz ······································· 12

2. Antique Fair ·· 23

3. Visit of the returned guests······························· 38

4. To take a look at the oil paintings···················· 49

5. Insurance inspector ··· 63

6. Several kinds of information ······························ 75

7. Fox Hole ··· 82

8. Café Sforza ·· 92

9. Holiday in Florence ··105

10. Café Sforza again ··113

11. Secret of Robert ··125

12. Santa Rosaria···132

13. Surburbs of Vienna ···137

14. Night hearing ···148

15. Helilifting ···153

16. Mistery at Research Facilities Collection of Hynrich ···163

17. Colletion of Heinrich ··175

18. Festival of flare and Heinrich ·······························189

19. Voyage to Japan ··203

20. Antique Festival in Kyoto ·····································213

21. Operation Rosalia ···221

22. Inspection of Rock Crystal Ball ·····························226

23. Painting transference and next order·····················237

24. Identification of Maria ··250

25. Guessing each other's intentions ·························270

26. Talk with Josef Brunner ·······································286

27. Request from Simon ···306

28. Interrogation of Bernard Gambino ·······················311

29. Palazzo of Romano Sfolza ···································330

THE END of I .Passo Romano ·································338

SS SHADOW EMPIRE

CANON

I. Passo Romano

1. While listening to Jazz

All roads lead to Rome is a popular phrase. Here the writer wishes to tell you the readers that all sources of this story originate from Rome. The era of ancient Rome rose in the fifth century B.C. and went to ruin after about one thousand years. In the world empire with Europe in its center there has been no such country ever existed that prospered beyond the Roman territory nor was any country that could keep a longer period of prosperity than Rome. Even Calthage which was located in the north African region alongside the coast of the Medetirranean Sea was perished by Rome, used to have a big bath and athletic field in the open space called Foro where the Roman military road and water supply line from Rome were connected.

This fulfilling history of Rome is shown in its thickness of the geological formations of Rome which still remains in the current human era. Urban areas in ancient Rome were burnt out many times and reconstructed at once many times. When Rome came into its imperial period, public buildings were gradually changed to buildings made of stone. Among such buildings, there is a building called Ara Pacis. Part of this building was found in the 18th century. The full-blown unearthing work was carried out from 1937 to 1938. This historic landmark was an offering by the senate made to Augustus commemorating his pacification of Spain in 13B.C. The construction of Ara Pacis was completed in 9B.C.

This name given to this building means the altar of peace. The whole building is covered by releafs of which there is a releaf of the family of Augustus. The one which was severely damaged was the statue of Goddess of Rome which was meant for the goddness protecting the city of Rome. The characteristics of this goddness is that she sits on the weapons that were derived from the enemy as we see it on the Roman coins. This designing is meant for the concept then of the peace of Rome was the peace obtained by force of Rome as it is called Pax Romana. Augustus let those people who did not have the citizenship of Rome admire both the temple of Roman gods and the temple of his own by building those two temples next to each other. For this reason, it is no wonder that the gods of Rome were utterly destroyed by the enemy. The relief that was carved on the whole surface of the buildings are separated in halves of upper and lower parts. That the line between the two parts was divided by the series of Manji signs which appeared in Europe at a rather early stage is not a very well-known fact to the public.

There did exist relationship between ancient Rome and the symbol Manji. On a side note, NS (the Nazi Party) took up swastika (Gyakumanji) as their party flag in 1920, while excavation of Ara Pacis in earnest was started in 1937 and was continued till the following year.

Incidentally, the Roman towns suffered from fire many times but every time the burnt towns were embanked and new towns were rebuilt on them. People nowadays there are actually living on the earth level higher by several meters than the level in the past.

Many people may think that there has been not much change of present Rome from a thousand years ago, and few recognize a complete change of ancient Rome to the modern time Rome. To

— 13 —

raise an example, Benito Mussolini did not realize till at a later date that his condominium has been built on a noble's condominium which was called domus in ancient Rome. As you see from the above because it is not easy to quickly understand

what the space under the earth had been used before, such sealed mistery exists in many places.

Even the ancient Rome's St. Peter's Basilica which place Vatican took over in this modern age had been located several meters under the present level of the structures of Vatican. The place which is now used as an underground road had been a road running on the ground. This fact explains why St. Peter who is remembered as the first pope of Vatican and had been buried in a stone-made coffin wearing a purple color clothings could be digged out in 1939. At a later year of 2009, a close research of inside the coffin was undertaken and the research witnessed and reconfirmed purple color linen fabric embroidered with gold threads and human bones of the first century. As St. Peter martyred around 67AD, this reconfirmation tells that this person's historic existence certainly matched to the oral tradition.

In the Mussolini's era in Rome, while various unearthing practices were being done, some underground of bombproof shelter constructions was secretly carried out against the sound of steps of the coming war. Rome as world's sightseeing spot would have no benefit to publicize such practice. In Rome, wherever you dig you can find the ruins of the ancient buildings. In those ruins, quite a few empty spaces of useful sizes were found and because of the good sound-proof quality there, these spaces were changed and reconstructed to be such as live houses. At the edges of the places where in the day time many sightseers from all over the world are busily walking around, brightly lighted places appear at night as if the spirits from the past were still there and happened to come out from their coffins and to wander about there. The veil of darkness is hiding something bottomless.

In such places as described above, the jazz club which is going to be the stage of this story is included. This space supported by an arch which, showing the best performance of the construction technology of ancient Rome, is older than two thousand years. Instead of the torch light, slightly thick and short candles are lit and fluttering on several tables. And there, waiters wearing such fabric as called toga of ancient Rome are serving the guests. They are secretly watching guests who are comfortably sitting at the tables through the shade of potted foliage plants.

Facing a grand piano in a dusky jazz club, an old man wearing a shirt and a jacket was playing a piano piece in a jazz style. He appeared relaxed in playing his piece in casual clothes without a tie. This jazz pianist is nobody but Romano Sforza of the head of the radican ethnic faction or the leader of the old-fashioned name of neo-fascists. A tall guy who looked like a German approached the pianist coming into the spotlighted area in front of the piano. He was Josef Brunner who is addressing his name as Alois for a certain reason which is in fact his father's name.

Then, when the piano was elegantly changed to 『Come Prima』 ,a slightly plump man taking three other men who looked like serving him came into the spotlight. He was Bernard Gambino, the Don of Mafia which was representing Sicily. As he approached the aged pianist, he stopped playing.

Bernard   [Hi, Romano, Long time no see. I have stopped ordering fake paintings for a while so I didn't have a chance to see you for quite a long time.]

Saying so, he and Romano, the jazz pianist, held each other's shoulders.

Bernard   [···then, may I ask who this person here is?] Gazing at the face of the man of a German look besides him as if he were tracing his memory of Alois in a photo that he might have seen before somewhere, he asked Romano.

Romano also stood up and came between those two in a formal manner.

Romano   [This is Alois Brunner, and this is Bernard Gambino.]

The two men who were introduced to each other by Romano shaked hands, then Bernard continued.

Bernard   [I heard my friend was cared by you very well during WW2.]

Hearing this, Josef who was introduced to Gambino by the name of Alois asked smiling.

Josef   [Is he still alive?]

Then, hearing his question, the tone of the voice of Bernard changed and he became to be neuvous.

— 16 —

Bernard [I will show you so come with me now.]

On hearing this conversation, each of the men who looked like under Bernard took a pistol out of their pockets.

Then what happened was in a moment the three men were pinioned by carabinieris from behind them and one of them was hit at his nose and was dripping blood. Bernard did not even have time to take his hands out from his pockets having his arms held tightly and bound at his back. At the end of this very quick arresting show, one big carabinieri called out.

Chief Carabinieri

[Done. Don't hit on the face up for the TV showing!]

Hearing the chief's order, other carabinieris having taken up the pistols from the three stopped hitting them. Confirming it, He, too, came into the spot light and talked to Bernard.

Chief Carabinieri

[Santa Rozaria, namely Bernard Gambino, you must come with us for a talk. Do you understand?]

Bernard who was seized the initiative in one moment kept standing bolt-upright.

Bernard [Entrapped am I.]

He frowned and became silent.

Romano [You are perfectly trapped. You now see we are sick and tired to be manipulated by Mafia.]

With a triumphant air, Romano stared back at vexed Gambino

— 17 —

and asserted. When they were taken away, chief carabinieri turned back to Romano and clicked his heels taking a posture of standing at attention in front of Romano. Then he raised his right arm and made a Roman fashion salutation (salute Romano) and issued words in Latin.

Chief Carabinieri

[AVE SENATUS POPULUSQUE ROMANUS!] (Honor to Roman Senate and Citizens!)

Returning the salute, Romano also raised his right arm and following him the other two including the man of German descent took the same posture and joined the salute. They did look alike the warriors of the ancient Rome. The Roman warriors used to hold a shield by their left hands and a sword called gladius, which is double edged and is of the length similar to the short sword, by their right hands. This fashion, except holding gladius by their right hands, was meant for salutation.

Everyone   [AVE ROMA!] (Honor to Rome!)

They chanted as if they were taking an oath to Goddess Rome who also stood for City Goddess. In the ancient Roman language, U and V were all shown by V. It happened only in the later times that use of U and V came to be separated according to the difference in pronunciation. In ancient Rome, this difference was not as clear as nowadays.

Regarding the word AVE, the pronounciation must have been just in the middle of U and V with slightly nearer to V.

When the three men finished their chanting. Romano spoke to the person smiling whom Bernard introduced to Gambino just then as Alois. Alois Brunner was a remnant of SS (Nazi SS).

Romano   [Good thing you look just alike your father, Josef.]

Once again, they hugged each other and spontaneously began to walk upstairs

The upstairs of this building was facing to a rather narrow one-way alley, a bit off into the alley from the place. The outlook of the building was not too eye-catching but as its location is near to the fashion streets, for those men who do not have any particular interest in fashion clothings or the like, it was a handy place for them to hang out while thir wives were shopping. A long counter was running between the entrance leading to the underground space and the entrance facing the street. Number of tables were counted about twenty or so. Down from the ceiling, old fashioned style chandellias made of tubular shaped copper with about twelve lights equipped which might be similar to what was used at old castles in the middle ages were hunging from about six places of the ceiling. On the wall posters of art deco style or sepia photos of popular sightseeing spots were pasted. As the height of the ceiling is quite tall, a couple of ceiling fans were in action.

Show Taro Hayashi who was left for the time being on the ground with Ave Maria, the astrologist, decided to bluntly ask her questions to which he had been failing to find the answers.

Show Taro [By the way, the first name given to you when you were born cannot be Ave Maria, can it? What is your legal name, may I ask?]

Maria [My true name is Michiko. Michi is a Chinese character for Street in English.]

Show Taro [That sounds like a word in the bible.]

Maria [You're quite right. Enter through the narrow gate.

— 19 —

My sir name is Tsuchimikado that means a gate, so I am to go through the gate.]

Show Taro [But your name used in American must be not only that.]

Maria [It is a taboo to inquire the true name of the person that uses the Demon.]

Show Taro [So you mean you have several other names as well.]

Maria [I will leave it to your imagination.]

In such a country as America keeping the principle of territorial jurisdiction, newly born babies in America become the citizens of that country at the moment when they were born. On the other hand, the dual nationality of America and Japan which case is more observed with Japanese born in America tells the fact that Japan is following the paternalism in nationality which is based on the concept that a child of Japanese parents is to be a Japanese. In many cases babies born in America reserve the right to be identified as Japanese by going through the established procedures to retain the right of Japanese citizenship at the Japanese Embassy or Consulate.

Talking about Maria, she was born in America with more than three names. However, when her parents had her birth registered at the Japanese birth registration offices, they registered just the sir name and the first name of their newborn baby. For example, if a baby of the full name of Donald Taro Paul Cortes Tanaka is born in America, Paul, the Christian name and the mother's name Cortes are normally to be used as a compound sir name which is also reflected on the Japanese certificate of family register, however, if the parents add a clause to the registration documents that they will register the first name as Taro only, the baby's first name is to be registered on the Japanese certificate shall be simply registered as Taro. To add a bit more information about this naming rule, the name given to the new-born when it was born is naturally taken and used as a leagally authentic name and is used at the hospital where it was born. At American hospitals, it is a common practice that as soon as a baby is born a sister visits the hospital and bapticize the baby giving it a Christian name.

Taking a glance at Romano and Josef who came out from the inside of the place, Show Taro Hayashi sitting at a table besides the on-the-ground counter felt that the scene he was then seeing was somewhat similar to what he had seen recently and tried to remember what it was recalling what happened in the past several months. Yes, Mafia was arrested and carabinieris showed up..Jews ran and SS (Nazi SS) showed up…History repeats itself, while undergoing a shift and progressing to the tide of the time.

The flow of the history built bals many hundreds of years ago on the ash- covered ruins of ancient Rome, which turned to be a bar and the place where was a harness maker's shop changed to a boutique selling branded garments as time went on. From an overall viewpoint based on the flow of the history, this ever-changing drama is going hand in hand with flow of time. To make it short, history repeats reproduction of consumer city, contents of which has little difference to each other regardless of flow of time.

The catalyst that had Show Taro involved in this time's turmoil was, if he remembered it correctly, the antique fair which was held a few months ago.

But it could also be said for sure that this catalyst did make him somewhat excited.

2. ANTIQUE FAIR

In Japan, many companies make the period from the end of April to the end of the first week of May a long holiday season called Golden Week. In the period of season many of Chinese companies in China are making it a holiday week, too, so this custom is offering a good vacation to workers of each of the two countries. During this holiday period of time, sight-seeing business and retailing business come to their peak selling time, so that in the antique business area in Japan, quite a few events called antique fairs that are programmed by the party of antique merchants are programmed and opened which attract people who have not had an experience yet to purchase antiques. Some of such events charge an admission fee to be paid at the entrance of the fair site whereas some are free of charge. This difference seems to depend on the policy of business that the organizers are aiming at to perform.

In the site of the event, many small booths which are 4 meteres wide by 2 meters deep are provided so the antique retailers participating in the event can use one booth or two booths depending on each retailer's needs. There also is a single booth which is shared by several merchants shifting the salesclerk amongst them. Way of display is also different to each participant. Such booth that is displaying western antiques and Japanese or Chinese ones mixed on the same shelves has a purpose of offering a convenient one place selection of the goods especially when they receive a designated purchasing group so such group of buyers do not have to walk around in the site to find here and there what they will need. And on the other hand, those booths that are grouping dolls, toys, oriental or western goods respectively are attempting to consider the visitors' convenience to find what they specifically want at one place without wandering about in the whole fair site. At the edges of the site space food and drinks are provided where antique dealers and buyers can relax and talk after the negotiation of their business is completed.

At such corner places, politic visitors are on search of professional sellers or the dealers called conjurers that do not use booth to sell their antiques. However, there is a risk to come to deal with those dealers who intentionally rumor ill information to secure the left-over goods of good value on the last day of the event. In other words, unless you build up your own knowledge and discerning eye, you shall not be able to get antiques of any good value.

There is an expression of 'have a sharp eye' but in order to get the 'sharp eye' it is necessary to take a calculated risk and spend your money to some reasonable extent. When you start this practice, the best way is that you have a good guide, but otherwise, second best way to study this merchandise category is to purchase some specific items only, after buying books and studying them fully, and buy more antiques of the same kind and make a careful quality comparison. For example, you buy buckwheat noodle cups alone, water containers alone, Kokeshi alone, and glasses alone and having studied relative books, you buy more of the same line of antiques and do the comparison work. Here you be careful not to be confused by wrong information which such antique dealers that do not have professional ability may emphasize their wrong opinion to mislead you.

In this way, if you target at a limited number of items and keep pursuing these spending several years, little by little you will become to be able to understand how the atmosphere of the time or the location are influencing the items in your hand even if briefly. Such people that have gained this knowledge in this way would make it a habit to go out towards daylight and arrive at the site to be the first to look for the items to their liking. Among such group of people professional conjurers are mixed. They scramble for getting items of value and such cases can happen that as soon as they buy quality items they resell them putting their profit on to their antique dealing customers who are visiting other events in the same timeframe.

However, whatever may happen, those conjurers are supposed to act subject to the condition of "pay in cash and return unacceptable". Actually, among common purchasers, those authentic collectors are making it a rule not to return what they have once bought. They know they must engrave their mistake of getting cheated on their mind, otherwise they would most probably repeat the same mistakes in the future. On the other side, it may develop this way that once they might think they were cheated, they might happen to find it a unique item of value at a later date. Also, the result of the unearthed antiques may at a later date prove the age of the item you purchased could be assessed to belong to a much older age than you thought.

For about two hours after the opening of the antique fair, the atmosphere of the site is usually highly exciting in the whirlpool of greed and the bid quotations. In there, those dealers who receive lots of ask quotations may be averaged two or three. They will not become able to stop laughing. They put themselves in a great haste to contact other dealers by cell phone who are not participating at the same site and try to negotiate with them for them to turn the items over to those winning dealers.

Exhibitors of antique fairs at the site provided at the first-class hotels in Tokyo have to spend very busy time in the early morning of the opening day of the fairs. They load into a car the parcels which they packed on the previous day. If they fail to complete the loading in time, they have to use a courier service for a specified time delivery. Into the small antique containers which are to be used at the site both for sale and for display purposes, they skillfully pack smaller antique pieces wrapping each small piece with thin wrapping paper. This work has to be done by their own hands otherwise accidental breakage can easily happen when the container is opened at the site. Ceramics are easy to break, especially beaks or legs of a bird statue and glasswares are exposed to the risk of peeling off if a shock is added. Those amateurs or people who are not used to purchase of such antiques are oftentimes very peculiar and demanding about small defects or scars. Some of this kind of people tend to make unreasonable demand such as ordering to have the scar mended which was made several hundred years ago. They bluntly say they would have bought it if the scar were eliminated.

Also, some people speak up that they would buy the piece they are interested in unless the mending method called restoring were not added on it. No one has ever heard that people that make such impossible demand have formed a good range of collection. Reason why restoring was done is very clear. If furniture that was produced before the 17th century which has the fallen off part of inlay work left unrestored, or the bottom slab which showed sponge like appearance with worm holes left unstrengthened by filling resin into the holes, which requires the same high level of restoring techniques to be applied on cultural heritages, so that such repairing is impossible to be handled by common people. At the same time, it is not always a good solution to further try mend the trace of mending that was done many hundred years ago of the legacy of a family of note of olden times. Talking about the old Iga pitcher 『Broken Bag』, the mender was that famous Oribe Furuta so it does not make sense if a collector of the later era dared to mend it again. Concluding, those people who believe in industrial products which is free from any scars or damages will come to waste their money on well-made fakes.

Morning of the first day of the fair is another battle field, but deliveries are divided in plural appointed timeframes in accordance to the location of each booth whereto the antiques are to be delivered. However, as trucks or delivery cars cannot afford to wait and see till the appointed time comes because if they did so, such delivery tools as hand carts or the like shan't become available, so all rush to the delivery entrance to get carts at least half an hour before the time. If they come at the appointed time, they will only find such useless hand carts as with half broken wheels or broken iron stopper which is needed to safeguard the loaded antinues on the cart .

Taking just about a bit less than a quarter of hour, they unload their antiques off their cars or trucks, they pass the unloading place to the next group and move their cars or trucks in the parking area seeking shades of trees. By securing such tree shades, they can shift the booth watch work and take their lunch that they bring with them. Finishing this they are to open up their packages with the largest one first, but before they proceed to this work, they have to go to the stockyard to secure a table which is necessary to unpack the antique pieces off the packages. They cover the table top with a big wrapping cloth of 180cm square in the neat way. They spread the wrapping cloth to make one side of the sideof the edge of it drop facing the side from which angle visitors will come and see the merchandise. Next, they quickly clean inside of the rental showcase and place the middle size antiques in there, while exhibiting the small pieces surrounding the showcase. This is the rough explanation of the preparing procedures. In the drawers of the chest type furniture, small glass jars or jewelries are placed for visitor's observation and selection.

When the preparing work comes to this stage, they could visit the washroom and change T-shirts to dress shirts and fasten ties. They change shoes to leather shoes so they will be all prepared. But at that step, many exhibitors have not finished placing small pieces in neat order. They try hard again and somehow manage to finish re-checking of the merchandise and price tag putting work. Though this depends on the decision of the fair organizer, it is taken as common exercise to show the retail price at such fairs which is majorly meant for the public people or sightseeing visitors from overseas who expect a department store like fashion display. The authdox method of determining price after the face-to-face meeting with the visitors has the risk of inviting doubt regarding the transparency of pricing or reliability of transaction.

In this hustle and bastle, announcement of opening the fair sounds and waves of visitors rush into the fair site. Lots of people flow into each booth but those visitors who know what they want leave such booths quickly when they do not see what they are looking for. It is almost meaningless to try to hold those visitors. Also, it is a useless exercise to call to those who do not have any plan to buy any particular thing. The most troublesome visitors are a group of visitors who maintain their own barriers against others. They tend to disturb the negotiation going on between antique dealers and visitors who have serious intention to procure what they want, or otherwise they tend to touch and handle the merchandise in a very rough manner. Those who seriously interested in antiques that they may buy are always trying to hold the goods carefully wrapping them with both hands. The last impossible visitors are those of the age under middle age showing absolutely no reaction to all what they look. It is useless to show what you treasure to such visitors who will not show any hint of what they want. It is a popularly known trend that many of the recent IT work related people do not care about human relationship. Under such circumstances the wave of visitors flows away.

Having finished the delivery work that was started early in the morning, Show Taro Hayashi, the antique dealer, came into the time when he could relax a little bit. Two full hours from the opening of the fair is the time zone when real curious and therefore serious collectors and professionals decide on what they will purchase. If they find a rare article they are not allowed time to seek similar article and make a comparison. They have to make a decision on the spot. However, even that generous time zone after the first two hours is also nearly coming to the end. At the fair this time, the opposite space called both was seized by a well-known antique dealer in the antique business field for his a bit off-the-forcus atmosphere. The old man there was befuddling his visitors talking in a very mysterious way. He did not miss the sight direction of the eyes of one of his regular customers.

Name of this old man is Kanji Yamashina, but people called him 『Speculator-like』. Of his name Yamashina, 'Yamashi' is pronounced as same as 'speculator' in Japanese with 'na' as 'like'. Many antique dealers are the type of just sitting in silence, but in case of Yamashina, his flaud-like talking is symbolizing his business and it sounds like that his fans are not few at all. Those customers who have a biased view may prefer this old man's business tactics.

Yamashina [Well, well..this sake cup is the one that Laozi was gifted by Confucius before he went out through Hangu Pass. It was the same sake cup that was used for the sake party when Laozi met Buddha at Tenjiku. You can read the story written on the side of that wooden box.]

On the side of the old cedar box there surely is written some words using a brush in ink. As the old man said the written letters were showing aged blackening that might be possibly resembling such article of the Edo era.

Customer

[Old man, what I bought from you last time was told to be a fake at another place. Are you sure this is authentic?]

The old man seems to have been receiving similar complaints from his other customers in the past for many times, so he replied quite unmoved.

Yamashina [Isn't the one he showed you an unquestionably obvious fake, wasn't it? As long as you keep yourself deluded by the nonsense of such fledgling, you will never be able to get the hang of antiques. I may concede with the price if you really want it. What about ¥150,000 instead of ¥200,000?]

In the antique business field, dealers are often getting in each other's way, insisting the goods that the dealer sells are always authentic and what his competitors sell are all fake. They are very keen to prevent the customers from buying their competitors' merchandise and to try to push customers to choose what he will buy from his selection. On the other hand, it is also a fact that there do exist customers who are expert appraisers. Those people will not tell the dealers their honest opinion and they do the pricing by themselves. They are entirely different from such buyers who only buy at auctions following the judgement done by others who are raising their hands to a bid price. Such expert antique researchers do exist mixed in so-to-called antique lovers.

Customer [Don't be silly. My price is ¥100,000 and no more.]

The old man noticed that the customer's face was getting flashed and his way of talking getting rough. He felt it might be about time to decide.

Yamashina [I'm scared of the anger of my old wife if I sold it at that price.]

The old man tried to raise the price avoiding to propose his desired price over again.

Customer [¥120,000!]

Voice of the customer was loudly raised to shut the old man's mouth. The game seemed to be over. The customer took a wallet which looked thick with the notes in it and took ten bundles of ten thousand-yen notes and added two more ten thousand yen notes on the bundles. He pushed these notes to the old man's hand to shut his mouth. Negotiation thus ended. He grinned ear to ear and packed the Chinese Tenmokuyu sake cup by his own hands and quickly pushed it into his bag and went away. He seemed to be well aware that the nonsense explanation written on the box was an outright lie.

The antique business field may be kept maintained by such expert customers who will never tell his secret of antique appraisal technic to his dealers.

Yamashina [Spank you.]

He said this 'Spank you' in the tone that sounded he was still worrying about possible complaints of his old wife. After seeing this skilled antique shopper off till he vanished away from the passage, Show Taro started to talk.

Show Taro [Congratulations for the first sale.]

Yamashita [Haven't you got any yet?]

Show Taro [yaa⋯]

He replied a bit sloppily.

Yamashina [Okay, then, here's celemonical water for you.]

Saying so, he took three steps nearer to him and handed a tinned juice over to him.

Show Taro [Thank you.]

As the visit of customers became slowing down, he opened the tin and took a sip.

Yamashina [Oh, that is the ancestral rock crystal ball of Matsuoka family..It is the one that Yosuke Matsuoka took to Germany when Japan joined the Tripartite Pact. It is written on the note Hitler was gazing at it with much interest for a few minutes.]

Customer [⋯⋯..]

Without issuing any word, the customer turned around and looked around the display of the booth of Show Taro. He looked like he noticed that the majority of the displayed antiques are western made but the range shown was not what was obtained through auctions.

Customer [You are going to Europe to purchase these items?]

Show Taro [Yes, as I have a close connection with those dealers who have access to castles.]

The customer picking up one of Show Taro's business card off on the top of the showcase asked.

Customer [What does Palais Flora mean?]

Show Taro [As our office is located in Nihonbashi Muromachi, it is a translation in French of 「floral Palace」 of Muromachi Shogunate. Palace can be translated as Palais and the goddess of flowers is Flora.]

The customer nodded once and looked at Show Taro and asked.

Customer [May I keep this calling card of yours?]

Show Taro [With pleasure.]

Customer [Do you stay here all the time?]

Show Taro [That on the card is the address of our office, so in most of afternoons of Saturdays I shall be there. During the week days I am usually out of office, though. But I wish you to ring me beforehand so I won't miss you.]

Customer [I will pay you a visit next time.]

The customer told him in pretty polite way.

Show Taro [I will be expecting you.]

Then, this customer put the card in his pocket and went out. After seeing him off till he vanished away from the passage, the old man of Ippin-do opened his mouth and said.

Yamashina [You think he is hopeful?]

Show Taro [Next time means no chance. You know that well, don't you?]

Yamashina [Yah, but they say 'something unexpected can still happen', so be optimistic and take his word as it is. That will make you feel better, don't you think so?]

It was philosophy of the old man Yamashita who was a veteran of many battles over the past forty years.

Show Taro [You're quite right.]

Having said so, he dried up the tin of juice. Those visitors that were wandering about at this time zone were either carrying his purchases at the other booths or still missing what they were looking for. Show Taro stepped out for a couple or three steps to Ippin-do and asked.

Show Taro [Please let me take a look at this rock crystal ball.]

Yamashina [No problem.]

Show Taro put the rock crystal ball on his palm and took a good look at it. There was a cold feeling against his palm which would

— 34 —

mean that the ball was not made of glass or plastic. He also saw his fingers through the ball and confirmed that one string of his dawny hair on his finger seemed doubled. Double reflection is a characteristic of rock crystal ball. Looking into the ball, he confirmed the inside of the ball looked slightly hazy. Using a magnifying glass, he enlarged the inside of the ball and saw though vaguely the growing line of the quartz of crystal. He reckoned that the rock crystal ball was a natural produce. In recent years then, artificial crystal which was made by growing the quartz slowly with powdered crystal getting melt, so it was a fact that it was getting difficult to take the measure of the quality of crystal.

In the next place, he checked the box that contained the rock crystal ball and confirmed that the sticker pasted on this time-worn box reads The Matsuokas. The box itself looked like one that was made before the Taisho era. The trace of the string attached to a box of paulownia wood came to be slightly whitened making a contrast against the somewhat darkened brown wood box. Yet, only with those appearance it was not enough to determine that was the long-stored property of Yosuke Matsuoka. Out of the box, a writing paper with some letters on it came out. On this stationery paper, the word [Letter Pad of The Matsuokas] was marked which could be useful to enforce the credibility of this rock crystal ball.

He read the paper and found the statement written on it which read [This is to divine Tripartict Pact. Leader Hitler examined this for a few minutes. Yosuke]. Possibility of genuinity of this as the old man explained came to be high. Another point is that the inside of the box that was touching the projected part of the ball perfectly fit

— 35 —

to each other, which meant that this ball was in this box from the beginning.

Show Taro 「Mr. Yamashina, what is your best settlement price of this?」

Stroking the ball Show Taro asked the old man but he looked away from Show Taro.

Yamashina [If you can offer some thing that has as valuable a history as this one, I may think about an exchange deal.]

Show Taro [If Ican sell some expensive stuff, I will ask you again.]

Yamashina [What you mean is that you will never make it, right?]

They looked at each other and laughed.

Then, both kept silence but in their silence, they started wondering how to carry back the left-outs at the end of the fair. Unless expensive stuff could be sold, the only other chance was the last day of the fair when how many visitors would come back to beat the price and get a good buy would matter. Not many Japanese tend to buy furnitures and one of the reasons of this is the narrow size of Japanese houses. These days, at newly built houses furnitures are getting to be built-in type to prepare for earthquakes. In addition, collectors do a pre-purchase studies of prices checking the bid prices at popular auctions held in Europe and try to get furnitures at a lower price than those European auction results. Such people buy antiques for investment so their posture towards antique collection is fundamentally different from that of the collectors who desire to keep authentic fine arts at their hand for personal enjoyment so that such people will never show any interest in furnitures of 17th century or before.

The major reason why people will not buy furnitures of 17th century or before is because at the two large aution dealing companies in New York only two to three items at most are presented at their auctions so even such professional auctioneers find it difficult to determine a fair value of such furniture. Number of Japanese collectors who are dealing with auctioning companies other than the two large ones in New York is quite few so that customers that have an expert eye to determine what they should buy and can be the customers of Show Taro are extremely limited. The truly orthodox collectors are those who deal with antiques with sincere and exclusive love to antiques as they love women.

3. Visit of The Returning Guest

Tokyo is an urban city which was developed with Edo Castle in the center which is surrounded by the damp ground at the sea side. The damp ground alongside the sea was reclaimed and the streets were maintained with canal provided for a good control of transportation of goods from various places by vessels. This city, as same as Rome, had fires for many times. Every time it was burnt, goods and materials for reconstruction were delivered from other districts and restored. Difference in this regard from Rome is it was developed since after the end of 16th century so that, as this place had originally been the ocean, basically speaking there was no possibility of its having ancient ruins under the ground, and though it has well completed waterwork system called Tamagawajosui, it does not have a sewer nor multipurpose underground utility conduit.

This megalopolis Tokyo was burnt out as many as twice since after the modern era started. The first big fire took place in accordance with a big earthquake in the Taisho era. The second time was caused by carpet bombing using incendiary ammuniction of the attack by American air force which literally burnt the whole Tokyo area. As the majority of the houses in Japan were made of wood, use of incendiary ammuniction was more effective as well as cheaper than using the normal bombing. However, some unburnt areas did remain in downtown Tokyo and such small sites are scattered amongst big and tall buildings without being re-developed to be gathered into one large premises. On these small spaces low-height buildings of three floors at most are standing. The king of Arab who landed at Haneda International Airport was taken by car on the highway to the center of Tokyo viewing endlessly continuing two-floor wooden houses and sometimes appearing three-floor concrete buildings, questioned [when am I arriving at Tokyo?]. This was not that the king was joking but the reality of the scene of Tokyo. In Such capitalistic country as Japan, uneven distribution of wealth is a matter of fact of course, so that such scene that puzzled the Arabic king can happen.

The original Japan's capital city was Kyoto where Muromachi Shogunate had the condominium of Shogun also Government Office built. However, in Tokyo, names of towns of other cities are often times used to name the streets or areas in Tokyo since the Edo era. Reason why this happened is when Tokugawa Iyeyasu reorganized then the City of Edo a lot of workers or builders were summoned to Edo and those people who became residents of Edo named the areas they worked to organize after the names of their hometowns or their beloved places around their hometowns. Similar phenomenon is observed in Indiana or Illinois where the names of locations in Paris, London or Frankfult exist. What this means is that Edo was then the new world for Kyoto or the western part of Japan. In Nihonbashi of Tokyo, there exists the name of the area called Nihonbashi-Muromachi. This naming implies how much the common people who started to live in Edo were longing for the gourgeous 「magnificent Imperial Palace」 in Kyoto and wishing to make a name in Edo after the prosperous Imperial Palace of Kyoto. In this street in between big buildings Show Taro Hayashi, the antique dealer had an office at the semi-basement level of a building nearby the warehouse of the space of about ten tsubo (33square meters).

In such streets as Show Taro's office location narrow side streets that won't allow cars existed, but because of these narrow streets there were concrete-block walls on top of which street cats were leisurely having a nap even during the mid-day lunch time where few people were passing by. As a matter of fact, such apartments where the trainees of cooks of small Sushi restaurants in the neighborhood or the like live are located here and there. A quiet time and space of one block behind the busy streets is spread over there.

It was in the early afternoon of a Saturday two weeks after the antique fair. Having no appointment schedule Show Taro was leisurely waiting for some visitors to come, checking the goods that arrived newly. Then suddenly his cellphone rang so he grasped it and jumped outside. At his office in between the buildings it was necessary to receive phone calls outside where the radio wave reception was better than inside the office, otherwise, at the moment he took the phone up, the line would become disconnected.

Opening his cellphone and taking an interval of one breath, he confirmed that the line was on, so he spoke out.

Show Taro [Palais Flora.]

Customer [I am the one that received your calling card the other day. I wonder if I can visit you now.]

Show Taro [Yes, please. I will be waiting for you, but do you know how to come here?]

Customer [I have come so far here checking a map. I am in front of the convenience store nearby.]

— 40 —

Show Taro [I see. I will be waiting.]

Finishing the talk, he came into the kitchen and started preparing tea. A short while later, the visitor arrived.

A gentleman of rather elder age to be called middle age came in and took his business card from the card holder.

Suzuki [Hi, I am Suzuki.]

Show Taro [Yes, I am Hayashi.]

Suzuki [I already received your card at that time.]

Waiving his hand to show Show Taro he does not need any more card of Show Taro, he gave his card to Show Taro. Show Taro recognized him as the same person he had met at the fair

Show Taro [Please be seated.]

The man who gave his name as Suzuki took a seat quietly. Show Taro served him tea putting the tea cup on a teacup saucer.

Show Taro was also seated and read the visitor's card carefully.

Suzuki Shoten Co., Ltd.

Minoru Suzuki, President

By just reading the name of the company, it was not possible to understand what this company is trading.

Show Taro [What kind of items are you interested in, Mr. Suzuki?]

Suzuki [I am not here to do shopping today.]

Suzuki replied unsmilingly so Show Taro asked in a questioning look.

Show Taro [Then, what do you want?]

Suzuki [I wish to consult with you about a sale of an oil painting.]

Show Taro provoked more questions in his mind.

Show Taro [Won't you give me more explanation about that painting.]

Suzuki started explaining slowly about the painting and the related circumstances.

Suzuki [It was about one year ago, when I lent my friend since our undergraduate years one billion yen as short term loans as receivable. Unfortunately, this friend of mine by the name of Kiriyama went bankrupt in spite of his efforts and after that he disappeared leaving this painting in my hand.]

Show Taro [I think you had better try the galleries in Ginza. They may be easier to take it .]

Suzuki [No, that's not possible.]

Show Taro [Why not?]

Suzuki [About this painting there is a rumor that it was a painting that was stolen from a castle in England three years ago so painting dealers do not want to take the risk that might be arising and will not touch this deal. As I understand you are handling the goods of the castles, I thought you might have any good idea to help disposing this painting so I am here.]

Following this explanation, Suzuki told more in detail about that painting's historical trail.

Suzuki [Originally, this painting was one of the paintings that the ex- President Fujimura of South America purchased in Switzerland while he was in exile. This is one of the four oils that were brought into Japan. This one was what was resold to Kiriyama through mediation of Defence Minister Yoritomo Yamagata. When I come to make this explanation so far to this point, both Sunday Gallery and Callery Yoshinaga said at one voice they were not in a position to take it. Is there any way to convert it into money somehow or other?]

Having talked this far, he took about half of the tea.

Show Taro [It is an interesting story. By the way, can I take a look at that painting in question?]

Eyes of Show Taro were shinning but Suzuki felt that Show Taro was speaking pressing tone of this voice as much as possible to hide his excitement.

Suzuki [Any time.]

Show Taro [Where do you have it?]

Suzuki [It is in my company at the president's office.]

As Show Taro could feel Suzuki's strong desire to dispose of this painting, he pressed rather hard for an answer.

Show Taro [May I visit you there around 01:30pm on Wednesday, next week?]

Suzuki [I will be expecting you then.]

Show Taro [By the way, may I ask you since when you came to be interested in art objects?]

Suzuki [The start was⋯around the first half of 1990 after bubbles economy collapsed. At that time, it happened that I received a request to lend a loan to the president of a construction company which was one of my business contacts.]

— 43 —

Show Taro [So you purchased the art objects.]

Suzuki [No, what I did then was to lend him about 10million yen but at that time he deposited with me the key of his rental warehouse.]

Show Taro [I see, that's when you obtained art objects?]

Suzuki [This friend of mine ran away under cover of night when his company went into bankruptcy. But as the end of the tenancy reservation approached near, I went there to deliver the stocked items there out from the warehouse.]

Show Taro [Did you go there by yourself?]

Suzuki [I took my wife with me, driving a truck myself.]

Show Taro [Did you find any good art there?]

Suzuki [What was there which came to our eyes at first was ···a life-size figure painted by Yamamura · Tadashi. A gal wearing a mini-skirt, exposing most of her breasts is casting a flirtaious sidelong glance. What happened was that my wife got furious opening her eyes wide and said 「Oh, you are perfectly cheated!」].

Show Taro [But I guess the life-size figure painting could be sold at a fairly good price.]

Suzuki [At the beginning I was at a loss how to handle it, but an auctioning company with whom I consulted suggested me to put it up to auction. Concluding, I remember I got about 5 million yen for that painting.]

Show Taro [Was there in that warehouse anything more?]

Suzuki [Well, there was a scroll covered with dust···My wife's comment on it was 「Look, this paulownia wood box containing this scroll is all over covered by worm-eaten holes. I guess this scroll must be a cheapy junk』. But a few years afterwards I had it checked by a professional appraiser and learned the painter of this dirty scroll was a Chinese painter called Qi Baishi. I could sell it at 3.5 million in 2000.]

Show Taro [Oh, that was what is called the bigginer's luck, wasn't it.]

Suzuki [Yes, you're quite right to say so. There were some neatly stored scrolls of Yokoyama Taikan but these were appraised as the third rank value by the art dealer in Ginza.]

Show Taro [You mean those were well painted fakes.]

Suzuki [You're right, but they paid me half a million for those fakes. Both my wife and I were then made aware of the fact that even fakes have their own demand if they are kept neat and clean.]

Show Taro [Is that the reason why you came to be a lover of art objects?]

Suzuki [Besides what I talked about, there were several ceramic arts of each packed in pawlounia wood box. Those are products of a potter who was designated as Living National Treasure in the current century. In a few months time after this designation was publicized, the person who bought Taikan from me came back to me and took all of those pottery works in exchange of one million yen. I was able to sell most of art products of my friend, but these several leftouts were also

— 45 —

found to be of such value, which means my friend did have an eye for art products.]

Show Taro [I see. You mean that so far you have talked about to me, you were able to recover the loans receivable.]

Suzuki [You're right. Since then, I started collecting what suits my taste.]

Show Taro [What suits your taste?]

Suzuki [My wife seems to like pretty things. I myself am collecting whatever I find interesting. I then tend what I collect and study these whenever I have time. I collect anything and everything that I am interested in regardless of whether they are Western, or Japanese or Chinese. I also make no selection of the kind, so my collection ranges from paintings and artcrafts to tools of my interest.]

Show Taro [In other words, your taste seems to be omnivorous.]

Suzuki [You can call it so.]

Show Taro [May I have a chance to view your collection when I visit you?]

Suzuki [About half of my collection is exhibited at my office so you can see them at any time.]

Show Taro [That sounds nice.]

Then the conversation paused and Suzuki took the tea left in the cup which had gotten to be cold.

Suzuki [I have another appointment, so please excuse me now.]

Show Taro [Thank you for your taking trouble to visit me at my office.]

Having seen Suzuki off, Show Taro sat back and thought about what Suzuki told him. He understood there were several points that would need clarification. About that oil painting, who is the painter and how does the painting look like? How many years ago was it stolen? Would there be any possibility that it was secretly switched with the stolen piece? What were the regal provisions like regarding international dealing of stolen goods? What sort of difference between the purchase price of the dealers on the international market price and the retail price? Did Kiriyama buy the painting knowing it was a stolen piece? He thought about each and any possibility about this case.

In the first place, he checked Japanese and overseas legal provisions as regards stolen goods that were applied on the international wanted list. In Japan, the legitimate owner is deemed to hold the first right of repurchase for the period of longer than two years and less than ten years from the stolen day. Also, what he understood was that the Japanese police would start investigation on the notice from the person who had his painting stolen and would have the gathered information notified to the country where the legitimate owner lives. To his surprise, he had never been taught about such detailed regulations regarding Interpol notice at the Antique Training Courses that are open once a year. Judging from this fact, it may have been the case that Japanese police is not too ernest to develop the searching exercise of antiques stolen overseas. In case a Japanese purchase such merchandise knowing from the beginning that it is a stolen antique piece, regardless of the length of time since it is bought by that Japanese owner, the stolen piece is set to be confiscated and

— 47 —

returned to the country where the original legitimate owner exists. However, Show Taro now found out that cases that had happened till then were mostly such crime as practicing extortion to the person who came to own such stolen antique .

Such extortioners that secretly sell stolen goods to Japanese, then tell the purchaser that it is a stolen piece and blackmail such wealthy purchaser who cares about his respectability. Then let the legitimate owner repurchase it and let the legitimante owner pay the extortioner gratuity.

Japanese art collectors have been suffering from wrongs and contumelies. At time of bubbles economy, if Japanese buyers raised hands at the auctions, bid price was unreasonably jacked up and sold to the Japanese. At the fall of the bubbles, naturally, bid price fell down, too, and when the fallen price came under the European and American bid price, the profitable pieces only were re-purchased and those extortioners made profits.

In the countries other than Japan, regulations there are much stricter than those of Japan so that even if the purchaser does not have any evil motivation without having the knowledge that what he bought is a stolen piece, he is confiscated without argument of the piece he has purchased. In such countries, ratio of collectors who dare to buy stolen goods will be far below than that in Japan. Nevertheless, some obstinate collectors do exist and for that reason art theft groups keep prevailing.

By the time he finished his study and investigation, tea got completely cold. Show Taro dried the cup up and stretched his back and started preparing to go home.

4. To take a look at the Oil Paintings

The appointed day was a fine day so good thing was Show Taro could carry tools to check the painting without need of carrying these under an umbrella. Suzuki Shoten was located in a comparably convenient place to reach. The company was doing wholesale work exclusively to the home centers in that area of such merchandise as the full range of gardening materials and seemed to be doing fairly good business. One folklift was unloading gardening blocks from a truck that had come back from the port going through the customs. Slipping by the truck he opened the office entrance door and nodded to a middle age female clerk inside the office.

Show Taro [Good day. I am Hayashi. Is President Suzuki here?]

She showed Show Taro through to the president's office and served tea and went out.

Show Taro looked around the office and found that the whole space of about 33m^2 was filled with Suzuki's collection.

Excluding the working corner, it seemed that the place was roughly divided into three parts of Western antiques, Japanese/Chinese art objects and contemporary arts.

Sitting on a leather sofa, he looked around and noted that the world map hung behind the President's chair was the one showing the world before WW2 judging from the name of the countries or border lines. The one next to it was a map of the Edo era and not the current Tokyo. In addition, on the desk there an old-fashioned black telephone was put. It was a dial-system phone which could seldom be seen nowadays. Also, over the corner where the sofa was put, a light of Art Nouveau style was hung. On a cabinet next to the sofa a vase was put which was with the floral pattern of Barbotine of the beginning of the 20th century that was often used in the remote district of France. On the wall beyond the cabinet there were put together an oil painting with streets where a house of white wall was shown, and a poster of cabaret of the age of Belle Epoque.

Turning his eyes to a different corner, he saw handguards of swords, Kokeshi, and soup containers for buckwheat noodles being exhibited in mixture of all of these. On the wall, framed Ukiyoe and Chinese pictures were decorated and in front of those framed pictures, he saw statues similar to Buddha shape which looked like folkcrafts were sitting. Comparing with the other side of the corner, this corner looked fairly promiscuous. Among all these bits and pieces, a figure of beckoning cat was raising its right arm and was beckoning as if it were saying it was the newest in all of those things. The rest of the corner was filled with contemporary arts consisting of abstract paintings or a turning back figurine of a gal wearing a mini-skirt which was as big as about one third of a living girl which was showing a strong pink color. On the wall, emblems of cars that Suzuki had been using till now or signboards of shops in the Meiji era were shown one and the other without any connection to each other.

Show Taro was amazed wondering how Suzuki could come to collect such chimerical goods. Collectors of this type oftentimes showed totally uncoordinated collection like this which was a kind of collection that tired Show Taro to no end. In most cases, such collectors that could classify collected goods in good selective way and spent the first ten years for studying the best way of making selection could perform a collection worthwhile to watch. By taking such steps those collectors came to be able to feel and realize through their skin how the weathering caused by aging coming from continuous use of those goods or the handfeel of the rounded edges and the eyesight of the luster as results of the long-time usage could come to be appearing.

As it is said that the longest way round is the shortest way home, a certain high degree of researches and time consuming endeavors are indispensable for such collectors to arrive at the stage on which they would be able to determine what is good and what is bad. Those who are wealthy tend to waste money on unnecessary shoppings or to loose the attitude of making utmost efforts to do their research. It is not incorrect that they can collect goods of a certain quality level by spending a great deal of money, but when they come to get used to such practice, their judgement ability will go wrong, for example, if they are offered an antique for the price of five thousand dollars which costs no less than one million dollars if it is authentic, they will take it as just a wonderful luck and never suspect the reliability of such quotation and what it means. The simple unmovable fact of that professionals is far better to ascertain the true value of the goods than amateuers is moved away and that matter of fact is changed to matter of falsehood.

As a consequence, there appears such a person at the TV antique appraisal program that blantly says he paid only 100,000 yen to get an item that was price-tagged of 200,000 yen, which in his opinion is worth half million yen.

Suzuki   [Thank you for your coming. The painting we talked about is here in this box.]

Suzuki pulled a box out which had been pushed in between the cabinet and the wall and took the painting out of the box and leaned it against the wall.

Suzuki   [Kiriyama told me this is 「the Man with the Golden Helmet」 of Rembrandt]

There appeared in front of Show Taro was a painting, which is currently owned by Berlin National Art Museum with attribution of Rembrandt Research Project (RRP) as a painting produced at the Rembrandt Work Shop.

The painting that Show Taro was then looking at was indeed very much the same as the painting called 「The Man with the Golden Helmet」. It was a portrait of a little less than Size 40 of about 70cm tall and 60cm wide. The number of the paintings that Rembrandt painted had been said to be more than 1,000 paintings till RRP started to classify and discriminate them. After the discrimination by RRP was finished, this painting which is alike authentic Rembrandt's painting was come to be discriminated as a painting drawn at the Rembrandt's work shop drawn by Rembrandt's apprentices and not Rembrandt himself. These paintings painted by his apprentices do not have even a touch of Rembrandt, but these are not deemed as fakes. In the wordings of the modern times, these can be said as the paintings produced by the Rembrandt's work shop under Rembrandt's supervision.

After getting a consent from Suzuki, Show Taro firstly took out a black light and checked the paintings from the corner to the corner putting the light on the surface of the painting. In case some parts had been mended in the recent years, the black light could detect those parts as they were shown in whitish color. Show Taro, however, did not find any such parts on the painting. This means that the painting did not show any trace of mendment right before it came into Japan.

Next, Show Taro took a loupe out and checked the vanishing state on the surface of the painting and confirmed that the cracks shown of paints were not made by printing but were true cracks. The features of the face are different from those of the one in Berlin but if this painting is taken for granted as the product of the Rembrandt's work shop, this difference could be understood as same as the Japanese portrayals. To explain this further, of such portrait of Minamotono Yoritomo or Tairano Shigemori, the part of old ceremonial court dresses was painted in the same fashion for both of them but only the part of the face was described iminating each person. This painting method in Japan was practiced to express the dignity of each man of power, so that possibility of this kind of painting method having been taken by Rembrandt at his work shop under his supervision could well be thought of.

Then the orderer of the painting made a pose before the apprentices who cooperated to paint part by part of the costume and the background leaving the sketch of the face to the last part of the work. They made it a custom to ask the orderer before they completed the painting if the orderer might like to change such jewellies as rings to different ones. This painting seemed to Show Taro to be the kind of paintings which was intended to show decorative accessories to show off the painted person's dignity at the saloon or the like.

Those jewery accessories were painted larger than actual and the portlait in the painting was painted younger than actual which was reflecting the painters' mindfulness to their ordering customer. Needless to mention, oftentimes features of the face were painted slightly more attractive than actual. Like what Michelangelo said, more than several hundreds of years afterwards, the stone statue will become to be taken more as the fact than the deceased. The statue of Ramses II of ancient Egypt cannot faithfully be the same as the real Ramses II. Those men of power must be altered to look like true men of power. That is the very reason why the statue of Caeser of ancient Rome is not showing a bold head and Augustous as we all know him must show strong figure at the young age of 30th which looks like he was ready to lead his army anywhere in the world. Suppose they had made a statue copying the true outlook of them, the invation of savage tribes into Rome might have been advanced by at least 300 years.

Next, Show Taro, getting permission of Suzuki, took a look at the reverse side of the canvas. Thinking such information might be needed later on, he measured the vertical and horizontal lengths of the canvas and wrote these in his notebook, and also counted how many linen yarns per centimeter were woven into the width of canvas cloth. He also noticed that the wood of the canvas frame was quite aged so checked the wood carefully expecting to find any words or marks on it but failed to find any. Next, he took the painting off the frame and took photos of both the front and back sides of it by his digital camera, and put the painting back to the frame and again took photos of the both sides. He did all what had to be done except the age determination that could be done by component analysis of the oil paints, infrared film taking and X-ray photographing. The age determination test of the oil paints can show a crue to discriminate the peculiarity of the region where the paints were produced and refining process of pigments used in the paints. These are the inspection items exercised at national museums or the like at time of purchasing pictorial arts.

Also, if the cloth that is used as canvas at the painter's work shop is produced at the same cloth manufacturing factory, plural number of paintings drawn on the same quality canvas can exist, in which case other such paintings and this particular painting can be proven to have been painted about the same period of time in the history.

Wood frames that makes the base of the canvas, too, can be a crue to determine that the painting was drawn by that particular painter of that particular country of that particular time of the history if the place where the painting was drawn and the time when the wood was purchased and the place where the wood was harvested can be confirmed.

Finishing the set series of inspections, Show Taro put the painting back to the cardboard box, when he noticed a napkin which was the kind of being served at a tea parlour was hooked on the corner of the box. As it was apparently not the part of the painting, he took it off the box and put it in front of Suzuki and questioned.

Show Taro [has it been in the box from the beginning?]

Suzuki [Well, as you say so, yes…why?]

Show Taro [Can I take it as reference?]

Suzuki [Yes, please take it.]

Suzuki granced at it wonderingly and showed no more interest.

— 55 —

That napkin had a word Passo Romano and did not look like Japan made.

Show Taro quickly inserted the napkin in the clear sheets sat down and wiped his hands with the wet towel served on the table and sipped half amount of the tea.

Show Taro [Do you understand some other paintings exist of the same subject matter made by the Rembrandt work shop?]

Suzuki answered showing in his behavior that he had been received the same explanation about this matter many times from his associating painting dealers.

Suzuki [Yes, I heard from Kiriyama it is a famous painting.]

Show Taro [As this is a production of the Rembrandt Work Shop, it cannot be transacted for a price as expensive as that of Rembrandt's original painting.]

Suzuki [Yet it must be worth for some value I guess.]

Shw Taro [Right. By the way, as regards the channel of acquisition of it, can I understand that Minister Yamagata directly took it to Mr. Kiriyaka?]

What Show Taro was interested in was not this painting only. There must be a hidden route of acquisition channel of similar paintings hereafter as well.

Suzuki [Dealer involved is 「the nine-tailed fox」.

Hearing the name of phantom of shape shifter, Show Taro reflectively asked back.

Show Taro 「the nine-tailed fox?」

Hearing Show Taro whose voice became a little louder, Suzuki thought Show Taro was a person that was not familiar to Ginza at

— 56 —

night.

Suzuki   [Don't you know the name? What I mean is Akemi Kitsuregawa. She is a female business person running an apparel shop in Ginza called 『Perfect Beauty=Kyubi=nine-tailed fox.』

Show Taro did remember that name of the competent business woman in her 30th of age.

Show Taro [Do you know Ms Kitsuregawa?]

Suzuki   [I saw her several times at restaurants in Ginza.]

Show Taro [With whom was she then?]

Suzuki   [Sometimes with Minister Yamagata and other times with an overseas⋯musician or else.]

Show Taro [Does she do good business?]

Suzuki   [You seem not too familiar with fashion business, correct?]

Show Taro [Yah, maybe not.]

Suzuki   [What I gathered is that in some movie or else, 『Perfect Beauty (Kyubi)』 branded bag or necklace was used which incidence is rumored that some powerful spirit made it happen.]

Show Taro [So that means her brand was taken up on top of other famous European brands?]

Suzuki   [Therefore, it is rumored that there should have been some kind of a backroom deal.]

Show Taro [Now I understand... Some overseas musician and Yoritomo Yamagata. Surely I, too, smell some politics going on about it.]

Suzuki   [And⋯I also heard that the nine-tail fox means a daughter of a popular Geisha in past, though this information has not been confirmed at all.]

Show Taro [What is the name of that Geisha?]

Suzuki [Well, it doesn't come to me now.]

Show Taro [If it was after WW2, it sounds like to have some relationship with GHQ or else.]

Suzuki [Judging from her age, she belongs to a later generation···it may be the time of Vietnam War?]

Show Taro [Haha, Vietnam War···]

Suzuki [I frequently visit Vietnam for procurement of blocks for my business so I know there were various goods from japan flowing in so Japanese industries kept sending their members to Vietnam for tending the after service for the American troops.]

Show Taro [She may be involved in such sort of rights.]

Suzuki [I have never thought in the way you just told me. You have an interesting idea.]

Show Taro [By the way, let me explain the procedure to dispose this painting. Can I tell you now?]

Suzuki [Does it not good just simply to sell it?]

Then, Show Taro started explaining procedures he thought about as to how to do the disposing business of the painting. Suzuki carefully listened to Show Taro to grasp the whole scheme that he constructed.

Show Taro [At first, you contact the castle that lost the painting or the insurance company which suffered damage. Next, on seeing the painting, they distinguish it as fake at once, then that's it. It is the end of this matter so it will become extremely difficult to sell it and get paid. However, if they think there is a possibility of it being authentic, they will wish to check the actual painting. Here, it is important that you will not take the painting out of Japan to show them.]

Because you are the bona fide third person, in the period starting more than two years after the theft till the end of the following ten years, the original owner of it has the first purchase right as set by the international pact which Japan is participating in. Therefore, I am intending to do trade negotiation at one billion yen plus 10% commission to my company which equals to 1.1 billion yen. In case they will not agree to purchase it at this price, they will send us a written notification to that effect. Or they may just call us on telephone and tell us that they will not purchase it back, in which case I will record it on tape. If we can get this evidence either in writing or by recorded tape, it becomes clear that they have abandoned the first purchase right, then you can sell it in public and can lawfully protect yourself from unreasonable threatening if any of such as that you must have obtained it knowing it is a stolen painting. One other suggestion I would like to make is that you had better not be too concerned about the amount of the purchase price. The original owner will choose the loss to be covered by the insurance company but you must set a proper market price otherwise you may lose the selling chance.]

Looking at Show Taro, Suzuki slightly nodded his head and said.

Suzuki   [I understood. I will wait for the reaction from the original owner. Incidentally, do you know the reason why blocks made in Vietnam are selling well?]

Show Taro [Is it anything to do with the change of the demanding trend?]

Suzuki [Living quarters in the recent days in the urban area are now being changed to condominium. At a condominium the highest price is set for the penthouse on top of the Condominium. But those living in condominiums hate to be watched from other high-rise condominiums. Therefore, they wish to cover their quarters using blicks or tiles for both purposes of shutting the eyes from outside higher condominiums and decorating their condominium. This is the reason of increasing demand of blicks. On the other hand, regarding independent houses, the age of traditional Japanese garden where Dads' duty is to clean the garden on Sundays is now going to pass away.]

Show Taro [Is that because size of gardens is getting smaller?]

Suzuki [In Tokyo, car port is now becoming a part of the garden, so, people pile up blicks to hide the sight from the car port. Also, space where in the old times such big trees as gardeners had to struggle with have lost the space in the garden to grow.]

Show Taro [I thought the best selling line must be European style tiles. Am I wrong?]

Suzuki [Tiles from Europe are mainly used for bathrooms, or the entrance area, and the mantlepiece area. But for those more spacious places such as the border area between car port and lawn, quantity needed of tiles becomes much more so Vietnam-made cost saving tiles are suited. Cost of transportation is less from Vietnam, too, so tiles from there are quite cost competitive. In addition, ample labor power there can respond to our urgent request of production increasement. Mexico-made tiles tend to be of slightly uneven quality perhaps reflecting the gayful temper of the race, but are still cheaper than European tiles. Tiles from Spain, Italy and France are highly suitable for use in the area around the fireplace, but delay of delivery often takes place from Italy. Rumor tells us such delay is caused by the theft led by Maphia at the loading port in Italy.]

Show Taro [That problem is with us, too. Loss of our cargos in Italy is a matter of our concern.]

Suzuki [How are you combatting with that problem?]

Show Taro [Deliverers of the cargo to the airport watch the loading into a cargo flight till it is finished.]

Suzuki [Do you have to be that watchful?]

Show Taro [I learnt that a certain art dealer had a whole folklift lot lost at the Roman airport, though this dealer could get the total amout of the damage back using the insurance coverage as the cargo was not the antiques that are not replaceable.]

Suzuki [Well, that kind of accident is not happening with Vietnam of these days. Vietnam people are delligent people and in the southern part of Vietnam the trading morale of the original capitalism is still there which seems to be well activating.]

— 61 —

Show Taro [So you mean that good trading habit is reflected on the increased importation of Vietnam-made bricks.]

Suzuki [I wonder how many more years this Vetnumese boom of importation will continue? I hope it will continue as long as possible.]

Show Taro [It is difficult to guess, but if Japanese yen becomes stronger, import will of course be eased.]

Suzuki [Right. That's the common sense.]

At that time, the Grand Father's Clock rang out.

Show Taro [Isn't that clock pretty precisely working.]

Suzuki [That clock is one of the items that I firstly imported. It is a German made, but is pretty precise.]

Show Taro [Thanks for your time given to me today.]

Suzuki [Likewise.]

In this way Show Taro finished checking the actual painting. He was convinced that Suzuki could be a reliable customer judging from his honest way of talking and the fact that he was actually doing business. Should he have been a con man no visible company office would exist. Also, there are such time-killing visitors who just enjoy teasing the dealers without having any intention to purchase any products.

5. Insurance Inspector

A few days afterwards, Show Taro printed both the front view and the back view that he had taken by camera and taking these copies he went to the front desk of the British Embassy.

Receptionist [Are you for visa application?]

Show Taro [I came here to make a reference to a stolen painting. As I received an oil painting that is rumored as a stolen painting in U.K. about three years ago.]

The female receptionist who heard the reason why the man came knitted her brows once, then answered.

Receptionist [I am not sure about such a matter as neither visa application nor any diplomatic issue···]

Then, Show Taro decided to use all the means in his hands to convince this receptionist of the importance of what he was concerned about. So, he took the digital camera photos out of the bag. However, he kept taking a rather low profile on this conversation with the receptionist so as not to miss her assistance.

Show Taro [I am leaving these photos with you, so, will you kindly refer these back to Scotland Yard or any suitable organization?]

She, putting a somewhat embarrassed look on her face, did still stay to answer his request.

Receptionist [I will anyway ask my superiors what we can do for you, so, please write your request on this writing paper and leave either your business card or contact details. Today, Ambassador is out of his office and···

— 63 —

please understand as your request is not related to diplomatic matters I am not sure if we can be of help.]

One week after his visit to the Embassy, an e-mail message arrived at Show Taro's hand. He returned his e-mail enclosing those digital camera photos, and on the following day he received a reply again which stated a request to show the painting to an insurance inspector whom they would send to Show Taro. He was reasonably satisfied with this progress.

He rang Suzuki and obtained his consent to borrow the painting out from his office to meet the appointed date after the arrival of the inspector in Japan. It will be necessary that Show Taro must accompany with the painting all the time till when he would be able to return this painting to Suzuki. Meanwhile the insurance inspector arrived in Japan from England.

The inspector handed his business card to Show Taro and said his name was Robert Grant. He said he was in charge of buyback of insured paintings that had been stolen. He was a rather tall and slim gentleman except his stomach which is a bit too fat. His face was cleanly shaved but he was storing a moustache.

Robert   [I haven't come to japan for quite a while since my last visit.]

Show Taro   [So you mean you have been here before?]

Robert   [When I was a college student, I went on an overseas study program for one year in Japan.]

Show Taro   [What did you major?]

Robert   [Modern history.]

Show Taro   [Of Japan?]

Robert   [No, regarding the influence that Japan gave to

— 64 —

European modern history.]

Show Taro [It was a rather unusual subject.]

Robert [Japan and Germany brought a huge change to the world by giving rise to WW2.]

Show Taro [And the end of the era of colonial domination?]

Robert [I was surprised Japan didn't teach its nation precise interpretation of the world history. Especially such facts as that Japan's attack of Pearl Harbor made America turn outward which had been facing inward following Monroe Doctrine, and Barbarossa of Nazi Germany made Soviet also turn outward till when Soviet had been fully occupied with bloody purges inside its territory. These big turnarounds broke out together with the inability of colony maintenance of England and France.]

Show Taro [Robert, I can now say your choice of the job at an insurance company is not a very wise choice.]

Robert [Research of history is a lofty hobby⋯as it won't make money.]

Show Taro [If that's what you do, I also have such lofty taste.]

Robert [What is it?]

Show Taro [History is matters happened in past, isn't it. But my hobby is related to future, too.]

Robert [Interesting.]

Show Taro [Reading of 『Les Centuries』 written by Michele Nostradamus. For instance, the part which refers to the world after WW2⋯]

Show Taro took a pocket notebook out and started to turn the

— 65 —

pages.

Show Taro [Let me see⋯2-89

The first line can be read as 'one day two powerful countries come into friendly relationship'.

The second line reads as 'their strong powers will get stronger'.

The third line as 'power of the one at the side of the new world will reach its peak'.

The forth line is difficult to be deciphered, but if taken as alliance of America and England, it already started in WW2, and if for America and Russia, it will become a situation that will arise in future.

Robert [I now know here in Japan a researcher does exist.]

Show Taro [Nothing more than a hobby, really.]

Robert [I am also interested in the prophecy of Nostoradamus, as I have heard in past my grandfather was in charge of interrogation of Nazi prisoners of war.]

Show Taro [Was your grandfather positioned at one of the prison camps?]

Robert [As he was a doctor, he was engaged in medical checkups of the prisoners.]

Show Taro [As I remember it, such is written in 2-36. A paragraph that states the one who intercepts the book of the great prophest is outwitted and gets into a mess ⋯This part can be deciphered as 'Nazi used 『Les Centuries』 as their propaganda which was outwitted and they got cornered'.]

Robert [There certainly seems to have been many there In

NS, namely Nazi, who were doing deciphering of Nostradamus. Heinrich Himmler, and also, Rudolph Hess were the ones, but in the speeches, Josef Goebbels looks to have quoted a lot from what Nostradamus had written.]

Show Taro [One of the reasons why Nazi・German troops attacked France was in order to peruse and inspect the prophecy that was stored in Archieves Nationales France.]

Robert [Well, well, this is the first time I met a Japanese who told that history to that extent.]

Show Taro [In the high officials in Nazi such person as Helmann Goering who was an art lover, but on the other hand, there were not few officials who were interested in occultism like Rudolph Hess. It was an easy matter to confiscate the libruary if only they asked Heinrich Himmler. Rudolph Hess, especially, deeply deciphered the prophecy and that must be why he flew to U.K. by himself before the great military results of Barbarossa took place.

Robert [Talking about that Rudolf Hess, as Adolf Hitler and Josef Goebbels announced that he had gone insane, my grandfather was appointed as the diagnostician of his mental status.]

Show Taro [And what was his diagnosis?]

Robert [My grandfather's test result was he was totally sane.]

Show Taro [You, too, are deciphering the future.]

Robert [I am progressing my research on my own way, but

— 67 —

am not yet confident enough to be able to decipher the future. But in Europe quite a few researchers still keep validating the evidence from various angles of viewpoint persistently. In this regard, Japanese seem to be easy to heat up and easy to cool down.]

Show Taro [Because they do not believe that kind of happening will not fall on their own selves.]

Robert [Les Centuries states that Europe was going to be affected, even if this matter is happening on the reverse side of the globe to Japanese.]

And again, Show Taro started to turn the pages of his pocket notebook and Robert was curiously gazing at his action.

Show Taro [Well, ···then···2-100.

The first line states terrifying disturbance will take place. The place could be England, but could also be Japan.

The second line states only the bellicose goup of people are heard. When the situation develops onto this stage, it comes to be alike the situation in Japan before the outbreak of WW2. Assassination of important dignitaries by coup d'tat. Then following this···

The forth line They form a great alliance and in that part of the sentence, in addition to the phrase of rangers will agree such phrase as the troops line up is recorded. This means military alliance. If this is what is meant for, this psalm would mean the triple alliance of Japan, Germany and Italy.]

— 68 —

Hearing that far, Robert was interested in how Show Taro was pigeonholing the psalm.

Robert   [I reckon you have quite deeply researched Les Centuries. Won't you tell me what happened in japan of any kind of this sort.]

Show Taro [Well, to answer you in the best way will be 5-81.

The first line The bird of the King, namely, the eagle flies over the city of the sun. This means American fighters fly over the Japanese urban area.

The second line During the seven months of time, ill-omened auspicium is revelated. This can be taken as the expression of the night attack starting in February, 1945 till August of the same year.

The third line The eastern wall falls down and thunderstorm and the crack of thunder roar. The word wall often means power, so this part can be translated as power of Japan is lost. However, the word tonnerre has a meaning of thundering noise and if that is the word to be meant, it could be taken as a huge explosion power which is uncomparably bigger than the sound of the night attack. I personally take it as the atomic bombing on Hiroshima and Nagasaki. Also, this word tonnerre has meanings of underwater mines or torpedoes so that in this meaning it can be destroyal of commerce by American troops, namely, torpedo attacks by submarines and blockage of sea routes or harbors by mines. It may be understood that this expression represents the high level of expressive power of Nostradamus.

The forth line Taking seven days, the enemy ..portes.. This word can be translated as a gate but can also be read as a harbor. There the enemy makes a rush. Seven days after the atomic bombing on Nagasaki of August 9 means August 16, so Nostradamus was observing the Japanese Emperor's acceptance of Potsdam Declaration that was broadcast at noon of August 15.]

Robert   [I understand you have been soring psams or the like into groups of the similar contents and bunching them together, aren't you.]

Having said so, then for the first time after the start of their conversation they took the tea cups up and sipped the tea.

Show Taro [Now, let me show you the oil painting.]

He stood up and took a cardboard box out from the place where he was storing his merchandise per category. He had the painting lean against the wall making it to face Robert.

Show Taro [This is The Man with the Golden Helmet.]

Robert gazed at the painting for about thirty seconds and then carefully looked around the reverse side of the painting. He seemed to be looking at the wooden framing on which the canvas was stretched.

Robert   [May I take a look at the inside of the box, too?]

Show Taro [Yes, please.]

As he did not find anything in the cardboard box, he looked a bit disappointed and asked.

Robert   [Was there in the box anything when you received it?]

With a little bit smug look on his face Show Taro took the thing out of the clear sheets.

Show Taro [Is this what you expect?]

He showed the napkin marked Passo Romano. Robert looked at it for seconds and looked up at the ceiling and said in the muttering way.

Robert [So this was in here, too.]

Show Taro bent himself forward in curiosity.

Show Taro [Did the same one as this come out elsewhere?]

Robert [Yes, in Chicago. But on that one of Chicago the letter C is marked while this one shows B.]

Show Taro instantly asked Robert back.

Show Taro [Is that one in Chicago drawing a different figure?]

Robert [The Man with the Golden Helmet.]

In a flash, he asked again.

Show Taro [Is one of the two a fake?]

Robert [Both are fakes. Only A is authentic. By the way, do you have enough information to make a trace of the route of this painting till it arrived in Japan?]

Then, Robert took over the roll of a questioner and started questioning about the matters of his concern. He wanted to find out if information that Show Taro could supply is worth using.

Show Taro [This painting was bought in Switzerland by ex-President Fujimura and took it into Japan and asked the disposal to Minister Yamagata. The dealer who undertook the work was that one with nine tails.]

Hearing the word Switzerland, Show Taro thought he felt Robert's ears twitched. At least, his eyes suddenly became piercing.

Hearing the word of nine tails, Robert leaned out.

Robert   [You know the name of that person, do you.]

Show Taro [Yes.]

Wondering for a few seconds, Robert opened his mouth.

Robert   [Alright, then please lend us your cooperation to recover the authentic painting. As a fight money we will provide you with £5,000 per month for a contract period of 12 months. Such necessary expenses as transportation, accommodations and meals are all cheageable to our company. Also, if the extention of the work becomes necessary, we will extend the contract validity three months additionally per extention.]

Show Taro [What about the incentive?]

Robert   [£50,000 for procurement of the authentic painting. Here is the outfit allowance.]

Show Taro quickly read through the presented contract sheets which were whitten in Japanese and surely confirmed the conditions Robert talked about were listed in there. He also read several lines of the English version written next to Japanese and confirmed they were exactly the same in the meaning, so he went ahead to put his signature on the documents.

Show Taro [Incidentally, what does Passo Romano mean?]

Since he finished signinig, Show Taro expected Robert ought to give him such information that he wished to learn. Robert asserted that the authentic painting is nothing but A. But he shook his head.

Robert   [We do not know it, though I know several people tried hard to find what it is.]

— 72 —

Show Taro [So no crue has been found to date, has it.]

Without giving him any answer, he continued a very business-like explanation.

Robert [When you come to Europe, use this travel agent under this name. Use this same name for your movement in Japan, too. For taxis and other transportation expenses, we will mail this card later to you for your use. This cell phone is to be used. Any question?]

So, he questioned about another tracker whom he was curious about.

Show Taro [The person in Chicago. Is he also tracking Passo Romano?]

Robert [Yes, Gabriel is tracking, too···he arrived in Switzerland last month.]

Show Taro [You are doing this tracking pursuit embracing a considerable amount of expenses.]

Without replying this question of him, Robert stood up and packed his bag.

Robert [In any case, please do not forget to send me a mail at a set time every day.]

Show Taro [Okay]

Seeing Robert off, Show Taro went out to return the paintings to Suzuki. Hearing those were fakes, Suzuki dropped his schoulders.

Coming back home, Show Taro perused the contract once again. The condition of the contract is not bad at all, but he came to be aware that to pursue Passo Romano would mean to help investigation work of a front organization counterfeiting stolen

— 73 —

authentic paintings.

However, he self-scorned thiking he could not say No when a £ 5,000　check was presented in front of him as an outfit allowance, but on the other side, he admitted the fact that this amount of money attracted him specially when Japan was in a depression period. A few days afterwards, the information so far gathered about Passo Romano was received by e-mail. Robert seemed to try hard in his busy work to translate it into Japanese.

6. Several Kinds of Information

It was a confirmed fact that the napkins with the word Passo Romano were found together with the same pattern as what were stolen from the castles or such.

To date, several of such fakes were discovered in the world, all of which have such a corresponding feature as that they were made to exactly the same size as the authentic paintings. In past one authentic painting was found and the attached napkin was marked A. As regards B and C, several napkins each of B and C were found to date which were all fakes with the corresponding size feature.

Regarding the used oil paints, some are the paints produced in the 18th century and others the 19th century. Frames of the wood base on which canvas is stretched out seem to be a re-use of the aged roofing wood of the farmer's house in the latter half of the 18th century or thereabout. Also, using some kind of technic cracks of the paints are copied on the fakes to be alike the authentic paintings, keeping the nature that does not react to black light.

Concluding, there must exist an organization consisting of more than several members, that was equipped with a range of oil paints and other drawing materials so as to be able to produce and sell the fake products in a large scale. One thing that must be noted is that in past about three art dealers who cooperated with the search of such organization seem to have been out of contact in the areas such as Switzerland or Italy. The art dealer of Chicago called by the insurance company Gabriel as nickname is not an exception and for the current three weeks or so contact seems to have been lost with him.

Reading the provided information this far, Show Taro felt something cold was creeping down on his back. Recalling what Robert told him, the nickname that Robert created for Show Taro for the communication purposes was Tom Boe. Robert told him reason why he chose this name was because the trade mark of the Show Taro's company was tomboe in Japanese, but Show Taro could not see whether this was the true reason of this naming or not.

However, it also was a fact that antique dealers were often using such nicknames for their customers or friend dealers even for the common commercial deals in order to prevent the leak of information on such occasions as business talks being done at coffee shops or so on, which in a sense might be reflecting the character of those people in this business.

In this meaning, 「Nine-tailed Fox」 of Akemi Kitsuregawa could be taken as showing her character fully with her gallery name. Before he made an approach to her, he visited an art gallery called Gallery Kumamoto run by his acquentance. Aunt Osanai who kept the gallery and he were face acquaintances to each other with her for as long as ten years, so this gallery where there were many female visitors as well as male was a good place for collection of information.

This gallery crammed its exhibition of Japanese antiques facing towards the street. In one prefecture in the western part of Japan those dealers who owned the market access right were mostly dealing within their prefecture when selling their stock that they had bought as a whole stockhouse lot except when they had some assured deal that offered them an opportunity of quick chance to get cash and the higher market price. In such cases only, they transferred their stock to Tokyo.

They are making it a rule to participate in an event somewhere in Tokyo once a month at least including an open market under a big roof or a special sale programmed by department stores. They show their merchandise at those events in the first place and after the event is over they continue to exhibit the leftover of the event at their gallery in Ginza for about half a year. During this exhibiting exercise of a long period, they can expect visitors and purchasers of not only Japanese but sightseeing visitors from China.

Such item as a set of Senchado utensils has a more chance to be sold to Taiwanese or Chinese dealers than Japanese depending on the situation. Regarding such a set stored in an aged paulownia wood box or cedar wood box, if the note of authenticity on the box is readable, the produced time of such set can be determined such as around when of the Meiji era or of the Edo era, and such additional information as the history of the change of the owners of the set from which family to which family can be known. This means the set was changed into a kind of time capsule so that by checking the box that contains the set, people can understand that the set inside such box can never be a recently made fake. Because of the fact that there exist so many imitations, namely, fakes, the Japan-made aged wooden box does have its value.

Among those traditional Japanese antiques, items that are popular with Chinese buyers currently are such as Nambu iron kettles which are pretty heavy but no such kind of things exist in China. One point that is corresponding with China and Japan is because in both of the countries the traditional extended family system has collapsed so that such set for the use of twenty people is often split into five by four sets and sold.

For this reason, at such event sales unless the buyer checks the number of the set inside the box, it can often happen that only half number of pieces are contained.

Show Taro entered the store through the side of the cupboard placed there. Tables that are placed there are being different from time to time but at this time Show Taro found they were the same tables as three months ago. In this store, western-made antiques are sometimes being brought in which came out in the countryside as such items cannot be evaluated at the local dealers' auctions.

In Japan, different from Europe, auctions called exchange events access to which is for dealers only are going on. The good point of this event is that the purchase price can be hidden from the public and the short point is because number of the participants is limited, when there happens to be present only few professional dealers, extremely cheap auction price may result. Show Taro arrived at the good timing just after the other visitors were gone. In such auctions in Tokyo, such aged people as secretaries of politicians or election counselors are killing time by looking around. But when Show Taro arrived it was near 5 o'clock in the late afternoon, so club hostesses or men in black suits who were the escorts of those hostesses began to be out on the street. Show Taro was thinking he would do and finish the collection work of information in about thirty minutes from then.

Show Taro [Good day. Haven't seen you for a while.]

Osanai [Oh, Unusual visitor. Have some of this. It is a gift of that visitor who just left.]

Saying so, she quickly made tea and served him with the teacakes. Whom she called that visitor looked like a business man somewhere from the countryside. A country style sweet bun was put on a small plate, which was two to three times bigger than the Kyoto style Wagashi

Show Taro [I have a question to ask. Do you know anything about Ms Akemi Kitsuregawa of 『Kyubi』 developing the brand business?]

Osanai, the shopclerk, looked at Show Taro who asked about Akemi Kitsuregawa who is popular as a fair looking woman.

Osanai [Have you received any request of any kind from her?]

Show Taro [No, no such thing⋯but I wish to learn what sort of person she is as regards her career or family or whatever.]

Osanai started talking about what she had learnt through the social conversation with the business visitors. Apart from her antique business she was not too caucious about what she was chattering.

Osanai [She is a child between a Shinbashi Geisha and a certain businessman and was grown up the hard way. What I heard is after graduation of a women's college or the like, she worked for several years as a low rank clerk of some apparel firm till she started an independent business on her own at her age of 28. She named her shop 『Kyubi』. What was lucky about her was an Italian actress placed her order of the small bits and pieces with 『Kubi』 ,that were to be used in the movie in which the actress played her roll and this contributed greatly to 『Kyubi』 business. But that could happen thanks to her father's help and backup though I can't tell who her father is as I don't know him. She must now be in her middle thirties so she must have her partner. I heard next week she is renting the gallery on the opposite side of this shop and is showing her new collection, so, why don't come and take a look? But I gather men do not particularly like her as she is a woman of moods⋯you seem not care about this character of hers, correct? It may be permissible she being a beauty.]

Osanai spoke as if Show Taro had a thing for her.

Show Taro [No, no, I'm not feeling that way⋯]

Osanai [Well, I do have the invitation card here, so I will take you with me then.]

Osanai was a nosy woman in a positive way. Show Taro did not have any connection with Akemi Kitsuregawa till then but all of the sudden distance between the two started to get shortened in one breath.

While they were talking to each other this way, his cell phone rang so he excused himself and went out of the shop.

Show Taro [Yes.]

Robert [I did not hear from you for the past three days. Are you alright, Tom?]

Show Taro [Oh, Robert, Looks like I am seeing Kitsuregawa next week.]

Robrt [While I am in Japan, make it sure you give me a call once per week.]

Show Taro [Understood.]

Robert [Hunt for the beautiful fox. Good luck!]

The line was suddenly cut. Show Taro felt Robert grinning. Then he returned to the shop when he heard Osanai saying as follows.

Osanai [Isn't that cell phone of yours got cut off often? I changed mine to a different model, then that trouble stopped occurring.]

Show Taro [But it doesn't work in the countryside, does it.]

Osanai [You're right. Cell phones that work in the urban areas often become useless in the countryside or hilly places.]

Show Taro [Correct. Kamakura is a troublesome place. There, rather than to say is the place where there are many mountains, many small valleys called 「Yato」 or 「Yatsu」 are located where radio waves do not easily reach.]

Osanai [Oh, by the way, yes, I will introduce you to her but mind you to get worn in a better clothes as clothes make the man.]

7. Fox Hole

Show Taro visited the gallery again on Friday of the following week where Osanai dressed in Kimomo clothes showing a look better than usual was waiting for him. Her kimono sash belt was of gay colors just acting her age.

Osanai [While I am taking the trouble to introduce you to her, how come you are even without a tie.]

Show Taro [Look, I am at least wearing a jacket, you see?]

Her shop is usually kept opoen till 7 o'clock in the evening, but on that day she closed it at half past five in the afternoon. Then both went into the gallery on the opposite side of the street.

Osanai [Hi, good day, I understand you were very busy yesterday.]

Kitsuregawa [Today's not that busy.]

Oyamanouchi [Will you meet Show Taro of Palais Frolas.]

Show Taro [Glad to see you, my name is Hayashi.]

Oyamanouchi [This is Ms Kitsuregawa of Kyubi.]

Kitsuregawa [Nice to see you. I am Akemi Kitsuregawa. How are you interested in our merchandise line from the viewpoint of an antique dealer?]

Show Taro [From the designing view point your line looks like a revival of art deco and rococo if I understand it correctly. Colors are brighter than in the past.]

Kitsuregawa [You are right. As I am co-developing the line with my Chinese friend⋯The Japanese color taste looks a bit too unobtrusive so I changed that part in this way making the pattern a little larger, though not as big as for the goods meant for America.]

She was an average built person but her skin which is as fair as can be inherited her Geisha mother's white skin. The way she carried herself was smooth and elastic which let others feel her intellectural refinement worth being called as a fox to get to the bottom of the beauty. The part of her face from the cheeks to the corners of the eyes were faintly light and the skin of her face looked almost transparent which did not need any make-up. The wide-spread legend of her having denied offers of support from several investors and yet made a success in this very competitive business field deserved to convince people of the validity of her success.

Show Taro [You must be visiting Europe on your own to procure products there. Are you visiting old castles or such?]

Kitsuregawa [I'm curious about you···Oh, by the way, I am planning to go to Switzerland and Italy from this monthend. If I can match my schedule with yours, shall we meet somewhere in those countries?]

At this sudden proposal, Show Taro was somewhat embarrassed, but it was a very timely offer to him.

Show Taro [Please tell me your visiting schedule in detail so I can match mine with yours.]

Hearing his words, Akemi Kitsuregawa turned towards her secretary who was standing at the corner of the room and made a sign raising one hand up in a half way.

Kitsuregawa [Fetch the purchasing schedule list here, please.]

After a short while, a woman in black dress in her thirtieth of age opened a notebook and showed a page to her.

Secretary   [Here it is.]

Kitsuregawa [If it is possible at all that you meet your schedule with this one of mine, I hope you will please show me to antique shops.]

Show Taro [With pleasure. But I do not visit too often clean highclass shops. Is this acceptable?]

Kitsuregawa [I understand oftentimes in such dusty warehouses products with designs which came out too early to time the trend may be stored and sleeping there, so I would not care to skip those highclass shops.]

Osanai   [Let me excuse myself now. I'm leaving you here.]

Osanai had the sense to leave them alone and quickly withdrew herself. It must have been her principle not to be too nosy.

Then, on that day, Show Taro dropped at the president's office of Kyubi once and was taken for dinner by Kitsuregawa from there. No need to say, he has a lot of questions to ask, so this invitation was a real good luck to him. One thing that could be said was that this whole situation was developing in her pace, she must have some specific purpose to be with him. In that evening, they went to an Italian restaurant with her driving her car, and they toasted with white wine taking grilled Shrimp Scumpi. She seemed to be seeking some new field other than the extension of her current business field, where she will make an injection of her fund. In other words, she was providing him with a convenient phase of situation in which he would be able to make questions abour the field that he kept investigating till then.

— 84 —

Show Taro [By the way, talking about your new business development, is this programming the deal of paintings?]

Kitsuregawa [Where did you get such information?]

Show Taro [What I have gathered is that a painting of which Defence Minister Yamagata took a role of mediation to sell it to a certain businessman was actually handled by you for handing it over to the businessman and collecting the payment from him.]

Kitsuregawa [Oh, that case is, I acted just as a helper having been asked by a female owner of a company who is a supporter as well as a lover of ex-President Fujimura.]

Show Taro [Then, do you know why this Passo Romano marked Napkin was packed in the box together with the painting?]

Giving a glance to the napkin that Show Taro took out of his bag, she looked a bit puzzled at his question which is nothing to do with the ongoing conversation between them, and taking some wine, she replied.

Kitsuregawa [It was already in the box in Switzerland.]

It was an unexpected fact to learn that she went all the way to Switzerland for what she said 'just as a helper'.

Show Taro [In Switzerland? I thought you had seen the painting for the first time in Japan…]

Kitsuregawa [All what happened was that I was handed over two paintings from Fujimura in Switzerland which I brought back to Japan to comply to Fujimura's lover's

— 85 —

request and visited the businessman of their designation and got payment in cash. That's all and nothing more.]

It was a good chance for Show Taro to trace the flow of the routing of the paintings.

Show Taro [Won't you take me to the place where you received the paintings?]

Goggling her large eyes, she looked up at the sky and replied showing such expression as if she came to hit upon some good idea.

Kitsuregawa [If that's all what you want me to do for you, okay, I will cooperate. But in return to my cooperation, I expect you to escort me in full time. This is my condition to take up this deal.]

She smiled pleasantly and grasped the bill for the dinner.

Kitsuregawa [This dinner is mine. Instead, won't you drive me back home? Can you drop me on your way home?]

He thought she might be such a type of person who wants to seize the initiative over any person of her association. When he parked her flaring red colored car in the underground parking area of her condominium she offered him tea at her living quarter. That condominium is a pretty new building and the security measures seemed well provided as shown by the system that a key is needed to enter into the building from the parking area. The mail posts for residents were equipped at the side of the marbled hall. The interior in the mediterranian fashion was providing the residents a superb hospitability. Coming through the entrance door of her quarter, taking highheels off she hokily staggered and leaned towards him. Show Taro wondered this might be the reason why she was called nine-tailed fox. Shown by her, he sat on the couch and the scene of night time Tokyo Bay jumped into his eye sight.

Show Taro, sinking into the white leather couch, noticed a painting of flowers of approximately size F20 showing vivid flower colors under the shadowy light of the downlight. Next to the painting, an about 25cm tall brown color vase of Royal Doulton stoneware of Lambeth Kiln which is now closed was placed in which about five white Casa Blanca lilies and some pale color small flowers were put together. It seemed she was decorating those flowers to refresh herself. On the side board, well polished small size silverwares were put in a casual way. A few of silver made figurines of wild game called gibier in Europe were mixed in those figurines.

One thing noted was the place lacked the lived in feeling of the atmosphere that should tell her every day life being spent there. One of the reasons may have been that she might not have much chance to dine there as her business might be making it necessary for her to eat out. Talking about goods for everyday life, one big scrap book like a teacher's mark-book containing cut-out pieces of dress fabric or the like was thrown on the table.

Those scrapped fabrics were of old and casual patterns which were similar to those common peoples' wears like the ones that many people at many places in Japan were wearing and walking on the streets in the old times. He wondered if she might be thinking about reviving these old and almost forgotten patterns into her merchandise.

The lamp shade from which shade a pale beige color light was shining was placed on the wooden side desk.

There on the same desk, a magnifying glass with a well polished lense was casually placed. He felt this was a thing that was to early for her to need.

Then, having made coffee, Akemi Kitsuregawa brought it there.

Show Taro [Nice room.]

Kitsuregawa [I have been living here alone for a long time. I have no one to live together since I lost my mother four years ago.]

Show Taro [I see. That's why I do not feel much feeling of everyday life here.]

While he was looking around in this room sinking into the Cassino couch of Italy, he already noticed there were few small goods which had the life feeling. He then understood the reason.

Kitsuregawa [By the way, how many sugar cubes?]

Show Taro [Please give me straight.]

She tried to serve black coffee to him but carelessly split coffee on Show

Taro's knees stumbling at something.

Show Taro [Ouch!]

Kitsuregawa [Oh, I'm sorry.]

She hurriedly wiped his pants with a dish cloth.

Kitsuregawa [Why don't you dry it taking it off.]

Show Taro [Well, but..]

Kitsuregawa [No one is here, so don't care.]

From the conclusion first, they agreed to dry his pants. When he was hunging the pants on the backrest of the couch, he felt her white hand wrapped from the side of his back to his waist.

Kitsuregawa [Please don't go home tonight⋯]

Show Taro [I guess there has been no man around here in this room all the time.]

Kitsuregawa [One of my supporters when I made myself independent establishing my own company, suddenly stopped meeting me and even refuced to take a call from me at the moment he came to learn that my mother was a Geisha. I guess probably he thought my father was a gang guessing from my mother's occupation or otherwise he might have faced his mother's objection···Isn't it a terrible story. But you are different.]

Show Taro [But, relationship of you and a president as well as owner of the new rise IT industry was rumored several years ago, wans't it?]

Kitsuregawa [When I first made a date with him, my Roadster made a spin on the motorway and the metal parts that were attached at the side of the truck caught him in the neck..That accident was screamed about in weekly magazines···but he and me were really not meant to be together. But you are different from any one that I have met till now.]

Show Taro [How am I different?]

Kitsuregawa [We were together before···so I feel.]

Show Taro [Most probably we may have been together before··· but I cannot recall it.]

Kitsuregawa [Did we pass each other somewhere?]

Show Taro [At least not this world.]

Kitsuregawa [Do you remember your previous life?]

Show Taro [Not so obviously, but perhaps we may have reincarnated many times.]

On the following morning, Show Taro was roused by the whistle of a ship. It was already after 8 o'clock. After all, he stayed overnight at her place, and he got up on the bed hearing the rattle of the frying pan with which she was cooking ham and eggs in the kitchen. On the dressing table placed next to the bed a photo of a man and a woman of the eldery ages. The woman looked like the mother of Akemi Kitsuregawa who used to be a Geisha. Contour of her face looks was identical to Akemi. She also had the man's eyes in the photo so Show Taro reckoned he was her father but he also thought he might have met this man somewhere before. He tried to remember who he was but failed.

He recalled she was saying her father stopped visiting her after her mother passed away.

Akemi [Good morning. Time to wake up.]

Show Taro [Good morning.]

Akemi [Are ham and eggs and salad okay with you?]

Show Taro [Thank you. This smell makes my hungry···]

After washing the face, he sat at the table when a glass of orange juice was served first.

Akemi [Which do you like, coffee or tea?]

Show Taro [Straight tea for this morning···can I take that Darjeeling?]

Akemi [What about a slice of lemon in it?]

Show Taro [No, thanks. No sugar either.]

Despite the fact that they met yesterday for the first time, such morning as if they had been spending mornings of many years together was starting. On a completely plain white plate, butter which was pasted thickly on sliced white bread was shining. Rays of morning sunshine were so amply filling that living room facing the canal, so inside of the room was dazzlingly bright. After the breakfast she sent him to a station nearby driving her car. This time the car she drove was a different car of pastel color from the car she used yesterday. She explained to him she had to try to be sensitive to the fashion trend which was apparently including cars she owned.

The sun of this morning was yellower than usual.

8. Café Sforza

Obtaining the ticket at the travel agency that Robert of them Insurance Company designated, Show Taro waited for Akemi in Switzerland where she was supposed to join him. It seemed she was always discentralizing part of the profit she gained in Japan to Europe and America.

Meeting up with her, they strolled on the side street off the main road, more precisely saying they wandered around to no destination.

In the show window of the first shop they visited together, a polished-up set of silverware was exhibited together with a Meissen full dinner set. Plates of Meissen had a thick 24 karat gold hemming. A simple design but nice and not too showy, however the full set for the use of twelve people is just unnecessarily too big for the present day's Japanese life. Due to the increased number of neuclear family Japanese families have less opportunity to receive guests at home so that even a half dozen set is oftentimes too many to handle. They do find the set nice but do not have a reason to purchase it. The shop clerks seem to be aware of this situation in Japan.

The next shop they visited was a gallery where comparably wide range of paintings of the 19th century to the first half of the 20th century were shown. On the entrance wall of the shop an old grandfather's clock was leisurely swaying its pendulum. Next to the clock, several sticks were exhibited. A stick with grip of ball shape silver, or of dog or horse head shape ivory were there and such as

— 92 —

the one in the grip in which a watch or some pieces of ciger were stored was shown. The store looked like for male customers, and in addition to the above, there exhibited art deco enamel pipes which must have been used by the chic gentlemen in the past age.

People who used to be the owners of such sticks may have been out to Paris and enjoyed visits to Moulin Rouge. Those antiques are the ones that are showing the life style of the owners, but in these days smoking population is getting less so such instruments are also getting to be the relic of the past.

The next shop they floated in was decorated with a painting of Jesus Christ in the medieval era was crucified on a cross. This shop seemed to be specialized in handling religious goods of the medieval era and maybe for this reason the lighting in the shop was surpressed down in comparison to the lighting of other shops. The lightness of this shop was producing the world of candles instead of electrical light. Shops of this sort present some hesitation of the common sightseeing visitors to casually step in.

Show Taro spent the whole day that day leisurely taking Akemi around, and in half way it became already early afternoon. When they found a tea parlour nearby the end of the business streets, she spoke out that she wished to take a rest at that tea parlour. They entered the parlour and conversed picking some sandwiches.

Akemi [It was this place where the businessman who had a relationship with the lover of Fujimura handed me the painting.]

Show Taro [But as I see this place, this shop seems in no way related to Passo Romano.]

Akemi [This shop's name, Sforza sounds like Italian, doesn't

— 93 —

it.]

Show Taro [I checked it on the telephone book just then, but did not find Passo Romano.]

Akemi [Can it be a different profession?]

Show Taro [I did check the word by the telephone book pages of alphabet order but no result. It may have not been registered, or may belong to different streets…]

Having taken the last piece of sandwitch, she said in an interested look.

Akemi [Let's go out now. By the way, where is your hotel? Show me there for my information.]

Show Taro [Okay, but what for?]

Akemi [I am just curious. What kind of room would it be for a single man staying on his single travel?]

Show Taro [Alright, shall we go now?]

After walking about thirty minutes, they arrived at his hotel. Before he named his name, the room key of his room was handed over to him.

Front cleark [You got a letter.]

Show Taro [Thank you.]

Akemi, hearing this conversation, showed a wondering look.

Akemi [Who are you after all?]

Show Taro [Who? I am Hayashi.]

She said raising her voice.

Akemi [You're lying, that letter is addressed to Tom, isn't it? I glanced the name!]

Show Taro [Don't be so upset …In America, too, Taro in the long-ago stories of Japan is translated as Tom, isn't it?]

That word was just his quick cover-up but looked to have somewhat worked.

They then came into the room and again he was exposed to a storm of her questions. Honestly, this suite called apartman was too broad for a mere antique dealer to stay. Coming in opening the door, what caught her eyes was an extra high ceiling of almost four meters high and the ceiling which was raised up by plaster was painted in sky blue where an angel was scattering roses and in the center of it Bohemian cut crystal chandellia was hunging. Looking at all these, Akemi came to feel that something was strange about all this. On the fireplace in the salon, two Aquilaria Aloe wood jars were placed and between those two jars, with whitish enamel coated metal fittings of about 25cm high, there was a clock in solid gold color swinging its pendulum.

On the side of the wall, there was a commode with drawers in the shape of round front middle of which was making a curve and sticking out. On the middle part of the commode a pottery of about 40cm high of Bavaria (South Germany) made was placed which was filled with flowers. A welcome champagne bottle was ready there together with six glasses.

Akemi   [Oh, this place is getting to look more or more dodgy. What for do you have to stay at a suite for your single trip alone? You must be taking a woman secretly.]

Having said so, she suddently opened the closet and looked around but she failed to find any women's wear there. What was there was only the luggages of Show Taro. She then went into the bedroom and finding there a canopy bed she stepped up to the bed side night table and pulled out the drawer opened rather wildly. In the drawer only what she could find was a bible and nothing else. Having finished all this searching work, Akemi seemed to be getting a little calm. In order to soothe her excitement, Show

Taro tried to speak to her in a cheerful voice.

Show Taro [I asked my friend travel agency who gave me this room perhaps in return for what I did for him in past. Do you now understand and accept the reason somehow? It may have been my fault to talk about you too much so they became too attentive.]

As it may be no wonder to cause Akemi's suspition, the bed there was decorated with walnut-made head board and footboard on both of which alto-relievo of grapes and squirrels was added and other than that, the top of the commonde was furnished with marble stone. It looked like of the 19th century. The wardrobe was also decorated with the sculpture on walnut wood beautifully embossed to show grapes and squirrels.

Taking his jacket which was hung in that wardrobe, they ended up to go out to a restaurant with him escorting Akemi. In that letter envelope that he received at the front desk, there was a key of a rent-a-car showing Robert's adroitness to make arrangements for Show Taro's drive to Milan on the following day. Robert is too smart, Show Taro thought⋯

For Milan, Show Taro and Akemi started on the following morning and drove down to the south. Coming down from Alps where it was rather cool, the weather improved quite much in Milan. Leaving Akemi there who was planning to visit her fashion-related contacts there, he drove to Florence ahead of her. He was intending to visit a dealer of his contact there to gather information as he was concerned about the backside of 「The Man with the Golden Helmet」. Of course, he would not miss visiting antique shops without appointment in a couple of the countryside towns. He knew chance to find any good antiques amongst junks was few but he wished to do this practice to comvince himself.

On arrival at Florence, he went to the hotel which he had reserved and found the room was again a suite and he was getting to feel it was somehow too good for him to get relaxed. After he woke up on the following morning, he walked alongside River Arno and visited the store of Antonio Scicolone who was his long associating antique dealer. Antonio was a rather big and gayful Italian. He was the second-generation runner of that store. When he became 40 years old, he found he was no longer young enough to continue his career as a fighter rider, so he quitted the fighter pilot and came back home and took over the family business. He owned not only the store on the ground which was facing the street but the basement underneath it. He was also borrowing space worth the size of three houses which could be used as his warehouse or working space. Needless to say, he was doing the work in the space which could not be seen from outside street and never put valuable antiques in places where casual visitors could have an access to.

His behaviors looked like showing the wariness and cautiousness of Italians whose country had been divided and ruled by other countries from the 5th century down to the 19th century.

Show Taro [Giorno!]

Antonio [Giorno! Did you arrive here from Tokyo yesterday? This meeting is since after two years, isn't it? How is your father? How long are you staying here this time?]

This ex-pilot Antonio firing quick questions at Show Taro, embraced his shoulder.

Show Taro [I'm planning to stay for three days this time to do some investigating work.]

He whispered his answer into Antonio's ear.

Antonio [What the hell do you investigate?]

He steped one step back and looked Show Taro at his face.

Show Taro [If I remember it correctly, you were restoring anything and everything in the warehouse at the backyard. I wish you to show there to me.]

Antonio [Come and follow me. I will let you have a look. What do you want to see?]

He talked in the tone of 'let me worry about it'.

Show Taro [I thought you were having some underworkers make the frames to stretch cambas on.]

Antonio [Oh, if that is what you are looking for, I have one that was completed today. I will take it here.]

Show Taro [You will take it where?]

Antonio [Here, I mean.]

Antonio showed Show Taro only the frame which was set against the other side of the desk. Show Taro, taking the photograph from his bag and started to compare the frame with the one in the photo. Needless to say, it was an enlarged photo of the backside of the 『The Man with the Golden Helmet』 which was photographed at the office of Suzuki.

Show Taro [Yes, it is alike.]

Antonio [You think so? Are you saying my work is a maestro's work?]

— 98 —

He said it in the boastful sound. Then Show Taro took out the other piece of evidence from his bag.

Show Taro [Do you know what it is, Antonio? A napkin of Passo Romano.]

Antonio quickly looked around to confirm no family members of his or shop assistants were around and replied in a low voice.

Antonio [I do know it but don't wish to tell you.]

Show Taro [I won't tell anybody so please.]

Antonio [Well, never mind. After the lunch time break, I am taking this frame so you can come with me, but I expect you to do Salute Romano. We, people who had robbed by Mafia must hang tight.]

Saying so, Antonio rose to his feet, and straightening his back, holding his arm up diagonally to the right directon with his righthand palm facing downwards.

Antonio [Ave Roma! Ave Caesar!] (Glory to Rome! Caesar Live!)

Show Taro [That is Ecclesiastical Latin, isn't it.]

Antonio [In the ancient Latin it of course is Caesar. In republicanism, when a commander who had been back from a war front made a triumphal march, he should have been received with a call of Ave imperatore! After Caesar came on stage of history, the call changed to Ave Caesar. Now is Ave Italia! Ave Republican Rome! can well be used but if we revive and use the word which means the territory of Rome, people will call us too aggressive. So, when there is no outsider, our satulation is Ave Rome! without question.]

Show Taro [In English it is a Roman salute. With Nazi, Deutscher Gruss.]

Antonio held Show Taro round the shoulders and said in a didactic tone. Show Taro felt Antonio was getting worked up as a sticker as the proud survivor of the Roman Troops.

Antonio [Hitler just mimicked Roman salute. He changed the name only. Look, there are such ones who copied the great Roman Troops, but mind you, copies are copies.]

Just after 4 o'clock in the afternoon, they left Antonio's office. Italians take lunch break till around 5 o'clock, so it meant that they left though it was a bit too early. Antonio and Show Taro took about ten-minute walk and Antonio took him into one coffee shop. It seemed Antonio intended to kill some time there. Sitting down they ordered café late. After a while the order was served when the café spilled off Show Taro's cup a little on the saucer. Show Taro took up the napkin placed on the table and lighly wiped the saucer and the bottom of the cup and noticed that the name of the coffee shop was the same Sforza as he had seen in Switzerland.

Show Taro [There was in Zurich the same name café.]

Antonio [Oh, My, you did know it already.]

Show Taro [What do you mean?]

At this question, Antonio started to explain, rolling his eyes.

Antonio [I mean the owner of this shop is Romano Sforza, the jazz pianist. Now, it is about time so let's go downstairs.]

Show Taro [Does this building have a basement floor?]

Antonio [Yes, a hall for chartering.]

The two stepped down the stairs. There in the basement hall, an

— 100 —

old man of the age of about 70 was playing jazz.

Romano   [I guess every one is here, so let's start.]

He then conversed with Antonio in Italian and handed two pieces of paper to a young man.

After a few minutes, every one there stood up. Antonio gestured to Show Taro to stand up, too.

Everyone   [Ave Roma!]

Show Taro could somehow be in time to join the Roman salute though his action was one breath too late.

Antonio   [Let me introduce this man. He is Show Taro from Japan, and he is the great pianist Romano.]

In this way, Antonio introduced the two men to each other. The party continued about thirty munites picking simple finger food. Antonio casually showed a paper napkin which was there on the table. Though the room was dim, the word Passo Romano could be read. When the party was over, on the way back the two talked.

Show Taro   [So the canvas flame of the picture in Tokyo is the masterpiece of Antonio.]

Antonio was pleased to hear Show Taro's words and knocked his chest.

Antonio   [I made two of that. Don't you think I am a maestro?]

Show Taro   [Another piece is in Chicago, now.]

Hearing this, he dubiously asked

Antonio   [Why do you know that?]

Show Taro   [Inspector of an English insurance company came to me. By the way, where is the original one?]

Antonio   [My job is to process old wood pieces of desolved folk houses or roof materials of old fallen castles. I receive

— 101 —

the order at that place and create one frame, or two once in a while, to the given size specifications. Somebody just stretches canvas on it. No painter exists here. I have never seen any completed painting in the frame I made. By the way, Romano was saying he was planning to go out from here day after tomorrow.]

Show Taro [To where is the canvas taken?]

To this question of Show Taro, no answer came back from Antonio. They kept walking in silence.

Antonio [Now, we arrived your hotel.]

Show Taro [This time is not this one. That one is my hotel.]

Antonio [That one's number of stars is different from this one. Are you making some handsome profit?]

Antonio looked at Show Taro in his face in a surprised look in front of the two-star hotel where Show Taro had usually stayed.

Just then, from that five-star hotel, Akemi Kitsuregawa noticed them and was coming out waving her hand.

Antonio [Before I become a disturbance, I will go away, Ciao!]

Antonio who started to be suddenly half smiling, showed a convinced face winking.

Show Taro [Ciao!]

Departing with Antonio, he explained to Akemi that he had to shorten the two night stay there to one.

She agreed to this change of the schedule as she too received some orders, but she insisted him to take her together with him this time. It was his turn to accept her request. In that evening a phone call from Robert came to the room of the hotel.

— 102 —

Robert   [Tom, For what reason do you turn head over heels to Switzerland. Exlain please.]

He asked in a business-like tone.

Show Taro [Owner of Café Sfolza in Switzerland and that in Florence are the same Romano Sfolza and the name of the undergaround club is Passo Romano.]

Robert seemed to be much surprised at this information and changing the hand of gripping the receiver, seemed to start taking memo by his right hand.

Robert   [What is going on there?]

Show Taro [In Florence, only the order of canvas for copying purposes is being processed. On the day after tomorrow, Romano Sfolza looks like to leave here for Switzerland, so I'm going to stretch a net.]

Robert   [Do you have a photo of Romano?]

Show Taro [We took a commemorative photo today, so you can take a look at it. As he is a superb Jazz pianist.]

Robert   [I think I can match my schedule with you so on the day after tomorrow, I will join you there.]

Show Taro [Got it.]

Robert   [I will stay at the same hotel as yours, is it okay?]

Show Taro [Make it two rooms.]

Robert said in a little sour tone.

Robert   [You missed to escape from the witchcraft of fox.]

Show Taro [None of your business.]

Robert   [Leave the booking of rooms to me. I will book the room under the name of Tom Boe. Bye.]

Show Taro felt that he had been involved in a situation which

— 103 —

was never like happy go lucky, but the fight money given to him seemed good enough at least. He can spend the whole day tomorrow with Akemi playing around.

All expenses can be paid by the card given to him so there was no worry about this point.

9. Holiday in Florence

On the following day, they strolled about in the streets of Florence. These streets were formed up by sightseeing industries and industries in relation with art business. These industries were standing up alright supported by those wealthy visitors coming from all over the world who were visiting antique shops in addition to their visits to art galleries. On his visit to Frorenze this time, as he is accompanied with Akemi, he chose to visit the showing of a collection of Baroque Pearls of 16th century to 17th at Galleria Palatina.

Pearls in that era were ones that were harvested before Kokichi Mikimoto succeeded in cultivation of pearls so that those pearls do not have the pearl nuclei inside the pearls as same as Baroque Pearls in the contemporary age. In other words, those pearls do not show on X-ray film such nuclei made from the shaved shell fragment of round shape shells. This type of pearls is called Baroque pearls. Concluding, of the pearls that are called Keshi pearls, large size Keshi pearls were selected and transported via Arabian Sea in that era. Such pearls were then sealed into designed jeweries by the hands of maestros in Florence who assumed such misshapen pearls as the figures of sheep or gods in the mythology

In the age of ancient Rome, Baroque pearls seem to have been imported. At that age, Roman generals used to take a few of Baroque pearls in a leather-made bag with them to the war front when they were appointed as commanders of prolonging wars. Foods for the use of the corps that could cover the first three

— 105 —

months of the expediton for the war were prepared and reserved by the corps but the insufficient part of the food preparation was covered by the commander's private capacity. As compensation, out of the booty of the war, half was donated to the senate for restration to the government and the other half became the general' s possession of which further half of it was shared as an Imperial award between the officers whom the general took with him to the war front from Rome and also the mobilized Roman corp.

Each of the Baroque pearls that the general took to the war front was worth paying for the food for about 5,500 warriers which makes one corps so that Baroque pearls were most probably the highest value currency at that age. Thus, the triumph general using the Baroque pearls was called as Imperator and the Roman corps must have marched carrying the booty amidst loud acculamations of the crowd. And that came to create the meaning of imperatore as decorating with pearls…so Show Taro explained to Akemi.

Florence is a town located on the basin in the center of Toscana, where River Arno is running right down the middle. In the Building of Gallerina Palatina the Royal Palace was temporally placed after the unification of Italy, and it was functioning as capital of Italy for some time till when Rome was made the capital of Italy. Reflecting this history, on the streets besides the building, antique shops and repairing work shops of those antique shops are still quietly in operation. As these shops do not deal with spot-buying sight seeing visitors, when lots of Japanese visited those shops at the peak time of bubbles economy in and around 1990, those sightseers were totally ignored there. As evidence of this fact, no big collecter of Italian antiques of middle to modern ages exists in Japan. It could be taken for granted as hautiness of overnight millionairs from Japan would no way be able to be accepted by those proud Italian antique dealers.

In this area where workshops of antique dealers were densely crowded, wardrobes which were more than 2.7m tall so they could no way fit to any Japanese houses were dismantled and fully restored there, or doors of old palazzetto (mini-palaces) were being renovated, so that this area was a quite interesting area to visit, but they refrained from visiting this area as it was possible that they might see some acquainted faces so they gave up visiting there and chose to return to the old city area crossing the bridge, Ponte Vecchio (meaning Old Bridge).

The prehistory of this Old Bridge as it is so called was in the old ages there were many shops open on this bridge and the passers through the bridge were charged a toll and it still retained the traces of such scene. Even in the modern age, demonstration sales are going on there of goldsmith making jewelries. This techonology of neatly attaching grains of gold onto a golden base so that it can gain more complicated reflection of light is the one that has been inherited from maestros to apprentices for generations which is unable to be copied by craftsmen of any other countries. Also, the so-to-called 18 karat in Japan is mainly using gold mixture of plural number of metals or gold mixed with copper so it is called red gold, but in Italy, they use more silver to mix with gold and as a result their gold of this rank looks more yellow than red, threrefore their K18 equivalent gold is called blue gold in such an area as Okachimachi which is a jewelry town in Tokyo. However, as regards necklace chains made in Japan, those of the middle color shade called Chuwari (even mixture percentage) so that these can match necklace heads made either in Europe or in Japan.

As regards leathergoods, there are a fair number of stores which are equipped with own workshops. Among those, quite a few are manufacturing as subcontractors of brand-name goods which are wellknown brands in Japan as well. Such shops tell the reason why they work as subcontractors is because they are avoiding the risk of the case of failing to procure the good quality leather to continuously produce a commercially paying quantity using their own brand name, so that if such stable procurement of material leather which quality meets their satisfaction is not possible, they would rather prefer to lessen the risk and take spot orders from others. Show Taro took Akemi to one of such shops.

Show Taro [Come and take a look at it.]

What he showed her was an open side of the long wallet made of crocodile. He showed her the inside of the folded part and pointed out that that part was covered by another piece of leather in addition to the crocodile leather used on the surface of the wallet.

Akemi [Neatly sewn on, isn't it.]

Show Taro [Such quality technique has been precisely inherited in the apprentice system.]

Akemi [Why doesn't this shop's brand land in Japan?]

Show Taro [Suppose they receive an order of 1,000 pieces for delivery by next month for example, they come to be obliged to procure good quality leather material in time for such delivery date. They don't want to take that much risk.]

Akemi [Will they supply Kyubi?]

Show Taro [It wouldn't be impossible, but I think it would be safer just to purchase what is now available in their stock for a small quality such as 100 or so.]

Akemi [You are right to say that as it is difficult to ascertain the delivery date with business with Italians.]

Show Taro [A wholesaler of shoes whom I know was saying he had to face a three month delay of delivery of high heels of his order. He of course complained but the answer from the Italian manufacturer was that reason of delay was due to unavailability of leather that meets his quality standard, which sounds reasonable. Even in Japan, if you place an order with a craftman of traditional craftwork, it can happen that you can only receive it after you have forgotten what you ordered. This means if you deal with natural materials and wish to burn in or engrave your name on it can never be completed to your request if you allow too narrow a time for production.]

Akemi [Do you know any specific example that actually took place in past?]

Show Taro [If I raise an example,⋯a craftman manufacturing fountain pens to an ordered production at a workshop in Wajima. The orderer decides on the theme, for example, Tale of Genji , so the craftman produces several sketches. Then, of those sketches one is chosen and half of the contracted amount of money in cash is given to the craftman for the completion of products in half to one year lead time, then when the lead time exired and the merchandise is completed, then the balance of the payment and the actually finished merchandise are exchanged between the craftman and the buyer. What has happened is that ordinary Japanese have forgotten this way of transaction. In the old days, this style of deal was just fair and common transaction system. Too much industrialization has this common sense lost.]

Akemi [Anyway at this moment, I will take it.]

Akemi paid for the long wallet which she was holding in her hand.

That evening, they fully enjoyed the beautiful seafood dinner tasting the grilled scampi fresh from the sea. As Italy is surrounded by the sea at the three sides of it, that place had much ample and various seafood. Scampi with garlic makes people happy and wine helps them relax. After dinner they took a walk around the town area browsing souvenir shops which were selling local souvenirs and when they were passing near by café Sfolza, Show Taro took a sight of Romano Sfolza whom he had met on the previous day, but he and his group did not notice Show Taro at all and were gone elsewhere.

Show Taro [That old man who just popped into the car is Romano Sfoltza.]

Akemi [He is a juzz pianist, isn't he?]

It was a surprise to Show Taro that Akemi's reply came to him in a flash while he was about to proudly explain what Romano Sfoltza was.

— 110 —

Show Taro [You know him, do you?]

Akemi [His daughter Barbara is fond of Kyubi brand. I understand she suggested her friend in movie related business to use my brand in the movie scenes as stage props. She is familiar with this field of business as her mother is a sister of a world-famous movie actress.]

Reacting what she said, this time his eyes became shining.

Show Taro [Have you ever met her?]

Akemi [No···but I know her by face.]

Show Taro [How did you come to know her by face?]

Akemi [Don't you know she is the party leader and the assemblywoman of the political party called Alliance of Conservatives and Reformists.]

Show Taro [Hm. Then tell me who recommended Kyubi Brand to her.]

Akemi [I may introduce you to the person someday.]

Akemi surpressed her smile in a little misterious way.

Show Taro [I feel something dubious.]

Akemi [More misteries are more fun.]

Then they dropped into the hotel bar and Show Taro ordered Margarita. Akemi made fun of him for his order of Margarita.

Show Taro [Do you know in Latin, pearls are called Margarita.]

Seeing Show Taro who got tipsy already with wine, Akemi said:

Akemi [you are a very light drinker, aren't you.]

In fact, it must be Akemi that have a higher tolerance to alcochol.

Show Taro [Let's toast to pearls for the fact that the Roman generals were taking pearls around. And even Caesar got weak so he started to collect emerald of Egypt as

— 111 —

amulet of rejuvenation.]

Akemi   [Does that mean Cleopatra was stronger?]

Akemi smiling radiantly asked.

Show Taro [Yes, at least at night.]

She continued to ask questions. She looked to be wondering quite much about him.

Akemi   [Your room is too gourgeous while you don't look like earning that much to afford such a room. I hope you won't receive Cleopatra rolled by carpet by room service.]

Show Taro [If you are in doubt, why not stay overnight with me.]

Akemi   [Let me see.]

Show Taro [So you don't trust my power.]

Akemi   [I will leave you here for today. When do you plan to come to take me out tomorrow?]

Show Taro [Okay, then half past nine.]

Akemi   [Good night.]

Show Taro [Ciao!]

Akemi went back to her room, while Show Taro was wondering about a newly coming up question of who was the person that introduced the Kyubi brands for use as props. Akemi's human network was bizzarre and complex, too, and she seemed not simply a woman of sole proprietor of her business with an uncommon ability. On the way back to his room, he kept thinking who that could be.

10. Café Sfolza Again

Riding on a rent-a-car, they finished checking-in in the late afternoon. Room there this time was a connecting suite which connects her room and his. View out of the windows of his suite was just so-so, but as the base of watching it was ideal as it is not far from Café Sfolza.

On the following morning, Akemi went out of the hotel telling him she had something to do. Show Taro guessed she must be visiting a bank. As their stay was prolonged for a few additional days, she might need some more fund or might have to give instructions to her workers. In this regard, antique dealing business is rather easy. If needed he can change the schedule without caring about others.

In the morning of that day, some one knocked his door. Opening the door he found Robert there which was a re-encounter with him after quite a while.

Show Taro [What's happening? Did you arrive from London this morning?]

Robert started to talk abruptly.

Robert [Yes, something like that, but I tell you you had better not go to Sfolza.]

Show Taro asked back showing he was a bit shocked at such unexpected words of Robert.

Show Taro [Why you say that, suddenly.]

— 113 —

Robert gazed at him in the gesture to get Show Taro's more attention.

Robert   [Romano Sfolza being the Italian right wing related person, at the place where fakes are created, the original painting shall no longer exist. What I wish to say is, in order to trace the route of the painting, it is not wise for you to stay here as your face has been known by them. I will go instead of you.]

Show Taro [Do you need a photo of him?]

Robert   [No, I don't. His face is openly known in the public as a jazz pianist.]

Show Taro could not fully understand what Robert's words mean.

Show Taro [Tell me how that relates to danger.]

Robert toned down his voice a little bit, but spoke slowly and in a persuading tone.

Robert   [Yesterday, the body of Gabriel, the antique dealer in Chicago, was found.]

Show Taro felt the blood draining from his face.

Show Taro [Where?]

Robert   [In Australia. His full name is Gabriel Capone. Did you know what this means? Uncle of his grandfather is Alfonzo Capone known in Japan as 'A-Ru Ka-Po-Ne, the leader of the gang.]

Hearing so far and having felt he did understand the situation, Show Taro murmured.

Show Taro [So, as a Mafia, he and they must have had bad chemistry.]

Robert   [One mistery is the way of his death. He died a death which did not look like the result of being tortured by fascists in their usual simple way of torturing.]

Show Taro [What you are trying to say is that that murder was not by Italians. Am I correctly understanding you?]

Robert   [There is a possibility that Neo Nazi is involved from here ahead.]

For Show Taro who already came too far, there was no going back then.

Show Taro [As long as the contract stands, don't let me give up the chase for 「Tha Man with the Golden Helmet」. I declare I have no interest in such political association.]

In a tone stronger than before, Robert told Show Taro what had happened more clearly.

Robert   [Concluding, my partner will go to Sfolza today, so you, you don't go if you don't wish to die with your blood sucked like what happened to Gabriel.]

Show Taro [Is this the second brew of tea of the Count Dracula Insident?]

Robert   [Who knows, but blood was extracted in gallons.]

Show Taro [Wouldn't it have been the work of a beauty Dracula leaving a love bite on his neck? Like it was actually a case of sweet death on the beauty.]

Show Taro said making a bit fun of it, but Robert's eyes were serious. He shook his head in disapproval.

Robert   [No, no, I heard he had his blood extracted by a syringe.]

— 115 —

Even Show Taro could not find a way to get well along with the blood sacking forces, so he chose to make a counter offer.

Show Taro [OK. I did understand, so tell me at least the distribution channel of the painting. Remember I too have my own reason. I still want the fight money of £ 50,000.]

Robert [You're rest assured to get the money. And this is the hotel I am staying.]

Robert went away leaving the memo. After a while Show Taro went to the front desk to get that morning paper in English and German and reviewed them but failed to find any news about Dracula or murder of an American. It could happen that the local news of the neighboring country was not listed on this country's papers. Show Taro wondered whether Robert came to learn that news on cable television or he arrived from Austria this morning. Just to make sure to follow this matter up, he kept putting the news program of cable TV on for half an hour but failed to get any such news. He therefore thought Robert might possibly have come somewhere from Austria.

In any case, that he did not have to go to Café Sfolza meant he had to kill time at the hotel. But a little after 4 o'clock he heard some sounds in the adjoing room so he became aware of Akemi's return. Therefore, he got up and went to visit her room and found her there to his expectation.

Show Taro [Welcome home.]

Showing somewhat surprised look, Akemi came out. She had been thinking that Show Taro would naturally be at Café Sfolza so she asked him abruptly.

Akemi   [Oh, Show, Don't you have to play a role of a watchdog at the café?]

Show Taro [My friend is doing it so today is a holiday to me.]

  Speaking in a bit purring voice, she took Show Taro's arm.

Akemi   [Show, I have a person to whom I wish you to meet. Will you come with me?]

Show Taro [When shall we go?]

Akemi   [What about after half an hour?]

Show Taro [Done.]

  So they were to go out, but the place where Show Taro was taken was Café Sfolza where Robert told him not to go. Though he felt hesitant, there was no way for him to make an escape in the flow of the development of the situation. They then sat and were taking café late there when a few more than ten men came out from the inside of the café. Among these men there was an old man who looked like a Japanese. Akemi looked to know him and took him to their table and introduced him to Show Taro.

Akemi   [This is Show Taro-san, and this is my father, Ryosuke Kato.]

Show Taro [How do you do.]

  According to the business card Show Taro got in exchange of his to her father, he learnt that Mr. Kato was the chairman of board of Midori Manji, a major blood products manufacturing company called Midori Manji and also was the chairman of Euro Midori Manji then. He was already half retired in Japan making room for younger work force. He said his business was his hobbies then and that he was survicing this company as the last period of time survice in his life.

At start, Midori Manji was a name of troops which was led by Army Sergeon, Lieunant General Ishii. This army was called Army 731 which was in action in Manchuria in WW2. Ryoichi Kato who was professionally involved in preparing strategies against America at Army 731 later made himself independent and formed his company naming it after the name of the troops. As Army 731 was disguising its activities with the name of Midori Manji as processors to practice water treatment to remove polluted water or bacteria. Researches which were being done there in truth was those of human blood. For example, such researches as to study how the blood component would change according to different races or different living environments, or else, where in the blood the bacteria attacking system was hidden……would it be possible to determine the character of a human judging from the character of the blood… Those researchers were given chances to analyze various conditions from various angles. These chances were provided researchers who in normal times were havitants in the Ivory Tower and could talk only about theories with the most desirable research materials.

Materials for such experiements were the enemy's spies who were being caught every day. Reason why spies were used was simple.

According to the international law of war as specified by Hague Conventions of 1899 and 1907, an immediate execution was authorized against spies who did not wear the military uniforms. What's worse was in case spies were infiltlated into the common people, the waring nations were deemed to have the right to execute the whole group of people that included spies in it. By such thoughtless and impulsive rulers ignoring the existance of such international law of war, spies in civilian's clothes were sent out under the name of civilian clothed soldiers which consequently led to the instance of innocent civilians having been executed and derived the innocent citizens of their lives. During WW2, Stalin broadcast on radio stating [fascists are not human beings, therefore they are not to be treated as human beings.] Reacting this announcement of Stalin, Nazis retorted on the following day stating [As long as Soviet dare to ignore Hague Conventions, we Germany will not treat captured Soviet soldiers as the prisoners of war.] Because of ignorance of the ruler, the bill of their ignorance is always to be paid by innocent common people. Those, who are staying where no bullet is reaching them, they can complete everything on their writing desk. This is the same situation as statesmen of high educational background being utterly unable to understand the hardship that common citizens are undergoing in their everyday life.

The building that was the base of the activities of Army 731 was completely destroyed and the confidential documents were all burnt out in accordance with the order from the Imperial General Headquarters. The hostages were called logs and who were supposed to be used as the experiemental materials were all burnt to be killed, but this work was finished mostly in an instant as the number of hostages was much fewer than those who were housed at the extermination camp of Nazi. Soviet had been aware from the information they had already in their hand the existence of such research facilities there, but failed to obtain any information. By the time the Manchurian capital Shinkyo was fallen, all of the researchers and troops had retreated from there.

All related people were released from the dissolved armies and secretly returned to respective hometowns, when American troops in turn tried to contact those Unit 731 related people using the information they were able to acquire. However, those related peole kept shutting their mouths being afraid to be convicted as war criminals. America, therefore, tried to gain over Ryoichi Kato who was good at English. The conditions that America presented to Kato were as follows.

① The Unit 731 related members will never be procecuted as war criminals.

② The Unit 731 related members are to reveal the information that they have come to learn as result of the finished research, only to American Army.

③ The Unit 731 related members will never submit the data of Blood Capillary War (Biobacterial Warfare) to Soviet.

④ In exchange for achieving the above stated purposes, the American Government will have the Unit 731 related members funde d to fill the need of living expenses of such members.

Under such confidential agreement, a corporation which was established by people with Ryoichi Kato in the center of it was the pharmaceutical company by the name of Midori Manji. In such connection, most of those members who had been doing important part of the researches were called back with their income guaranteed. After the establishment of such company, they continued to keep the connection with the American Army. Therefore, part of the chemical preparation that were used at the

— 120 —

Vietnam war was the products of Midori Manji, but ostensibly those were delivered to Okinawa or Yokosuka through Japanese trading firms. This fact is what only the limited number of people know about.

At the Vietnam war, various weapons were used and consumed there as the place of experiments of the complex of the army and the industry among which there existed defoliant which is a notorious phermacist because of its characteristic teratogenicity. However, as same as this teratogenicity was delayed to come outside as a problem, most of the problematical charactors of other phermacists have been covered up. That the American Government could come to stock the knowledge of lethal dose of various phermacists would partly be due to the cooperation from the Unit 731 related members. Though the documents describing the results of the varous researches done by the Unit 731 were lost, the memory was remaining in the brains of the researchers and the result of the tatalization of such memories came out as a form of a corporation called Midori Manji.

The fact that medical science can exist separated from the human moral can be attributed to the reality of such part of the medical science being developing it. Suppose in the middle era no anatomy of human body had not been approved, the current level of medical science would have never reached the present standard. In line with this fact, the human experimentation also contributed to the progress of the medical science.

As Stalin failed to obtain such results of the medical researches, he must have had a sense of impending crisis about the delay of the medical science in his country, so it is rumored in the western block that he allowed researches based on human experimentation at the house of political offences, which rumor cannot easily be denied.

The elder son of Ryoichi Kato, the founder of Midori Manji, which had the afore-mentioned background story, is the present chairman of the board of Midori Manji, Ryosuke Kato. Kato was a person of average size and had somewhat whitish skin and showed an impression of a man who was all through the time confining himself in his laboratory. He looked to be of the character to analize any and every matter to the bitter end, wearing a skelton watch of Patek Philipe. Reason why he wears the gold watch was he was valuing his every second and minute to devote it into his researches. Life is short and the researches are endless.

Kato started to explain about the company he was operating. Commonly in western countries businessmen chose as a conversation topic their hobbies as it was less risky than to talk about the business they were involved in, but in Kato's case, his hobby might have been equal to his business.

Kato [Use of the company name Midori Manji does not pose any problem in Japan, but when I had my company launched in Europe in response to the request from the investor of South America, as this name may give a bad image there, I decided to use Euro Midori Manji and not to show the trade mark.]

Saying so, he completed his explanation about the genesis of the company name which is printed on his business card. In line with his explanation, the company logo was EMM in green color which was different from the logo he was using in Japan which was a green manji.

— 122 —

Show Taro [I see. I can understand how much you are exerting your consideration. Did you work on some business in Vienna today?]

Show Taro didn't overlook the printed address on his card was not Switzerland but Vienna. To this comment of Show Taro's, Kato continued to talk without changing his talking tone.

Kato [I sometimes buy paintings there through the introduction of my friend, but most of the paintings that I buy there are copies.]

Show Taro [What sort of percentage of availability of authentics?]

Kato [Maybe a couple or three. Rest of twenty or so are all fakes. But the company this friend of South America possesses has specialists to successfully reproduce even the crackings of the paints. If you can spare time when you arrive in Vienna, I will show those fakes and the technics added on them.]

Show Taro [Looking forward.]

Kato [See? That person who just stepped out is my friend I'm talking about. Let me introduce you to him.]

Kato stopped the old man who was about to be passing by.

Kato [Romano.]

Show Taro cut in in a flash and greeted to Romano Sfolza.

Show Taro [Hello again.]

Kato [My, you already know each other.]

Both Kato and Romano were surprised.

Show Taro [Yes, we met in Florence a few days ago.]

Romano [Didn't know you are Mr. Kato's friend.]

Romano suddenly showing his smiles and looked at Show Taro and Akemi.

Akemi had been in silence all the time but was a bit flushed and looked down.

Kato   [He is my daughter's friend.]

Kato was conscious of Akemi's presence there so he replied rather awkwardly.

Romano   [I am counting on you to sell those copies non stop into Japan.]

Romano knocked Show Taro's shoulder. As Antonio introduced Show Taro to Romano as an antique dealer, Romano looked to be expecting good helf from Show Taro.

Show Taro [Leave it to me.]

Romano   [When next we have a chance, I will introduce you to my daughter, though she is seldom available being too busy.]

Romano made a promise with Show Taro for him to introduce Show Taro to Barbara, the politician of the Conservative Alliance.

To such person that was on the upward wave of his power, certain level of spirits suitable for his power would normally gather, so to get acquainted with Barbara might give him a chance.

Show Taro [Looking forward.]

Romano   [I have another appointment for tonight, so please excuse me now.]

Show Taro [Ciao!]

He followed Romano with the smiling eyes.

11. Secret of Robert

The building across Café Sfolza used to be a mansion which was built by a noble in the 19th century and since renovated to function as a hotel since after WW2. It was a six-storied brick made building of which the top floor was used as a penthouse.

There were several men who bought out two rooms of this hotel and were watching the surveillance monitor among whom there was Robert. There gathered multi-national members of such language speakers as English, German, Italian, French and Japanese. In Zurich which is an international financial center, plural kinds of languages were flitting about.

Under the counter and several tables microphones were secretly attached to follow up the talks and actions of dubious charactors. In addition to the microphones, small size cameras were equipped of which one was watching egress and ingress of people into and from inside the hotel, one other watching the front and the left side of the hotel and the last one the right side. Needless to add, a man and a woman who were fortune telling with tarot cards, a man who was reading a nobel, and a man next to him spreading a sight-seeing guide map and was half asleep over it, those were all the multi language speaking investigators gathered at Europol.

In such a set up there was no chance for Robert to overlook the scene of Show Taro coming in with the guide by Akemi and seized a table around the center of the room.

Robert   [What the hell did Show Taro come here? I did stop him to come so adamantly…]

Murmuring to himself, he gazed at the monitor and listened to the voice that the microphone picked up. Then there came out some ten men from the door leading to the basement floor. As a matter of course, a man coming out of a car which had been parked on the road and the couple who had been playing tarot cards behaving very naturally started to follow them. There was a man who were carrying a large canvas under his arm who could be an artist to produce fake paintings. This man of course was followed by one of the investigators.

Needless to say, the extra large package must be a framed oil painting. This man who was carrying this package looked like an owner of a certain gallery. Unless the whole structure of their organization was clarified, termination of this organization as a whole was not possible. One possibility that had to be counted in was, if independency of each person was strong, such individuals might be separating the account and on that condition they might be forming a large combined association. If that was the case, it would come to be difficult to deem such whole association as one single criminal organization. Their action of stealing paintings was no doubt illegal, but is the production of canvases for use of fakes a crime? Such part of the flow of this kind of transaction came to be diffuclt to be ascertained as legal or illegal which is a different point from just to sell the stolen paintings directly to someone.

What so far Show Taro came to understand was the fact that Romano Sfolza was practicing the production of copies of stolen paintings systematically in a carefully considered way of showing no linkage between those copiers of the stolen authentic paintings and that part of the operational fund might have been coming from the right-wing political party to which his daughter belonged. But for Show Taro who was just an antique dealer and who had no interest in politics, as per the contract he concluded with Robert if the original painting could be got back, the promised reward of £ 50,000 could be obtained and that was all what he was concerned about.

Now that Show Taro could find out that Kato of Midori Manji was the father of Akemi and the sponsor of this deal and that reason why the small goods that Akemi was dealing with were shown in a movie was in relation with the daughter of Sfolza and the elder sister of his wife and such information was good enough for Show Taro to learn. However, though that much Show Taro came to find out by then, one thing which was not yet clarified is the transisional flow of 『The Man of the Golden Helmet』. He needed to clarify this point, as how much he came to know about such other facts, it did not come to have him get the £50,000 incentive. Though Show Taro was still not aware the true purpose of Robert's task to aim at, the every month expenses of   £5,000 had been transferred to Show Taro's account without fail.

That night, Robert came and visit Show Taro at his room just while Akemi was taking a shower in her room. Robert casually sank himself into the sofa, and spoke out with a stern looking face though in a low voice.

Robert   [Tom, why did you come to the café?]

Show Taro [I was taken there being told a person was waiting there to whom Kato wished to intoduce Akemi.]

Robert   [Who was it?]

Show Taro [Ryosuke Kato, her father and the chairman of the board of Euro Midori Manji.]

Robert [What for did he come here?]

Show Taro [He sounded like occasionally he had been buying some fakes on the social basis at Passo Romano on the basement floor.]

Robert [Why did he know that transaction was being done there?]

After thinking a few seconds, he replied.

Show Taro [He may have been introduced by the South American investor of Euro Midori Manji.]

Robert [Can you find his name out?]

Show Taro [I will try. One thing, Kato is to return to Vienna tomorrow and taking this occasion he is going to show us the office of Midori Manji and the East European factory. I wish you to make arrangement of the accommodations.]

Robert [You mean a two-room connecting suite.]

Show Taro [Of course, yes. By the way, did you come here from Austria?]

Show Taro made this question as he had since been wondering about this point and found that Robert looked like choosing words to answer.

Robert [I came from the Hague, Holland.]

Show Taro [Why did you come to learn the death of Gabriel? That was not on cable TV. Is that information with some unspecified reason?]

Show Taro tried Robert with the information he had gathered that morning, then Robert reluctantly leaked a bit of the

— 128 —

information he had gained.

Robert   [I came to learn it by the mail from our branch office in Austria. It was several weeks after contact was ceased to come from him. He was shot truth drug and at the last he was getting his blood drawn for at least one gallon.]

Show Taro [Don't you hide any more terrible kind of information?]

Robert   [What I just told you is all I know.]

Show Taro [By the way, the hotel is at the opposite side of the café, isn't it?]

Robert   [That's because we can watch it.]

Show Taro [Is the insurance company robbed of many millions of pounds?]

Robert   [Yes, many paintings.]

Show Taro [Why did you choose pounds for payment instead of Euro?]

Robert   [The painting of this time was stolen from U.K. so the insurance policy is made in pounds.]

Show Taro [If the original of this time is recovered and if my cooperation is further needed, I wish you will pay me in Eurodollars.]

Robert   [But, mind you, in such situation particularly it can happen you will have to run about in England or America.]

Show Taro [I reckon you may be right.]

Robert   [Bye.]

Show Taro [Good night.]

A few minutes after Robert left Show Taro's room, Akemi in the bathrobe came from her room adjoining to his, shining her eyes with curiocity.

Akemi [I heard a man's voice.]

Show Taro [You must be disappointed if you were expecting Cleopatra.]

Akemi [If Cleopatra, she would have been torn in pieces by me. Who was it, then?]

Show Taro [Robert the insurance man. By the way, Have you heard who is the joint venture partner of Euro Midori Manji?]

Akemi [No, nothing except that he is a business man in South America. But I wonder whether Robert is always stationed at the Hague branch of that insurance company.]

Show Taro [I understand he is moving around in Europe as his task is in charge of theft insurance.]

Akemi [Were you discussing something which you don't want to be heard by others?]

Show Taro [According to what he told me, the body of an American antique dealer was found in Austria. What's strange about it is this news cannot be confirmed by any medias such as cable TV, newspapers or internet.]

Akemi [Any other information about that?]

Show Taro [What he told me is that body was with blood extracted in gallons.]

Akemi [Can a mere insurance man get that much detailed information?]

Show Taro [I haven't heard any more details about this case, but a

— 130 —

painting worth a big amount of insurance premium has been stolen.]

Akemi [But only for that, this treatment you are receiving is too good, isn't it? Well, it's okay of course, though.]

Combing her hair, she rolled her eyes looking like she was trying to solve the riddle of the secret which Robert was holding.

Akemi [Oh, I am getting tempted to learn what kind of person Robert is.]

Show Taro [You better not. As long as he is putting the expenses in my account, he is a good customer of mine for that reason. In addition, this work that is assigned to me is a justifiable job. The contingency fee of £50,000 promised if I succeed in getting the painting back is also quite reasonably good.]

Akemi [But why had Gabriel his blood extracted? Is that because he could not keep living without you?]

Show Taro [That's a good answer. Thanks.]

Akemi [Go ahead quick and take a shower.]

Night of Zurich just started.

12. Santa Rosaria

At the Port Palermo in Sicily, the light of sunset was burning the sky in the golden color. One white yacht [Santa Rosalia] was elegantly floating on the water. On the yacht a man of the fiftieth age wearing sunglasses was lying buring the skin on the deck with a woman in bikini besides him.

The cell phone bell rang and the man put the glass of cocktail down and slowly took the phone trying rather hard to get his body up which was swallen due to too much drinking. This man was a business man by the name of Bernard Gambino. As he came to realize the profitability of the food serving business for sightseeing visitors was limited, he was waiting for the chance of recovering from setback the business which his co-worker got lost in 1996. That business is the sales of the stolen paintings which originally was an important source of collecting funds of Mafia. Bernald not only succeeded the Mafia but was feeling proud to protect the concessions of the Sichilians.

Bernard   [What?.... Did you find out who else was making a chase in Switzlernad?]

Underling   [They had identification cards issued by Europole, Don.]

Bernard   [How many did you hold?]

Underling   [Three. As they saw us in face, we will dispose them leaving one that will be our tool. Is this okay?]

— 132 —

Bernard [I think the number is a bit too many. As I will let the police to take care of them, just imprison them in the basement. They may possibly be used as a good bargaining chip.]

He hung the phone up once and meditated for a few minutes, then decided to ring Nicola Zamir who was his acquainted art dealer. This person is overstriding the wholesaling route in America since right after WW2 was over. Nicola's father was a cooperator of Mafia's landing in Sicily so that since then this route has been under the control of the Zamirs.

Bernard [I let my underlings chase the fascists for getting the painting business back to us, but there happened a problem.]

Nicola [You mean you need our help?]

Bernard [There were some other men who traced us to the hiding place of the faker. We seized them and found they were the Europole members.]

Nicola [Did you dispose them?]

Bernard [No, As Switzerland is not our base, if we disposed as many as three it would be too noticiable.]

There came silence between them for a while, and Nicola decided to straighten out their business routing back to normal.

Nicola [Okay, I got it. Let me make a negotiation. We will release those three men and tender the information of the Swiss route of the production routes of fakes of

— 133 —

the stolen paintings on the condition that the police will have no concern in our retaliation activities. In case the public people do not concern our retaliation, Europole cannot make a fuss about it.]

Bernard [At my side, our aim will be achieved if the stolen painting business route which was once annihilated when Franchesco was arrested in 1996 can be reopened.]

Nicola [By the way, are you alright not annihilating inside the country of Italy?]

Nicola getting a little concerned about this point asked Bernard, but Bernard replied after taking the tropical drink.

Bernard [Romano Sforza and his organization should have been contented with just doing the work of creating antique look canvases. Painters cannot paint without paints. If Swiss Group is gone, he will surely be back to get the work.]

Nicola [Aren't you happy-go-lucky. Are you enjoying the cool at Santa Rosalia as usual?]

Bernald [Good guessing. Wish if I could let you see the seagulls messing around here. Ciao.]

Primarily, Santa Rosalia was the name of the patron saint of Palermo. He chose this name as he was flattering himself as Don of Sicily. It was an amazing thought that he could let his people admit that he was the very guardian of them when the route that Mafia lost in 1996 was revived.

Sicily before WW2 was a land of poverty and no such large size factory as work place for the residents existed either. People had no other choice but to emigrate themselves dreaming the new life in the new world America. Those immigrants' jobs that were quickly available were port workers or dish washing work at restaurants. However, for Italians who immigrated after other nationalities into France or Holland of West Europe and Germany of Middle Europe, it was hard to get good job chances. That is one of the reasons why Italian immigrants became gangs like Al Capone during the prohibition era for example.

On the other hand, there existed Pennilessly poor social-class emigrants. They had no other choice but to stay in Sicily so there they tried to secretly operate gambling houses in such a town like Palermo or acted as procurers for sightseers and developed their organization. That was what Mafias were or in their own expression Cosa nostras were. Most of such gangs came to be thrown into the prison when Benito Mussolini came to rise up before WW2, but they cooperated with America at the time of the allied invation of Italy.

The reason why those gangs were imprisoned was for murder, gambling or prostitution, but such criminals were released under the name of political offences leading to allow them to get related to politics as the mayor or city counsel members. Benefited by such situation and circumstances, the revived mafia organization kept faithfully observing the code of silence called omerta so even the existance itself of such organization was not easily grasped.

The prime reason why the organization was taken under the sun was that the members of Mafia no way dared to tell others what they were because it meant that they were to risk the lives of their family members as well.

— 135 —

They stole art products out from charches, old castles or nobels' mansions and disposed these just in America. Among those stolen arts, many of unearthed pieces out of the ruins which did not have the formal export permit, or of stolen goods from treasure chests of churches existed. Part of the proceeds from sales was donated to the ex-president Andreotti and the politicians around him. This art smuggling route was completely destroyed in 1996, so robbers around the Sicilly area were forced to live very poorly. As a matter of course, there should have been the ways and means to earn money by gambles or prostitution but profit that could be gained by such means was far too short to fill the loss caused by the destroyal of the art smuggling route.

If this art exporting route could be revived, it could again be possible using such profit to send out into the Italian politic world the Mafia related politicians for the prime minister or the house minister positions. If they could be that much successful, they could once again put the police under their complete control. If all these could be achieved, all the Sicillian Cosa Nostra related people could not but respect Bernard as the top of the bosses. When that time would come, he could have the several of the best women at each of the night clubs there in Sicilly as his mistresses and could have his Santa Rosalia exchanged with a triple size yacht. Imagining the day when he could have his own page in the Mafia history, he smiled at seagulls and drank up the tropical drink.

13. Surberbs of Vienna

In the trees of the suburbs of Vienna, there stood a three storied manner house like small chateau look building with white walls. The roof was made of natural stones so the look was pretty plain and not much standing up. Size of the building was large probably containing thirty or more rooms. As the building was not surrounded by a canal, it seemed that this building had not been used as a defence base. At the entrance of the site, there was a gate where there was built a guard station. There the couple addressed themselves and were given two entrance badges. The guard gave one to Show Taro and the other to Akemi.

Show Taro put the badge on his chest pocket with the top part of the badge folded into the pocket and put himself back on the car and parked it in the designated position by the guard and helped Akemi to get off the car coming around the other side of the car. In Japan, such a manner could never be hit on to be done, but there, that was the common manner that had to be followed. The main building of Euro Midori Manji was not that modern type of the building but had a good and reasonable size. Proceeding to the entrance of the building, the both sides of the strand there hung the company flag showing EMM in green on the white background. There was one other flag on the opposite side but Akemi did not care about it taking it for the company flag of a visitor, but Show Taro took a glance at it which was fluttering a little then opened the door for Akemi to have her lead him.

Inside of the entrance was a space with an about four-meter high ceiling which was an European styled high ceiling ground floor but was without a stairwell. There they were received by an Asian look woman. She could well be Kato's secretary. They undersood her name was Tsuchimikado from the nameplate she was wearing.

She was a rather small woman with white skin and looked fragile.

She looked like about thirty years old and politely received them with thin voice which sounded almost weird.

They were guided by her to the bottom room in the corridor while conversing as follows.

Tsuchimikado [Welcome. Please come this way now, as the chairman is meeting another visitor at the moment.]

Show Taro [The atmosphere here is quite relaxing, isn't it.]

Tuchimikado [I understand this building used to be utilized as a detached house for the hunting exercise by a noble. In order to lessen the maintainance handlings I heard it was rented out while the noble was not using it.]

Show Taro [I like the size of the house is just good and not too big.]

Tsuchimikado [there are a lot of rooms which I have not seen as yet.]

Show Taro [There may be rooms that have a trace of spirits.]

Listening to this conversation, Akemi cut in. She wished to check and learn what relationship this secretary has with Kato.

Akemi [Excuse me. Are you a Japanese?]

Tsuchimikado [Yes, I am. My ancesters used to live in Kyoto till the Meiji era but lost their jobs in the transit of the age.]

— 138 —

Show Taro [So, you are a count noble, aren't you?]

At his question, Tsuchimikado showed a bit surprised look.

Tsuchimikado[How do you know that?]

Show Taro [I understand The Tsuchimikado family is originally the descendant of Abe-no-Seimei.]

Tsuchimikado [You know so well.]

Show Taro [All what I know is that the downfall of your ancestor which happened in the Meiji era was due to the failure of their objection scheme against the introduction of the Gregorian calendar.]

Tsuchimikado [My apologies if my question sounds rude, but is your profession something in relation with Shintoism?]

Tsuchimikado looked like trying to find some hint about something to do with him, and seemed to have felt that something.]

Show Taro [My ancestors may be of the family tree of a clan that had connection with Shrines, but my occupation is an antique dealer in Tokyo.]

Tsuchimikado [If you are an antique dealer, I am sure our chairman will place an order with you of a certain thing.]

Akemi [What does your father look for?]

Tsuchimikado [You will know it at your meeting him.]

They were shown to a room and in there Tsuchimikado made two cups of tea and nodding to them asked them to wait a short while and went out of the room.

This small room did not look like the main room, so the height of the ceiling was rather low of only about 3.5 meters, but comparing with ordinary family room in Japan that height could be said fairly

— 139 —

high. The wall was painted with white plaster and the wooden construction was uncovered so it had a presentation similar to wooden construction in Alps in a sense. There was no hanging light from the ceiling. Instead, one each stand was put at the four side of the room sending out soft light. View from the window could see bright outside in the center of the garden on the lawn, but in front of this room a big tree of about 200 years old was standing to shut the viewing eyes.

Akemi   [Don't you think that person was too young for my father?]

Akemi was suspecting that Tsuchimikado might be his lover so made this question expecting to get his agreement.

Show Taro [She is not a normal woman.]

Akemi   [How can you say that?]

Show Taro [Did you observe her carefully?]

Akemi, who could not understand the meaning of his question, instantly replied.

Akemi   [Yes, but the back view only.]

Show Taro [No, I mean this room, not her.]

Akemi   [Where of the room?]

Akemi could not understand what Show Taro meant, so she looked in his face.

Show Taro [We are pushed into the shielded boundaries.]

Without saying any more, he showed by gesture amlets were pasted at the four corners of the room.

Akemi   [So we cannot go out, can we?]

Akemi looked somewhat uneasy.

Show Taro [Of course, we can. Here is the inside of the

boundaries, so the outside of this room must be filled with aura.]

Akemi　　[Is that person not a secretary?]

Show Taro　[It can better be said that a mystic or a diviner is doing secretarial works. And remember she has said there are rooms that she has not opened yet? That can be well taken that she is not supposed to stay here for ever.]

Akemi　　[Where does she usually stay I wonder.]

Show Taro　[By the way, who do you think the person is who came here before us?]

Akemi　　[I don't.]

Show Taro　[You really lack concentration. Look, suppose the flag EMM which is hung in front of the entrance is okay, the other flag was Japan's Midori Manji. Here in Europe, Midori as color green has no reason to be questioned, but Manji of the turned-out swastika can possibly be problematical. Suppose the visitor is not a Japanese, can you guess who the person could be?]

Akemi turned her eyes round and started to think about it. After keeping silence for some time, she opened her mouth.

Akemi　　[If not Japanese, is the visitor a capitalist of South America?]

Show Taro　[Probably, your guessing is right. Won't you ask which country the visitor is from?]

Akemi　　[Leave it to me!]

Akemi turned her eyers round again and made them shine.

— 141 —

After some more time, Tsuchimikado came back again. This time she led them to the office of the chairman. His office was a large room with a high ceiling in the center of the building and is located at the second level of the building in the Japanese terms. In the well trimmed lawn garden a pond of the size of 15m wide and 50m long was spreading. In the pond, several couples of mother duck and child duck were swimming there. Further up on a small hill, an arbor was standing and further up from there it looked like that the whole view of mountain belt of Alps might be able to be sighted.

Size of the room looked like about 30 jo (49.5 square meters=540 square feet) in Japanese terms. There placed a walnut wood center table under the chandelier and on the table there placed a big Meissen flower vase filled with flowers. The table legs were lion's paws which were powerfully supporting the table top. Looking around the wall, there hung about 20 oil paintings of which some were landscape paintings of the 19th century next to Venetian paintings of Reneissance style. Other than those, there was a flower vase painted by Renoir. All those paintings came into Show Taro's eye sight when he was sinking himself into the sofa as being offered by Kato.

Having watched all those paintings, he asked with his eyes shining.

Show Taro [Did all these paintings come from Sforza's]

Kato [Most of them are fakes.]

Show Taro [But, can I take a bit closer look of this painting?]

Kato [Do enjoy it.]

Show Taro [May I take a look at the reverse side?]

Kato [Yes, please.]

Show Taro took the framed painting off the wall and check the state of the backside of it. Both the canvas and the frame were aged so it could at least be said these were not what Antonio of Florence was produced.

Show Taro [Sorry but won't you show me the cardboard box if you keep it.]

Kato [One of the boxes put between that cabinet and the wall. Please check yourself.]

He found a box which just fit that frame and took a paper napkin from inside the box and looked at it.

There, under the lettering of Passo Romano the letter A was marked by a pensil. He could not help stopping his hands that were slightly shaking with his excitement.

Show Taro [The original 『The Man with the Golden Helmet』. No doubt about it…]

Kato [In here, that one is the only one that is authentic. Well done. I knew you could make it.]

Hearing Kato's a little raised voice, his secretary turned anew to Show Taro and said.

Tsuchimikado [We have been waiting for you.]

Show Taro [Did you know I was coming here?]

Kato [It was not clear to me who was coming, but I did and do understand the person coming to me can meet the condition that is to be explained to you following this conversation.]

Show Taro [Then what you mean is?]

Kato [Please explain to him.]

Kato calmly instructed Tsuchimikado and she started to explain

— 143 —

slowly in a voice which was clearer and more comprehensive than the way she talked before.

Tsuchimikado [My observation of you tells me that you no doubt ought to obtain a certain 『thing filled with spirits』 distinguishing it is what you need. And if you will accept the condition of exchanging such certain thing with this painting, we will give this painting away to you.]

Show Taro felt at the long last the question he had been holding in his mind was solved.

Show Taro [So you are a medium as I thought you would be.]

Kato [If you accept this offer on this spot, I will proceed to explain about this matter further.]

Show Taro [What level of price do you have in your mind for me to get the painting?]

Kato [If you accept the condition of exchanging with such certain thing, you can take the painting free of charge. Taken for granted that Maria's prophecy is correct, you ought to know where that certain thing exists so you can take it over to me. Do you agree, Maria?]

Kato turned to Tsuchimikado.

Akemi [Ah, are you by chance the python 『Abe-Maria』 ? !]

Akemi hearing the word of 『Maria's prophecy』 blurred out the well-known name which often came out on women's weekly magazines. Hearing Akemi's words, the woman with the name plate of Tsuchimikado smiled and responded.

Tsuchimikado [you are exactly right.]

Show Taro [Now I understand why I had thought you were

— 144 —

unusual. I will accept your offer.]

Kato [Do the best you can.]

Akemi [Tell me why such popular python in Tokyo is here with you, Dad?]

Akemi now learnt that Tsuchimikado was no lover of her father, but this fact caused another question to her.

Kato [That's because I need her power.]

Akemi [In this era of science?]

Kato [In line with the progress of the science, metaphysical existence comes to appear in a shape for the first time. The modern age which is satisfied with all material needs filled is instead losing the ability to sight the soul as a compensation of its material fulfillment. Despite the fact I am no Christian, I am fearing that this world has already entered into the age of apocalypse. This is why I handed over my business to my son and am taking an ample time to study this theme in Europe.]

Akemi [Incidentally, the person you were meeting before us, is he a Japanese?]

Kato [No, he is from South America.]

Akemi [Show Taro, well done. Your guessing is correct.]

Tsuchimikado, who was listening this conversation of Akemi with Show Taro, was over again surprised at Show Taro's ability.

Tsuchimikado [So it can be seen by you, too.]

Show Taro [No, no, it's only coming from the calculated results of my attentiveness and fertile imagination. As I do not own such precognition as you have, all what I can is to

— 145 —

feel and to analyze my feelings.]

Tsuchimikado [Well, I understand, but despite your high sensibility, you do not intend to make a question about 『The thing filled with spirits』. And still you will not admit that you can see what ordinary people cannot see.]

Kato [I agree to what Maria said. You have not yet made any question about what it's all about. Maria says you will know what it is by viewing the thing I am showing you at my factory tomorrow.]

Tsuchimikado [This person is the one that can find an answer on his own of what is what he is in need. We will give you what you need for free of charge, but mind you you must never tell others who you met and what you saw. Do you fully understand what I said now?]

Show Taro [I understand.]

For that day, Show Taro and Akemi were to leave there, but was to return here on the following day and to move by helicopter. After the two went away, Kato asked Tsuchimikado.

Kato [What side does that man belong to, do you think?]

Tsuchimikado [He is not our enemy nor our side. Regarding the present case, he will be just a cooperator. He has a capability to be able to feel what I am. This capability of his will be useful to us in future as well.]

As Akemi was standing for Show Taro, Kato wished to learn about both of them together. Maria, feeling what he was thinking, spoke up as if she had already found answers to his question.

Kato [Is some spirit haunting on my daughter?]

Tsuchimikado [In addition to the deseased mother, a house wife of

— 146 —

a merchant in the Japan's middle ages. A madam of French Province or somewhere around there is also seen to me.]

Kato [What about that man?]

Tsuchimikado [Besides a warrior of Japan's middle ages, an old man in China, A noble in Rome, a clerk in Egypt···and some more.]

Kato [What do you think about those two?]

Tsuchimikado [I reckon they would not know how they had been related to each other in the previous world. At worst, their present relationship will continue as business partners.]

Kato [Thank you. Please add reward to your service today to your fortune teller's fee.]

14. The Night Hearing

In that evening, they returned to the room that Robert reserved for them and while taking tea with Sachertorte, they heard a knocking at the door a bit after 7 o'clock. That was Robert in person. Being shown into the room Robert greeted to Akemi, too. Needless to say, Show Taro never mentioned that he found the original 『The Man with the Gold Helmet』 painting. Should Robert inform this fact to the police and let them seize the painting as stolen painting, he would not be able to get even a penny for his work. Akemi, turning her eyes round, was showing her strong curiocity about the secret of Robert's.

Show Taro, sinking into the Neo-Baroque sofa, watching himself to keep very careful, slowly spoke out to Robert.

Show Taro [Today I made a visit to Kato of Euro・Midori・Manji.]

Robert [Yes, I know that. What did you find there then.]

Robert, getting prepared to take a memo on his pocket notebook, asked.

Show Taro [I saw a copied fake there.]

Robert [Anything else?]

Show Taro [Tomorrow, we are scheduled to be taken to a research installation somehere in Eastern Europe.]

Robert [What is there?]

Show Taro [Life would be easy if we knew that now⋯By the way, we saw a visitor there before us. He seemed to be a businessman from South America.]

— 148 —

He leaned forward a little and showed his interst.

Robert [Did you see him in his face?]

Show Taro [No, I didn't.]

Robert [Did you meet any one else?]

Show Taro [Though I think it does not relate to this investigation, his secretary was the prophest 「Ave Maria」.]

Telling so to Robert, he put Maria's calling card on the table. For some reason that he could not guess, the name printed on the revers side of the card read Ave, Maria. This business card was with the company logo of EMM and the address on the card was also the address of the company.

Robert [Ave・Maria…what a ludic name is it.]

Akemi [She is popular with the positive predictive value of her fortune telling. By the way, may I ask you one question?]

Robert [What is your question?]

Akemi [Regarding the news of Gabriel murdered in Vienna…I cannot confirm such fact either on the newspapers here nor cable TV. You said you gained the genuine information at your branch office in The Hague but I wonder if it is a true information. Are you truly an insurance inspector? Do you have a calling card?]

Receiving the shower of questions from Akemi, Robert showed somewhat embarrassed face and reluctantly gave his card to her.

Robere [Here it is. Do you have any question?]

Akemi [Research Department, I see. Is it okay I ring there?]

Robert [No problem.]

She started to ring the number on his card while Robert was

— 149 —

watching her. Her tone on the phone sounded like that of a bar girl, and the way in a Hollywood movie.

Akemi   [Hello, Robert please.]

Employee 1 [Robert, I see. Just a moment.]

A pose of time was telling he was sort of looking around the office.

Employee 1 [Sorry, but Robert is recorded to be on a business trip.]

Akemi   [Where has he gone--]

Employee 1 [He was supposed in Zurich till yesterday, but today⋯ wait a second.]

And a short while.

Employee 2 [Hello, I'm replying instead of our staff you were talking with. He was saying today he was going to Vienna for the investigation work of cultural assets in line with the fire damage. His schedule for tomorrow may be known to us in the morning tomorrow. Do you like to leave any message?]

Akemi   [Won't you tell him I・am・missing・him.]

Employee 2 [I understand.]

Then the telephone line was cut. Akemi looked enjoying watching how Robert was reacting her telephone conversation. Robert looked mortally afraid, swetting his forehead. Akemi staring at him and opened her month.

Akemi   [You're somewhat sketchy.]

Robert   [Didn't they say I was out on business trip?]

Akemi   [What is the purpose of your business trip?]

Robert   [For investigation.]

Akemi   [I'm asking what kind of investigation.]

— 150 —

Robert   [Restration work of cultural assets.]

Akemi   [Okay, if that's all what you can say, I will pass it just for today. But I know you are still lying…]

Then, after a few minites, the cell phone of Robert's rang. Akemi quickly derived him of his phone and put it on her ear. Angry voice jumped into it.

Employee 3 [Robert, you are neglecting your duty to keep contact and have a woman say 「I'm missing you」 instead. What the hell are you doing wasting expense budget! Isn't the expense of Tom's girl just a wastful spending?]

Akemi   [Thank you!]

Then, Akemi returned the phone to Robert quickly.

Robert   [I'm still at the office of the business contact. I will report back to you later.]

Akemi   [Seemingly you are likely doing investigation of an insurance company.]

Robert   [As it is my job.]

He wiped his sweat once again.

Akemi   [Instead I will kindly trust you, I will request a more quality food this time.]

Show Taro [And a handsome looking maid, too.]

Hearing his words, with a fierce look in her eyes, she stared the two men and lifted her voice.

Akemi   [Should you prepare such maid, you are to get a big punch.]

Robert   [Enough for tonight…good night.]

As Akemi was really crossed, Robert ran away.

Hearing the door was shut, Akemi started to talk this way.

Akemi [I admit Robert is his real name, but that he is an inspector of an insurance company must be false. Firstly, that this much expense can be afforded is very strange.]

Show Taro [Well, as this work is to get back a super expensive stuff, cost-effectiveness can be big.]

Akemi [As we fly by helicopter tomorrow, what wear will suit me, I wonder…]

Her concern had already been shifted to the wear for tomorrow

15. Helilifting

At half past nine on the following morning, they gathered at Euro · Midori · Manji where they were put aboard a helicopter. Besides Kato and Tsuchimikado, there was a German South American businessman to whom they were introduced. He said his name was Heinrich Hitzinger. He was a small man for a German origin and was wearing square framed sunglasses. For some reason he spoke to Akemi and the conversation between them were heard by others which were as follows:

Heinrich   [I am also a love child as you are.]

It sounded like he knew Akemi's background hearing it from Kato.

Akemi   [My mother was a Geisha.]

Heinrich   [Yes, I heard so. My mother was a niece of Felix Kelsten. She was a beautiful woman so I guess my father fell in love with her. She was a tender mother. It is regretful that I could not bury her next to my father.]

Akemi   [How is your father now?]

Heinrich   [He was killed in the war.]

Akemi   [Oh, I am sorry.]

Heinrich   [After my father's death, my mother went to South America by U-boat where she lived with help from others there. The U-boat that went around in Uruguay failing to get scuttled in July, 1945 was the same U-boat that had been used by the runaway

— 153 —

companions.]

Akemi   [I do not know much about the history, but they must be suffered very much. By the way, your English is very good.]

Heinrich   [Father of Mr. Kato established Midori Manji using the hidden fund of America. After that, Midori Manji funded countries in South America for students to study in America. I was one of such students. In America, I studied about agricultural chemicals and fertilizer as same as my father did and gained academic degree of doctor of agriculture. With this educational background, I now possess a holding company which is making the highest profit in the field of agricultural chemicals in the whole South American region.]

Listening to his talk, Akemi looked to be interested in him. Akemi feels that any talk about business is an interesting subject to her.

Akemi   [Isn't your business background superb!]

Heinrich   [While your father is active in business, why don't you come and visit any factory of mine located in several South American countries.]

Akemi   [Thank you.]

Then after he finished talking with Akemi, he started to talk to Show Taro.

It seemed whom he was most interested in was the ability that Show Taro possessed.

Heirich   [Show Taro, in the neighborhood of the factory

— 154 —

whereto we are now heading, I have my villa. We are going to stay there tonight. I heard from Mr. Kato that Miss Abe Maria is saying you have power to find out what we need. Therefore, I do expect you to show your power.]

Show Taro [What do you expect me to find?]

Heinrich [According to what she told us, you are able to find out what we are in need even if we do not tell you what it is. During when she was telling fortunes you arrived from Tokyo here and while we both are here, you came here and found authentic 「The Man with the Golden Helmet」. Therefore, if you will find out what we need, we will give you the painting in exchange of what you will find out what we need.]

Show Taro [Is there any one else other than me who knows about this painting?]

Heinrich [Some time ago, a Mafia related man came here and this man seemed to have succeeded to break the boundary which Abe Maria had founded. I didn't meet him so know not much about him, though. What I know is it was my subordinate who placed the order of the copying work of the two canvases with Romano. It needs a very fine technique for a German-Swiss painter to copy the painting in fine and minute details faithfully copying the touch of brush strokes of the original painting on the canvas which was carefully and precisely created by an Italian maestro to have it look exactly alike the original canvas.]

— 155 —

Hearing the explanation of Heinrich, Show Taro was convinced he could then understand what he had heard and seen till then, and dared to refer to the finished appearance of the paint.

Show Taro [With regards the cracking of the paint the chemical treatment which did not show any difference from those in the olden times through black light also shows a very high copying technique.]

Heinrich turned his question to Show Taro in the attitude that showed he then understood the behaviors of Show Taro.

Heinrich [Now I reckon you are able to see something. Mr. Kato was saying so, too.]

Show Taro [At a glance the crackings look natural to meet the age when the original painting was created, which would mean the chemicals used were characterized.]

Heinrich [If we get the paints patented so that they would be opened to the public, it would mean we loose the expected profit, which is entirely to the contrary of our purpose.]

Show Taro [Do you mean that more profit can be gained to sell the fakes?]

Heinrich [You can make more money to copy and sell the paintings that you obtained free of charge? What I am trying to say is the best profit we can make by a painting which was knocked down to us at one million dollars is 10% of the one million dollars to the at most when we sell it to our customer. However, suppose we obtain such a painting without paying any expense, even if we can sell it only for .8 million, we can get far

— 156 —

more return, so that the safe and still profitable way is to wholesale it at half a million still allowing us a handsome profit. But one thing we will not do is stealing the original. What we do is strictly limited to the sale of copies. Delivery to us of the stolen originals and sale of the copies that we produce are two separate business handled by completely separate groups of job categories.]

At the explanation of Heinrich exphasizing that his job category is not the stealing part of it, Show Taro threw his question about the issue that involved Germany.

Show Taro [In 1996, a group of thieves of Chizec Republic broke into Prague National Art Museum and took away more than twenty paintings including the famous 『Disproportionate Lovers』. They were killed at the firefight. Was that group also such specialized group of thieves?]

In reply to his question, Heinrich explained the reason why he would not touch the thieving part of such business raising actual examples.

In orfer to convince Show Taro the high risk of such scheme, he raised a couple of examples that happened in the recent years.

Heinrich [Gold-Tooth Kittler is just one of the forty or more groups of thieves and nothing more. In 1994, two paintings of Turner were stolen in Frankfult, Germany. Those were loaned from Tate Gallery in London. A member of armed forces in Serbia called Alkane tried to sell them but was shot at

— 157 —

Intercontinental Hotel in Beograd together with his two underlings. What I am saying is the two points of obtaining the targeted paintings and selling them are the life-threateningly dangerous points of the flow of this business.]

Show Taro [In the course of the reguest of creating copies, is there any possibility of firefighting to occur?]

Heinrich [Such instance has not taken place among us, but do you remember the case of Mafia selling paintings they stole starting in 1969 through to 1996 in the Palermo region which was disclosured through quarrel with each other. At that time, money as a political fund was sent to Julio Andreotti, the ex-prime minister of Italy. In other words, if there are those who cannot keep up with the rules, any organization will fall down.]

Show Taro [What is the reason why the stealing route of art products by Mafia could be active for such a long period of time?]

Heinrich [It is because they stopped selling the arts within Italy and instead sold them in America, besides completely destroying the betrayers. Those arts must have been sent to America aboard the vessel owned by Mafia and delivered to the Jewish Mafia groups like a pizza delivery. Mafia was released by the ground work of the Jews grew up till they came to get the important posts of many fields in America since after the occupation of Sicily Island. Therefore, in order to extinguish such Mafia occupation Romano keeps making his efforts.]

Show Taro [Is there any other selling route in America other than by Mafia?]

Heinrich [Do you know of the copying incident of Mona Lisa in 1911?]

Heinrich became curious to try to find out how much Show Taro knows of this kind of the matters so he took out an extremely aged topic to try him. If Show Taro fails to answer, he can determine that Show Taro's knowledge is just a superficial polish with which he is trying to approach Heinrich.

Show Taro [If I remember it correctly, a con man calling himself an Argentine marquis had a French faker, Yves Chaudron, produce six copies and sold such fakes to American businessmen for .3 million dollars per piece.]

Heinrich [This selling route remained after this case as an established distribution route of other copies.]

Show Taro [In other words, another 『The Man with the Golden Helment』 came through this route and was cast ashore Chicago. Correct?]

Heinrich was surprised that Show Taro referred to Chicago, and became cautious not to talk too much about this subject, so he felt it was not wise for him to talk about this subject any more.

Heinrich [Regretfully, I do not know the selling route. All what I know is the organization of counter feiters keep buying chemical products of our company paying very expensive expenses.]

He sounds intentionally changed the subject. Earler in the

— 159 —

conversation he sounded like he was actively producing fakes. At least, his talk sounded that actual copying work is being practiced somewhere in Switzerland or Austria and that transaction of such fakes were being exercised at the underground club, Passo Romano down Sforza.

Heinrich   [Maria, Has tonight's schedule been arranged okay?]

Leaving the question of Show Taro unreplied, Heinrich changed the subject.

Tsuchimikado [I should say tomorrow night would be better.]

Heinrich   [Is that the answer from the stars?]

Tsuchimikado [As I will collect spirits during the daytime tomorrow.]

Heinrich   [Alright, I understand.]

After that, all of them kept silence for a while, then the helicopter started to fly around making a big circle in the air and landed. There several guardmen were waiting for the arrival of the helicopter. They were wearing black military-look uniforms. When the helicopter landed, they received the heli members with the greeting of Roman Salute and opened the door of the car which was painted in black. The car ran around the edge of a ranch when Show Taro saw shades similar to those of a couple of Stuka and a couple of Messershumitt in a wooden hut, which made him wonder. In case what he just saw was kept in the condition ready for immediate use, he felt the existance of those fighters would be exceeding the hobby level. Would this road on which the car Show Taro was riding become the runway of those fighters if war took place? It was only natural such a question came up. Show Taro tried to ask Heinrich who was sitting on the opposite side seat in

— 160 —

the car.

Show Taro [May I ask you one question?]

Heinrich [What is it?]

Show Taro [We have just passed by a hut where I thought I saw the aircrafts which were used during the WW2. Are those real ones?]

Heinrich [You've got good eyes. These are restored real ones. Stukas were the ones that were left hidden in the mountain area of Poland and Messershumitts were the ones that fell on the desert of Libya which were restored.]

Show Taro [Do you steer aeroplanes by yourself?]

Heinrich [No, I cannot steer planes by myself. Those elderly people of about 70 years of age whom you will meet at my castle later on used to be pilots .]

Show Taro [Well, then, Are you programming an air show by those ex-pilots some day?]

Heinrich [Haha···This is the first time that I receive such a question. I guess it is an American idea to earn money by air shows but nevertheless I reckon such attraction could well be considered.]

Show Taro [Plane restoring is a costly exercise so I think it perfectly natural if you plan such an event.]

Heinrich [I will certainly keep your opinion as reference.]

Show Taro [Looking forward.]

Of the planes that Show Taro saw, the one called Stuka in German is a dive bomber with a distinctive shape of wing named Gull Wing. Looking at this bomber from the front of it, the main

— 161 —

wing once curved down below the body then rose up towards the front. This bomber is well known as the one that contributed to completely destroy the Soviet armed division during the beginning part of the German-Soviet war when Barbarossa was triggered.

Hans Ulrich Rudel (1916 ~ 1982) had a record of having destroyed more than 500 tanks and 800 armored cars. As results of the great activities of pilots as is reported on the astonishing military achievement records, the blitz tactics supported by Nazi German armoured brigade could achieve such a great success and came to be referred to the kill ratio of Barbarossa as 1 versus 56.

This figure means an astonishing ratio of that 56 Soviet soldiers had to die in order to kill one Nazi German soldier.

Also, messershumitt as Heinrich explained was meant for the combined defence forces of Nazi Germany and Italy. At the war front of these defence forces, there was the flying ace, Hans -Joachim Marseille (1899-1942). He was the one that left the record of shooting 17 enemy fighters down in one day and according to the researchers' report, he shot down one enemy fiter with average 15 bullets only. This record can also be said astounding. Probably even now the minefield was left existing in the desert of Libya among which under the desert sand such destroyed tanks or fighters may be buried. The fighters of Heinrich's possession which are said to have been restored shows those are in the fully serviced state so are ready for flying.

While they were continuing some innocuous conversation they may have finished running about fifteen minutes or so alongside the ranch spreading on the mountains, their car went through a forest ahead the ranch and stopped alongside the research facility owned by Euro · Midori · Manji. There again they were received with the Salute Romano salutation. It was an impressive scene to look at that a white flag with Midori manji together with the green EMM flag were fluttering. As this place was located where no outsiders could not sight so it may have caused no problem.

16. Mistery at Reseach Facilities

The chairman Kato arranged to have Tsuchimikado attend Show Taro and Akemi as a guide for her to give them explanation to questions from them, so they could make a tour of the factory to sight the process till the completion of producing process of the blood products. There was no single worker in the broard and clean factory so they could not understand why Kato showed them the factory to the deep end of it which was insulated from the normal visitor's tour route. Kato suggested them to make any question they wished to ask, but things and facilities shown to them were beyond their comprehension so they could even not raise any question.

Akemi [We are shown the factory where no one is working and are suggested to freely make question. I am puzzled what question I should make. This is waste of time, isn't it?]

Show Taro [No, no, we may feel some shadowy existence sometimes.]

Maria [So you have come to notice it.]

Show Taro wondered by which name he should call her, so he anyway started to talk to Maria in the following way. Magicians are not to use their real names at the place where they try to use spirits.

Show Taro [Incidentally, whichever you are, Ms. Tsuchimikado or Ms. Ave Maria⋯. Why do we have to visit and review the manufacturing process here?]

— 164 —

Maria   [We are just passing by this place in order to enter the next portion of the building. And one more thing is please call me Ave Maria hereafter.]

Show Taro [Is that request for your using Shikigami magic?]

Maria   [You are quick to understand, aren't you.]

Show Taro [Is there any other reason?]

Maria seemed to think that to hide the truth wouldn't work with Show Taro, so she started to explain.

Maria   [This place is where the force of the people who gave their blood remains. What I wish to say is, if such blood was a donated blood by normal and healthy people, there would happen no problem. But sometimes some people came to have no other choice but to pay their debts by their blood. Such people tend to lose power of resistence to sickness and are getting weak and shall consequently die. And such deceased people are sometimes apt to be wandering into this place.]

Sho Taro [So you have been employed as a talisman to protect people here from the evil, is this right?]

Maria   [You are half way right, ···I am also exercising fortune telling for the safety of the related people here. Please take a look at the things placed in the block where I am showing you now, and later review Mr. Heinrich's collection. Then choose what you need. My psychic reading is telling me that you could find out by your own power what you should present in exchange of 『The Man with the Golden Helmet』.

Akemi could not possibly think that with such an absurd story the mistery could be solved.

Akemi   [What will happen if he cannot find the thing?]

Maria   [My psychic telling is concluding he is the only person that can find it out.]

Maria said it point-blank.

Akemi   [Why and how can you know he can find it out?]

Replying Akemi's repeated question, sound of Maria's voice rose a little showing her irritation.

Maria   [Don't you understand I have been repeatedly saying that it is being seen by him.]

Akemi   [Is that what you mean?]

Maria   [Exactly.]

While such conversation was going on, they arrived at a door at the side of the collider where they were supposed to enter.

Maria   [This is the entrance of the block which I wish you to sight. As I ought not reply to any question from you here, please wait and hold your question if any till we come out from this block.]

Saying so, the door was opened by Maria. Sound of the steps of the three was following them. As the scene of organs being regenerated in big test tubes, even such person that did not know much about science could understand that there cloning technology was being researched. There, tails or ears only of mouses were being reproduced. Needless to say, such a scene was nothing but a highly uncanny scene to look at, so Show Taro and Akemi were lost

— 166 —

for words. Actually, Akemi had to try very hard to force back a shriek. They passed through that block and Maria opened the next door in silence. There they found themselves on the lawn where the afternoon sunshine was bright.

Maria   [That block which I showed you just now is the top secret of this factory. In short, technology to effectively restoring and reproducing arms and legs or the like that were lost, say, by traffic accidents, within a few weeks' time after such accident, had taken place.]

Show Taro [But for that purpose, you do not need anything filled with spirits, do you?]

Akemi   [I never knew that my father's company was doing such uncanny business.]

Akemi was just about to throw up.

Maria   [Such experimentation that you have just seen does not need any organ that is filled with spirits, as that technology is used just to exchange a part of a living body.]

Show Taro [Then, what is what you say your specialty?]

Maria   [I wish to keep it in secret for a while longer, but by what you have just seen you may have become aware of a bit of it.]

Show Taro [Will you allow me some more time to understand what you really are.]

Maria guiding the couple to show them to a small room at the side of the office. There, too, amlets were pasted at the four corners producing one shielded boundary. It also was a reality that they could calm down being in there. There, cookies and afternoon tea

— 167 —

had been prepared. They enjoyed cookies and tea and kept chatting.

Show Taro [Are we in Hungary?]

Maria [I will leave that up to your imagination.]

Maria replied in a highly gracious manner but was showing her couciousness not to say anything unnecessary.

Show Taro [In any case, for building a plant, it is indispensable that the approval by the official body is to be obtained, isn't it?]

Maria [Even if it may be called a plant or a factory, the size of it is no more than one classroom of a small size primary school and before talking about the size of the factory, number of the employees at the factory is no more than several ten people.]

Show Taro [Is that number of the employees inclusive of guarding staff?]

Maria [Yes, and even me the shaman is included.]

Show Taro [Is anything like ascetic practices being carried out here?]

Judging from what she told them about the necessity to create such organ filled with spirits, this question of his was quite a natural question.

Maria [No, but Mr. Heinrich looks like an enthusiast of the black magic as same as his father.]

Show Taro [Is what you mean another line from the Christchan doctorine?]

Maria [What I mean is they are versed in ancient Germanic religion before Christianism was propagated.]

— 168 —

Show Taro [I remember I read in a book that in past Nazi SS troops executed a ceremony copying the enlistment ceremony of the German chivalric order.]

Maria [Such celemory is still being practiced in this modern age.]

Show Taro [I learnt NS namely Nazi preferred to gather at night. Is the current gathering being practiced in the same manner?]

Maria [Yes, at dark night when there is scarcely no moonlight.]

Show Taro [Do you know for what purpose he is doing such gathering?]

Maria [I have never asked him why.]

Show Taro [On your receiving the fortune telling fee, is the payer treated as your customer?]

At this point, Show Taro clarified Maria's order taking policy.

Maria [Yes, you are right. Besides, I have not requested to work on any matter that relates to a crime.]

Akemi [Does Mr. Heinrich have some eye trouble? I notice he never takes his sunglasses off.]

Maria [I have seen him changing his sunglasses with a round frame glasses when he was to put his signature on the documents.]

And, at this time instead of Show Taro, Akemi started to ask Maria questions about Maria herself.

Akemi [Don't you take meals with us?]

Maria [While performing purification rites, I do not take my usual food.]

— 169 —

Akemi	[Does sumptuous feast disturb your fortune telling ability?]
Maria	[Though I take secred sake, I don't take it so much.]
Akemi	[You are always staring at Show Taro. What of him makes you so curious?]
Maria	[No, I do not look at him that much.]
Akemi	[Then, are you taking care of my father?]
Maria	[No. Male staffs seem shifting the duty of taking his daily life care. Whie he is asleep, one staff is always guarding him standing at the entrance door.]
Show Taro	[What does that strict guarding mean?]
Maria	[Mr. Heinrich is consigned a research work from your father. In orfer to prevent this technology getting leaked and also for the sake of his safety, he is protecting himself using one guardman and one chamberlain working in shifts day and night.]
Akemi	[What is the purpose of my father continuing this research?]
Maria	[He said to me he was continuing this research of his as it is partly for your mother's sake.]
Akemi	[You mean that research does good to Mr. Heinrich, too?]
Maria	[I understand it also does good for Mr. Romano Sfolza.]
Show Taro	[What I have understood so far is the contents of the Kato research will be useful both for Heinrich and Romano. What sort of success possibility does the research work have?]

Show Taro's attitude seemed that he already came to realize

— 170 —

something even not needing Maria's explanation about the contents of the research.

He would soon find out the reason why the wishes that Romano contained in his mind was diffuicult to be met.

Maria [Regarding the level of the chrone technology, the success of realization of the research will be more possible with Heinrich or Chairman Kato. However, success depends on whether they would be able to gather all of that something. In regards those inherited things, lots of erroneous factors are included so such research has a rather high risk of encountering unexpected obstacles.]

Akemi [Do you, Maria, know about the contents of the research work?]

Hearing that much from Maria, even Akemi seemd to become aware that Maria must know something more.

Maria [No, I have not asked any question···but my sensibility caught some part of the contents for me to understand it.]

Akemi [Do you see other things randomly?]

Maria [As Ms. Akemi already knows, I am a prophecy, so that if I am paid for the fortune telling fee, I am in a position to see whatever things per my customer's request, and to tell my customer what I have seen.]

Akemi [Will you tell my fortune next time we meet?]

Maria [Yes, I will take your request, however, at the moment I am bound by the weekly basis contract with Midori Maji Company so you will have to wait till I become free from the current contract.]

Akemi   [Do book me in your forward reservation list, please.]

Maria   [What do you wish me to tell?]

Akemi   [I will tell it to you when you are ready to work my request.]

Akemi spoke in a tone as if she knew Marie already realized the content of Akemi's request.

Maria   [Okay, is a couple of hours sufficient, I guess?]

Akemi   [Done. Thank you.]

Akemi and Maria exchanged their business cards.

Show Taro [Just let me take a look at Maria's business card.]

Akemi   [Here it is.]

Saying so, she covered the cell phone number on the card with her right hand thumb and showed the rest part of the card to Show Taro.

Show Taro [So the job description is Medium of Love, I see.]

Maria   [I am consulted without distinction of the consultation, but as this way to put my job description somehow seems to appeal to young women.]

Show Taro [But those who can pay more will be company owners of the middle age and up, is this right?]

To Show Taro, Maria did not look like dealing mainly with such customers that could not pay good sum of money to her.

Maria   [But on the whole, the most number of the consultations is seized by business women regarding their love affairs.]

Show Taro [Are their consultation in relation with marriage?]

Maria   [Half is adultery.]

— 172 —

Show Taro [For what kind of consultation?]

Maria [To oust the opponent.]

Show Taro [Scary obsession, isn't it.]

Maria [Yes, as jealousy is another form of love.]

He then dared to ask Maria a question answer of which he had been seeking a while.

Show Taro [Why do you have others call you Ave Maria?]

Maria [Firstly, I want to use the ancestral sir name, and secondly, my real name may cause me danger in the present world.]

Show Taro ⌈Yes, I understand what you say, but the word Ave means 'Glory to'in ancient Latin.⌋

Maria [Yes, I know that.]

Then, there returned Kato. Next action was to make a move by a car that Heinrich hired.

They drove about 30 minutes to reach a dense forest where they drove in and ran further ten minutes in the forest. Crossing a bridge there they saw through trees a building which looked like an old castle located on a hill as the extended part of the mountains. The car stopped in front of the repeatedly iron riveted gate of the castle-like building. The gate was opened with a heavy lingering sound and the car parked in the courtyard. There again a group of people in black military look uniforms received them with the Salute Romano greeings. Precisely stating, there they surely heard a chorus of Sieg Heil by that grouped people, so they must be saluting by Deutscher Gruss (=Nazi Salute).

A grey-haired elderly man who looked like the captain of the guard bowed respectfully and opened the door of the car for them.

— 173 —

Stepping out of the car, they saw the grand chamberlain at the side of the front door. He, too, wore grey hair and looked like around the age of 70.

Grand chamberlain [Welcome to Neo Black Cameron.]

17. Collection of Heinrich

Entering the old castle, Kato and Show Taro alone were shown to the salon of Heinrich Hizinger. Heinrich was wearing the square sunglasses as always. The room they were shown in was the broardest of all the other rooms which looked to seize nearly 50 jo in Japanese terms (nearly 83square meters=1,800sf). Height of the ceiling would be close to 5 meteres. The width of the fireplace looked to measure almost three meters, one side of which books with the leather spine were fully lined up. The chandellia looked like Checoslovakian Bohemian cut and in addition, to give the room more light, at the four corners of the room one each stand was placed which was falling a soft beige color light on the thick deep red color carpet. On the wall opposite the bookshelf, a large size picture of the mythology-based drawing was hunging and next to that, one other painting which seemed to show the scene of the triumphant return of Napoleon was hung. At a corner in such an office Heinrich was placing a large desk at the windowside nearby the fireplace. The chair was leather-covered and the style of the chair looked like the Gothic Revival. Regarding the chair, Show Taro knows from his use experience that those made in the modern age were more comfortable than the ones of the previous ages.

Heinrich stood up and spoke to Show Taro over again.

Heinrich　　[I think here is a thing that you will be in need in order to obtain 『The Man with the Golden Helmet』. If

— 175 —

you can obtain what I need, I will give you as an exchange deal any item out from my collection which is located here at this Neo Black Cameron. I presume this condition of the deal I am offering is a very good condition for you to accept. How do you think?]

Show Taro [Thank you for your very generous offer.]

Of his collection, the first item that caught Show Taro's eyes was an ivory pistol. The grip of that pistol was made of ivory and on this grip the Nazi crest of the design of an eagle on the swastika was engraved.

Show Taro [Is this the pistol that Hilter gifted to Hermann Goering?]

Heinrich [No, this is a Ruger P08. It is not Walther.]

Show Taro [Is this a model before the WW2?]

Heinrich [Amazing you have that much knowledge. It is the one that was given to the SS high rank officer. Is that what you choose?]

Show Taro [No way. It cannot be taken into Japan. I need something else.]

Kato [So what you are saying is what we need is in Japan.]

Moving a few steps ahead, Heinrich pointed to a flag to Show Taro.

Heinrich [Maria was saying that if you see this flag, you will come to learn what you are seeking.]

Show Taro [What sort of history does that flag have?]

Heinrich [This Swastika was the one that was covering the body of Hilter during the time since he killed himself by a gun shot till the body was cremated. After the

— 176 —

delivery was comlete, it was exchanged by a bloodless new flag and he was cremated being seen off with the Deutcher Gruss salutation.]

Show Taro [I now feel what I am in need.]

Heinrich [You can please take any thing but this flag.]

Show Taro [The owner who owns what we are talking about won"t accept anything that lacks story.]

Heinrich [Maria was saying the same thing.]

Next to the pistol there placed a celestial glove which looked quite an old one but as he did not feel any kind of spiritual air about it he thought it would be the one coming out from a small size mass production. Looking into the next shelf he saw a dagger which looked like the one that was used by knights of the middle era. This again was not allowed to be taken into Japan. Next to it there was a cabinet-on-stand. Those cabinet-on-stands made in the 17th century in Italy had many drawers so it was called by another name of collector's cabinet. It seemd to be used by the castle lord for a sorting box of the castle lord's collection.

The inlaid front panel of the falling front had been already opened. The small drawers or small doors inside the box were showing as if they were ready for inspection by Show Taro. In there, such small goods that are of no use for the common people or no value to them, but that are to meet and satisfy the nobles' intellectural desire.

To Show Taro it looked like to contain many small things that would be easy to be taken by him to Japan.

Show Taro [May I take a look at the goods inside the box?]

Heinrich [Please.]

Show Taro [Allow me to open the drawers.]

He firstly opened the middle door using the key, and drew out the hidden drawer inside of it. Heinrich gazed at Show Taro's such action for a moment, but Show Taro did not care about him and opened the leather bag that was contained in that drawer. There came out a red color precious stone with big cabochon cuts. Show Taro immediately checked and confirmed that through it he would see his finger hair doubled. If it was ruby with double reflection, it could be said it was a fairly rare article. If what he saw showed him just a single hair through it, it would mean the stone was of single reflection so it could be concluded that it was a Barlas Ruby which is applicable to most of the traditional rubies, namely spinel stones as minerally called.

Show Taro [This seems to be a spinel. Fairly large. It would have been needed to feed one army.]

Heinrich [Do you need it?]

Show Taro [This may be needed by you but it was of no value for my negotiation partner.]

Heinrich [That is good to me. This is a talisman which came out from an Austrian noble family and is a kind hard to get.]

Show Taro [This too has spirits in it but those spirits are better utilized by you than me. I suggest you to make good use of it.]

Show Taro then gazed at bloodstone and amethyst for a few seconds. Those were the ones that were also contained in that drawer. The amethyst was embossed with a crest of a double-headed eagle and looked like being used by a high rank noble.

— 178 —

Heinrich [Is it what you need?]

Show Taro [This looks like the property of a noble who used to have military convocation rights which had a stronger power than those owned by the margrave of Haus Habsburg. However, I am afraid this is not good enough to move the opponent.]

Heinrich [Do you think your opponent would prefer something that relates to authority?]

Show Taro [I cannot say for a fact but somehow can't feel it is right.]

Then, he drew out the bottom drawer in a casual manner and started to look around inside the drawer. Both Heinrich and Kato kept observing that scene in silence. Show Taro grasped and pulled out something like a long pole.

Show Taro [What is it?]

Heinrich [A half-made marshal's baton. It was a baton which was prepared for use of the army marshal. Name engraving is not completed.]

Show Taro [This deep red color would mean the blood color of the army. This does not contain even spirits.]

Heinrich [You mean that is not the thing either.]

Show Taro [Regretfully, yes.]

Heinrich [It indeed is an unusually rare thing, though···]

Show Taro [What matters is not whether it is a rare thing but the spirits in that thing are good enough to attract the present possessor of something.]

Heinrich [I see.]

Next, Show Taro opened one upper drawer on the left side and inspected the contents of the drawer.

Show Taro [This is my only second time to see this sort of the thing.]

Saying so, he took domino cards out from a wooden box

Heinrich [What is the reason why you say there are rare?]

Show Taro [In here, the largest card is double · nine. Mind you, the present days domino cards' the largest card is double · six.]

Heinrich [As you say so, you are right, but I never thought they were odd as I have been seeing those cards since from my childhood. Is that set of cards what you want?]

Show Taro [Regretfully, no, not this one either.]

He again pulled out another drawer at the right side of the former one and checked the inside.

Show Taro [These cards are quite old Tarrot cards, aren't they.]

Heinrich [Yes, you are right. These are of the age of the early 18th century. So these are extremely ragged.]

Show Taro [This card is with the drawing of burning tower··· which has no good meaning.]

Heinrich [I have no idea why this card is here.]

Show Taro [Most probably, people did not want to draw this card.]

Heinrich [How come could such a thing happen?]

Show Taro [Well, everyone has a mental state to wish to avoid odd things. Though it is an unnessessary addition, all rulers desire to have their names engraved in the history as wise ruler or a noble minister. But reality is such a lot of rulers left their names as feeble-minded politicians against their will. Destiny often brings the result to the contrary to what was intended in the first place.]

Heinrich   [What do you think about Adolf Hitler?]

Show Tara [Are you aware that he was bespoken by Nostradamus of his emergence?]

Heinrich   [Yes, I do, then what?]

Hearing this reply, Show Taro took a pocket notebook from his pocket and said.

Show Taro [That was shown in 『Les Centuries 3-35』

Line 1 At the bottom area of West of Rome

Line 2 A baby is born at a house of a poor family

Line 3 His speech will attract a large political party

Line 4 He will become even more famous in the orient.

This prophecy exactly meets the fact that Adolf Hitler was born in a poor house in the countryside nearby the origin of River Rhine and after growing up to be the leader of NS or so-to-called Nazi party and made his party grow big to attract the public notice and was more valued in the orient, namely, Japan.

This fact was also been noticed by Rudolf Hess or Heinrich Hemmler. Even such Adolf Hilter was not able to evaluate himself in the big flow of the world history. Even Napoleon whom Hilter respected could not foresee that his body came home through the Arch of Triumph which he had constructed. On top of this fact, it has to be noted that a deed which was a bad deed during a certain era could be evaluated as good in the following era. What Napoleon performed could be taken as compulsion to the people of French sense of values if the angle of view is changed, but one thing for sure is that was Eroica. I presume reason of that is inclusive of the fact that Napoleon's behaviors had never been recreant.]

Heinrich [You have a talent with which you can see through future.]

Show Taro [This is my hobby and nothing more. In addition, to interpret what happened in the past in this way is far easier than to refer to things that are to happen in the future.]

Heinrich [I fully agree with you.]

Show Taro [I presume that NS, namely Nazi high rank officials should have been able to make a guess of what would happen in future, but the biggest mistake was they put the happenings in an incorrect order. The representative example showing this fact is 3-57. Taking it for granted that the poems of Nostradamus ought to be read each of the first half and the second as two separate groups, so the first group can be read as the period of time when U.K. people experienced the seven time change of forms of government and the second as a separate period, but when with intervention of Germany leaving Poland in the state of derived freedom took place, the two groups of the period was connected and as a result the attack to U.K. did happen. Suppose this reading and understanding are correct, U.K. ought to have been fallen.]

Heinrich [But they were not aware of that mistake.]

Show Taro [Hess did notice this error, so he flew to U.K. by himself alone.]

Heinrich [It is an interesting viewpoint indeed.]

At that moment, Show Taro seemed to hit upon some idea which was unknown to others and moved his hand and reached in one second the left top drawer of the cabinet.

From there what came out was a bracelet made of Core-formed glass and with the bracelet there was a four-time folded paper. Though no one could not guess why, Show Taro took a keen notice of that piece of paper.

Show Taro [This is Syrian glass, isnt't it.]

Heinrich [It was unearthed from the cemetery built in the last era of Pre-Umaiya period of the 8th century.]

Show Taro [Were you in Sylia then?]

Heinrich [It was given by Alois Brunner who was my father's friend.]

Show Taro [That name sounds familiar to me.]

Heinrich [He used to be an SS commander. As he was not a Catholic, he could not obtain a departure permit from the Vatican Cardinal. However, as the then Sylian government expressed acceptance of him he joined the intelligence office of Sylian troops, where he spent his weekends unearthing the ruins as his hobby work.]

Show Taro [I see. So he unearthed this glass there. This glass is not that type of finish which would show the strong silverification to make the glass appear older than actual using chemical treatment.]

Heinrich [You have an amaging knowledge.]

— 183 —

Show Taro [Unless people study copies which are on the Japanese market for sale at a cheap price and come to be able to understand what fakes are and look like, they shall for ever never be able to obtain a good discerning eye for which are fakes and which are authentic. People who have failed to ascertain such difference and have been incurred a loss can become to understand the valuableness of the authentic art.

There are a number of antique and art lovers who have not experienced any failure in choosing authentic antiques or arts. They are either purchasing from the first-class art dealers at a decent price or otherwise⋯ they shall get dead exhausted to seek one authentic item amongst millions of fakes. That they buy fakes believing what they buy are authentic would mean they are paying a necessary lesson fee. Also, depending on the situation, there are copies that were made by faithfully copying the full details of the supurb quality authentics in an endeavor to acquire the top class tecniques. Such copies have to be dealt differently from junk copies.]

Heinrich seemed to introspect he was also the same side of having been cheated for quite a lot of times with fakes, so he grinned and said.

Heinrich [I, too, have been paying tuition for fakes.]

Show Taro [Well, my sympathies. By the way, can you guess the vintage of this Syrian glass?]

Heinrich   [Not really. One thing I know for sure is it was stored
                 in the coffin of a princess of the 8th century.]

Listening to him so far, Show Taro started to tell Heinrich his opinion about the imaginable introduction of this glass.

It was a question that could be answered based on the piled knowledge gained from continuous studies even if he had not physically sighted the object in question. In actual fact, life of things is far longer than that of human being, which fact can be rephrased as things are attending human beings on their death. Taking Japan for example, such things as tea-ceremory utensils are seldom used as grave goods, so they are being passed down to tea ceremony lovers of later ages and as a result the utensils came to acquire unique atmosphere nourished by such tea ceremony lovers over the long period of age.

Chinese men of letters treasure art objects starting with bronze ware or the like. In Europe, too, nobles after Reneissance period happen to collect various antiques of the age before Christianism was introduced.

Show Taro [That one you are talking about was produced in the
              AD 1st century. It then was passed over to various
              princesses of honorable families and finally came to the
              hand of a princess who lived before the fallen
              Umayyad reign.]

Heinrich   [It's amazing that you can see through that much in
                 detail.]

Show Taro [It is the way to enjoy antiques in the true sense.]

Heinrich   [So you wish to have it, don't you.]

Show Taro [Yes, indeed.]

Heinrich [Then, take it please.]

Show Taro [Yes, I will, but I will soon take what you need to you.

Heinrich [I'm counting on you.]

Show Taro [I have one other favor to ask you.]

Heinrich [What is it?]

Show Taro [Please give me an export permit or such equivalent document issued either by the Austrian government or Sylian government together with that Sylian glass.]

Heinrich [Okay, I make the arrangement.]

Heinrich · Hizinger took up a bell off the antique inkstand of the 19th century on the desk and sounded it in a leisurely manner. Then, the door of the adjoining room opened and the butler came in.

Butler [What can I do for you?]

Heinrich [Please call Maria here.]

A little while, Maria and Akemi came over there.

Heinrich [Will you check and tell me whatever that can be seen on this bracelet?]

Heinrich was still a little suspicious about the Show Taro's talk.

Maria [Let me take a look.]

Maria received the bracelet on her palm from Show Taro and lifted her palm with the bracelet up at the height of her eyes and closed her eyes and started talking.

Maria [This bracelet itself was firsly owned by a daughter of a certain wealthy merchant. Later she married into a noble's family. After that, it was relayed to more than thirty female owners. But it doesn't mean the bracelet was used by those owners every day. It was used only on special occasions and taken out to a different family at every wedding ceremony. The last owner of the bracelet passed away just before she got married and soon after her death this dynasty was destroyed. And finally, a German related person unearthed it.]

Kato [Now I see what our diviner saw and the antique dealer saw corresponded to each other.]

Kato who was watching the entirety of talks made by those two, was over again impressed. He looked at Show Taro and Maria alternately. When his eyes caught Maria's, Maria spoke out as follows.

Maria [No, not exactly. His ability is to feel the truth but not perfectly well. Incidentally, may I ask if you can convince the owner of the painting in exchange of this bracelet?]

Show Taro [Frankly, I am not sure, but probably⋯]

What Heinrich just observed made him convinced that he can trust Show Taro.

Heinrich [I do hope so. We need your cooperation for us to achieve our researches.]

Heinrich was offering his hand to Show Taro.

Show Taro [I, too, am in need of 「The Man of the Golden Helmet」 , so I will not spare any efforts.]

Heinrich [Has Maria gathered enough spirits?]

Show Taro [Thanks to you. And, where is the thing?]

Heinrich [Take her along.]

The butler guided her into an ajoining room. Voice reciting a spell sounded there.

— 187 —

Show Taro [What is she doing?]

Heinrich [She is sealing each of the spirits which draw out loyalty. Tonight, we are having a meeting. If you can promise me that you will not tell others what you see, I will arrange to have you see what will happen at the side of the tiered platform.]

Show Taro [Thanks. I will take your offer.]

Heinrich [One only condition. Will you join Deutscher Gruss, as you joined Romano's Passo Romano.]

Show Taro [What I joined there was Salute Romano.]

Heinrich [Okay, take it easy. What we will say is Sieg Heil.]

Show Taro [What kind of gathering is it?]

Heinrich [Such members that have been newly appointed as the managing staff are coming to this gathering from each country in Europe. At this gathering they shall be given the skull badge of Teutonic Knights as a testimony of the glory. This is the Festival of Flames and is a huge spectrum so I hope you enjoy it by all means. Astrologists and magicians other than Maria are participating there.]

18. Festival of Flare and Heinrich

Starting a bit after 11 o'clock midnight, the open space of the south side of the castle came to be filled by some handreds of people. They were in uniforms and were standing in a row. Show Taro wondered when in such a short time so many people could gather, but as things had been set this way already, he decided he would stay still and watch carefully what was going to take place. Marching began with the blowing sound of a trampet and a group of people carrying lit torches appeared from no where, and the recomposing of the lines of people was done. Groups of several ten people each raising swastika in the ancient Rome fashion were keeping in step and letting the sound of military boots out.

At the stands, Romano Sfolza slided in just to make the start of the festival. He pointed the marching lines and whispered to Show Taro.

Romano [This is Passo Romano. This is Goose Step.]
Show Taro [I know, I know.]

The touchlight parade of large group of people was bringing about a strange atmosphere. Smells of burning wood hung over the place. Were they replicating the scene of the parade of new conscripts executed by SS(Nazi SS Troopes) before WW2? Or otherwise, was it the reproduction of Nuremberg Rally? Show Taro wondered. Searchlight was flushed straight up to the sky creating poles of light in the dark while plural number of touchlights were producing a big Gyaku-Manji on the ground. In this way, the demonstrations were shifting one after another matching the music.

Show Taro remembered he had read a long time ago that Heinrich Himmler, secretary of Nazi Security Service gathered the SS main members at an old castle in Germany to hold a ceremony by German Chivalric Order which had been lasting since the middle era, however, he was not sure if the big spectacle which was developing in front of his eyes was copying that ceremony. With the roaring of trumpets and the sound of drums, excitement there was all the more swelling.

Meanwhile, when Heinrich appeared in the center of the stage, from the left side of the tiered stand a group consisting some tens of people was marching on, each holding a touch in the left hand. The flag bearer leading the group was holding up the flag insignia called Standarte. That flag insignia was showing a crest of a golden hawk grasping swaltika with a black mark board with some letters marked on it underneath of which a red 70cm square cloth was hanging. As this group was approaching the tiered stand, music began to be blown.

And, almost at the same time, this group turned their faces to the stand and sticked out their right arms to Heinrich.

Romano who was sitting next to Show Taro whispered him at the ear.

Romano [Salute Romano.]

Show Taro [I know. Is that group consisting of Neitherlanders, by the way?]

At this word of his, Romano looked to be surprised and tried to explain as follows:

Romano   [Don't you know this? The anthem of Netherlands and the SS anthem use the same melody. What's more is that of Netherlands was enacted later than SS anthem.]

Show Taro   [Anyway, who is the tall old man next to Heinrich?]

Romano   [He is the man named Alois Brunner. Mossad of Jewish Agency are chasing him.]

Show Taro   [Is he still chased after?]

Romano   [They are as persistent as snakes. Maybe tonight or so, some Mossad members shall be hanged.]

Romano winked. Talking about the afore-mentioned group, they had in the meantime changed direction and stood in a row. Heinrich who had been resaluting with his right hand up took off the square sunglasses which he usually wore, and changed them with round shape glasses. Heinrich wearing the round glasses looked exactly alike the historical figure. Show Taro thought there was no way that Heinrich could deny he had absolutely no relationship with that historical figure.

Romano   [He is a duplication of Heinrich Himmer. He is quite alike.]

Show Taro   [I am absolutely consternated.]

Romano   [That one is the son of the niece of Felix, the exclusive massager of Hilter. Her mother when she was plegnant went to South America with financial help by Count Forke Bernadotte who belonged to Swedish Red Cross after the war. It was no way impossible that the refugees on the U-boat which stranded in Uruguay in July, 1945 could keep themselves hidden without any help until the anti submarine patrol net of The Allied Forces ceased its action. Utilizing that route, the gold nuggets and treasures of NS (Nazi) and the key SS members made an escape.]

Show Taro [Was the collection of Hermann Goering inclusive?]

Romano [Even I don't know that far.]

Show Taro [Most of the Goering Collection is missing.]

Hearing it, his eyes showed a pierce look.

Romano [You, if we find them, shall we take equal shares?]

Show Taro [Let's.]

Romano [Aren't you an interesting guy.]

Hermann Goering was of a character of an uncomparably strong collection mania and an extravagant spender reflecting his aristocratic lineage.

There, Heinrich Himmler had been forming up a specially assigned unit in SS for collection of art items. At the beginning, work assignment of this unit was selection for seizing purposes of the property derived of the jewish people in the Nazi concentration camp, but at a later date when Nazi German troops stampeded into France and East Europe, various plans were put into practice fairly deliberately and systematically.

At the French war front, they purchased some hundreds of copies of Michellin restaurant guide books for selection purposes and right after the French surrender, they confiscated for use by SS officers restarants and hotels of their choice which were located in the area that came to be under Nazi's control. In line with this action, such mansions as possessed by anti-Nazi nobles or wealthy level of people became the target of seizure.

The other people who are obedient to Nazi and not that much wealthy hid their family treasure in a place such as an attick of the hut in the countryside place of their possession showing arts of less value at their houses in an attempt to keep their treasures safe from the seizure of SS and entertained German commanders or the like at their houses where valuable arts had been removed. One thing that could be added was German Nazi was in a sense considerate not to dare to seize the portraits of the successive castle owners. That we can in this modern time world see that the portrates of such old castels are kept as is since then is because the old times gentelemen's agreement was thus kept.

In this sense, when the bubbles economy was flowering, a certain Japanese business woman bought a chateau in France once and resold it after a few years. What she did then was that she removed the chateau's successive owners' portraits and sold the chateau, which of action of her became an issue at that time. This can be determined as the deed by a new rich with greed blinded woman who did not understand culture. In addition, her father was a notorious miser so the writer, too, would not wish the name of such a person to be recorded in the history.

After then, German Nazi troops advanced to attack East European countries and there, too, an army for the exclusive purpose of seizing the Goeing Collection was formed in SS to enable removal systematically of all those art products in only one day even the size of the castle was quite large. In this part of the art seizing program, the Michellin Travel Guide must have been very usuful.

Regarding the Amber Room in Russia, the fact that the whole

interior decoration using amber of Bartic Sea only was plannedly divided, packed and taken out was found out after retreatment of German Nazi Troops. To date whereabouts of the most of amber interiors is unknown. Romors are telling that they must be hidden either in the mine pillars of a part of Alps or in an abandomed rock mine, and the majority part of them are still missing. It could well be considered that some people might have looted those like at a fire attributing the absence of those amber arts to the result of Nazi seizement.

In Japan, too, such legends as the buried gold of Toyotomi family or Tokugawa Family are still going on. This phenomenon may be construed that the dream has been expanded extra big beyond the reality. However, for such art lovers as Show Taro or Romano it would be more favorable way of imaging the roman that those art objects must have been secretly hidden somewhere waiting for the day when those could again come out under the sun, rather than believing they had all been destroyed into the ashes by the war.

Romano and Show Taro was whispering about the interesting subject of the sharing the Nazi seized treasures with each other, and suddenly came back to reality in which Heinrich was making a speech in German. Show Taro happened to cross the eyes with Akemi who was sitting at the opposite side of Romano and found that she was gesturing to show she could not understand what Heinrich was speaking about in his speech. Kato who was sitting beyond Akemi looked like the Heinrich's speech coming into one of his ear and out of the other.

Show Taro [By the way, do you ascertain who is the man sitting
  next to Maria on the tiered stand?]

Romano [That man is a doctor and an astrologist by the name of Luc Gauric. He is from the family of successive astgrologists for the several hundreds of past years in Europe. His grandfather was engaged in the work of librarian in Paris and was close to Rurolf Hess and Heinrich Himmler, but as that family is originally of Italian family tree, when they tell their astrology, they use the ancestral Latin name of Luca Gaurico. Needless to say, though, no one knows their true long name as it always is the case with astrologists.]

Show Taro [I remember I have heard the name Luca Gaurico⋯for ⋯]

Romano [Yes, I'm not surprised. Their ancestor of about 20 generations back in the past was the Cathaline de Medicis' exclusive astrologist. It is said that the Queen used to rule the court with help by prural number of distinguished astrologists.]

Show Taro [Now I see. That must be why I thought I had heard the name previously.]

Romano [Besides Queen Cathaline, among the ancesters of his, there were employed by that nortorious Borjas or the Estes who had brought about Reneissance. All of them were excerting Ecclesiastical Latin or ancient Latin. Besides them there are similar family trees existing. Is such also happening in Japan?]

Show Taro [Talking about family tree, Miss Ave Maria who is there next to Luc Gauric is of the similar family tree. The Abes are of the family tree as fortune tellers that has been continuing since the era of Heian in Japan. Their family tree has been producing fortune tellers in their many generations keeping characteristics that is pretty alike those of the exclusive fortune tellers of the Imperial Family. Apart from this instance, there exist fortune tellers originated in a school of Buddhism called Esoteric Buddhism or such extension of Japan's ancient mountain worship represented by itinerant Buddist monks in the mountains. The fortune teller whom high rank officials of Meiji Government were counting on was Kaemon Takashima, the wood dealer. His fortune telling method is called Eki fortune telling. He is said to have a special fortune telling ability.]

Romano [Did that man tell the fortune of the result of the war or the destiny of well-known people?]

Show Taro [After the first prime minister of the Meiji era called Hirobumi Ito became the elder stateman called Genro, this man stopped his planned visit to Russia as he said he foresaw danger in that trip. He was also believed to have successfully guessed the name of the assassin of Ito as 'Omone', and at the time of both Nisshin and Nichiro wars, he helped his superiors telling them the exact starting day and time of the wars and also the time of the end of the war. However, in Takashima's case, his children were not made to succeed their father's profession.]

Romano [Well, if that's what happened, I guess Japan might have a difficult time at WW2. If they do not know how to end a war, the war can be an endress war.]

Show Taro [Your guess is quite correct.]

Romano [Reason why Italy surrendered at quite an early time was because the high class officials around Benito Mussolini came to learn his fate had run out.]

Show Taro [Was Luc Gauric involved in that case?]

Romano [No, He is the person who ought to be called as Maestro Luca Gaurico in its formal Latin. When an astrologist is able to see through the fate is when some spirit is falling down which is not related to Christianism. Otherwise, he could never use the Evils.]

Show Taro [Has such an astrologist contracted with the Evils?]

Romano [No one has ever seen such a scene as an astrologist negotiating with the Evils, but according to what I guess···he may have the Evils grasp a fake bank check.]

Show Taro [So that's the way you guess.]

Romano [Well, before that, that the fact astrolosists are hiding their true names itself already means the danger of such deals.]

Show Taro [Sure you are right.]

Heinrich was busy to personally hand over the badge to each man as a proof of the member of German knights. His figure observed in the light of torches did not look like Heinrich Hizinger but did look like revived Heinrich Himmler himself over the time lapse of more than 60 years. Strangely, on the tiered stand the ex-SS leutenant colonel Alois Brunner alone looked extremely aged as if he had opened Pandora's Box. It is said history repeats itself but such an opportunity to sight the occasion would seldom come around to you.

After a short while, the handing ceremony of the skelton badge was over and Heinrich went back to the tiered stand, then once again the same melody as that one of the Neitherlands was chanted. Then again there was a short speech by Heinrich and finishing it, Heinrich extended his right arm and shouted at the microphone.

Heinrich [We've met before, now we meet again! And we will! In the future!]

Everyone [Sieg Heil!]

Reverberating sound spread all over the place but the ears of Show Taro did not miss Romano shouting [Ave Rome!]. Naturally, Romano sent a wink Show Taro with full smiles on his face.

When the gathering was over, everyone went back to the rooms allocated to each.

Akemi [Weren't you cold?]

Show Taro [Shall we get some coffee?]

When they entered the room, they asked the butler standing at the doorside to bring some coffee, and soon a coffee pot and several cups and saucers were brought in. Show Taro tried to tip the butler but was refused. Crossing with the butler, Heinrich taking Maria came in.

Heinrich [It was a bit cold, wasn't it. As the butler is stationed at the collider, ask him anything you need.]

Heinrich looked still trying to surpress his excitement.

Show Taro [It really was a huge spectrus.]

Heinrich [They made a vow to Standarte tonight and became the members of SS. There were .9 million SS members during WW2 but majority was seized by non-Germans. This situation is still the same with a large number of members coming from the East European area, Middle East or South America till just recently but now the number of Germans is gradually increasing. You may have already heared from Romano, but our situation doesn't necessarily match the one in Italy where fascists are again gathering raising an anti-Mafia policy against Mafias backed up by Jewish capitals.]

Heinrich looked to have satisfied with the result of the enlarged stabilation of the expansion of his party as the tendency in the recent years was showing. He also stressed the fact of SS acting beyond the border as same as in the past.

Show Taro [Acturally, it is rumored that Sycillian Mafias have been flowing the stolen paintings into the Jewish capitals in order to yield the political funds for many years. In return to this benefit, the secret of protecting the activities of Andreottie ex-prime minister had been kept which however was revealed at the court in 1996.]

Heinrich [Incidentally, when are you scheduled to return to Japan?]

Show Taro [I plan to make a return maybe tomorrow. I must ask you by what means I am supposed to contact you when I have got the thing.]

Heinrich [Please contact Mr. Kato of Euro · Midori · Manji]

Show Taro [Okay, understood.]

Heinrich   [Right, then, good night.]

Heinrich went out, but as Maria stayed there, the three had coffee together.

Akemi   [What is your role at this gathering?]

Maria   [To change the badge to a talisman.]

Akemi   [Yah, I agree. Skelton is just too evil, isn't it.]

With the amazed look, Show Taro explained the relation between the skelton badge and the knights.

Show Taro [The beginning of the use of skelton was when a cavalry started to use the skelton of the prophet John as a talisman.]

Akemi   [Is it really so?]

Show Taro [It is a legend. But I don't think why the Hospital Cavalries called themselves as Saint John Cavalries does not have any relation to that legend. This group of cavalries is now named Marta Cavalries and does still have an office in Rome.]

Akemi   [Are they defencers of justice?]

Show Taro [During the period of time when they were called Rhodes Cavalries, they were no less than pirates in the view point of the Islam side.]

Akemi   [Did they change the name so often?]

Show Taro [Names differed to the location of the cavalries, but the contents kept the same continuity. The original model is Saint John Cavalries.]

Akemi   [By the way, I notice this room too has talisman pasted at each corner.]

— 200 —

Maria told in the look of that Akemi was so slow to notice it.

Maria   [That is to protect you all from the evil spirits]

Akemi   [I am not an evil spirit.]

Maria   [No, no. Not that meaning. What I know is that many sorts of crying voice can still be heard here as this castle were used by SS in the WW2.]

Listening to this weird story, Akemi suddenly came to feel uneasy.

Akemi   [Did you hear it?]

Maria   [I have seen several times something floating in the air.]

Akemi   [Are there many of such places as here?]

Maria   [Yes, ···such places are not where laypersons can live. Mr. Heinrich can live here no problem as Luc Gauric of the family of astrologists whom his deceased father appointed as the family astrologist is protecting him. I have heard that grandfather of this astrologist was also the consultant of Rudolf Hess.]

Show Taro [Incidentally, Mary, If I return with what Heinrich needs, will he hand over the painting to me as promised?]

Maria   [Before you talk about that, your counterparty may snatch the painting away from you in Europe and will not pay you the contingency fee.]

Show Taro [Could such a thing happen?]

Maria   [Mind you, you should deliver the painting after you have brought it into Japan.]

Show Taro [Can it be so seen? To you?]

Maria [So feel, I do.]

Akemi [Robert is also a dangerous man, isn't he.]

Maria jumpily moved her ears and bent herself forward.

Maria [Is he calling himself Robert?]

Akemi [That's what I heard, right?]

Show taro did not wish to be asked.

Show Taro [I'm not in a position to tell you who my client is.]

Maria [On the enigma telegram which arrived at Heinrich, the clause of 'watch the Robert connection' is written. It came from the Hague. What I understand is that is a caution notice of the man from Scandinavia who has a habit of wasting his money.]

Show Taro [Blonde haired and tall man⋯No, I haven't seen such person. By the way, I wish you do me a favor.]

Maria [What favor?]

Show Taro [Will you ask Heinrich for him to arrange a round trip air ticket to and from Japan?]

Maria [Alright, and what do you intend to do?]

Show Taro [I will secretly return to Japan to get a thing.]

Akemi, expecting something interesting to happen, rolled her eyes.

Akemi [What do you do with the hotel in Vienna?]

Show Taro [If Mary can spare time, please use the room as you like it under my name.]

Maria [Okay, then I will tell Miss Akemi's fortune there.]

Akemi [Good on you.]

That night was ended then.

— 202 —

19. Voyage to Japan

On the following day, by helicopter they returned to EMM (Euro Midori Manji) in the surburbs of Vienna. This time, Akemi and Maria rode on a rent-a-car and returned to the connecting suite and were to stay here for about three days to wait Show Taro's return from Japan. Robert was relieved to learn Show Taro was alive by a mail from him after a three-day interval of no news from him. That mail told him Show Taro would not be able to return the hotel for about three days as he would be out to trace the painting.

Robert was settled down in a hotel which was located at the opposite side of the cathedral. Hearing the two women returning to Show Taro's hotel, he thought he would any way be able to meet them and gather whatever information they had. He was concerned about the fact that two of his co-workers that followed those men who walked out from Café Sfolza died accidental death and also, he lost the touch of the other three, consequently, those who safely returned were only the ones who reached the art dealers running their business in Switzlerland or Austria. They visited those dealers disguising in a sight-seers but though they showed the black card of the credit card, only what they were offered for their purchase were paintings with a paper napkin marked B so they had to try hard to decline their pretty frantical sales of these Bs. That was what Robert was reported by those who returned surviving from the chase of the Mafias from Café Sfolza.

That night, Robert knocked the door of Show Taro's room but as he failed to be answered, he then knocked the adjoining room and found there the two women.

Robert   [Good evening, I am Robert. Won't you tell me where Mr. Show Taro is gone?]

Akemi   [All what he said to us was that he was going to trace the cue of the painting.]

Robert   [Don't be so short. Please try to remember whatever can be a crue of whereabouts him.]

At Robert's earnest request, Akemi answered as if she hit on a good idea.

Akemi   [I may be able to recover my memory if I can take time.]

Robert   [I will buy you dinner down in the restaurant, so won't you remember what you have heard?]

Akemi   [We are two. Is it okay?]

Robert   [Leave it to me.]

Akemi   [We will go downstairs in thirty minutes.]

In this way, Akemi and the other two were to take dinner at the hotel restaurant, but Rober could not be aware of those two women's intention of searching the background of Robert.

After thirty minutes, the two women who were slightly dressed up showed up at the hall. In the restaurant, they of course seized a table in the non-smoking area.

Akemi   [Let me do the introduction. This is Miss Maria, the medium. That is Mr. Robert in Insurance business.]

Then, the two exchanged business cards. More accurately saying, both exchanged to each other a card of the insurance company and a card of a permaceutical company.

Maria   [At which office of your company do you usually

— 204 —

work?]

Robert [I am commuting between London and Hague quite often. As I am an investigator, I have to travel a lot.]

Maria [Are you familiar with paintings or art objects inside out?]

Robert [My favorites are the old masters in the 18th century to the 19th century.]

Maria [What about the impressionists?]

Robert [Being in charge of lost items, I am combatting with difficult recoveries with those arts.]

Maria [Do you investigate doubtful persons in a separate room?]

Robert [Our company is an insurance company so we do not do such type of investigation.]

Maria [But, there in your Hague office, Solomon's seal is observed.]

Hearing these words, Robert was at a loss as to why such a question was posed to him.

Robert [Our Hague office is an old building···but I have not heard anything odd about it. In addition, what is Solomon's seal?]

Maria [Some people are calling it the Star of David because of the compiled D's and Israel uses it on its national flag. But in true fact, it is a seal to seal off the evils.]

Robert [I see, but I have not seen such a thing in this building.]

Maria [Your work place in London seems to have been built after the war.]

— 205 —

Robert	[How can you see that?]
Maria	[I just see it.]
Robert	[By the way, have you been long here in Vienna?]
Maria	[No, just about these three years or so.]
Robert	[What is the main task of the assignment General Affairs?]
Maria	[Reception work of special guests.]
Robert	[From Japan or South America?]
Maria	[Countries are not specified.]
Robert	[How many languages do you understand?]
Maria	[On the spoken language side, They are Japanese, English and Spanish. On the reading side, Latin, French, Sanskrit, and so on.]
Robert	[So you do astrology as your hobby?]
Maria	[You understand me well. But why? Or rather I put this way that you, too, have an interest in the future and fortune telling.]
Robert	[As my grandfather heard and saw odd things.]
Maria	[Were those tellings of the future?]
Robert	[With conclusion first···those included the fortune telling of the future.]
Maria	[Was your grandfather's profession···a doctor?]
Robert	[Yes, how do you know that?]
Maria	[Just a coincidence. But that does not mean he saw the future.]
Akemi	[Wait, Had your grandfather come to know any or some prophecy of the future?]
Robert	[By coincidence.]

— 206 —

Akemi	[Don't put on airs like that. Just teach us.]
Robert	[What I heard of is around the year of 1941, Raphael Grant, my grand father was a doctor and one day he was put on a black car.]
Akemi	[Was it a kidnapping?]
Robert	[It seemed to be an assignment ordered by the army.]
Akemi	[Was it a confidential assignment?]
Robert	[He was taken to do the health check-up, or more precisely, the counseling work and the person counseled was Rudolf Hess.]
Akemi	[What is that Rudolf Hess?]
Robert	[NSDAP, known as Nazi, he was the dupty leader there.]
Akemi	[Is he a great figure?]
Robert	[Did he hold classified national information? Was he sane insisting on a negotiation with U.K.? What could his true target be⋯At that time The German Government was broadcasting Hess got insane and flew to U.K.]
Akemi	[The answer can be simple, can't it.]
Robert	[No, it was difficult. Germany and U.K. were in the war at that time.]
Akemi	[Why didn't U.K. have Rudolf Hess broadcast to Germany?]
Robert	[It is a totally unexpected idea! That is an unthinkable action to have No.2 of the enemy country broadcast by radio back to the enemy country.]
Akemi	[You mean what you said based on a chess game?

	Once a chessman is taken over by the enemy lines, it becomes the chessman of the enemy. So, if you seize a chessman of the player of Japanese chess, that chessman becomes your chessman.]
Robert	[Regretfully, there was no such idea in U.K. then. Raphael, my grandfather, was told by Hess a strange story about the future, and so he in turn was suspected he might have gone insane when he reported Hess story to the U.K. Government.]
Akemi	[And what happened to your grandfather, then.]
Robert	[He was urged to analize and explain what he had heard from Hess, and to try to worm out more information about the future from Rudolf Hess at the request by the U.K. highclass officials.]
Akemi	[But Hess wouldn't speak out any more.]
Maria	[No, no. I guess Rudolf Hess requested the original copy of 『Les Centuries』 which existed in U.K., am I right?]
Robert	[Correct! My grandfather arranged to have a copy made for Hess. So, he, too, did see the future. But what I heard from my grandfather, Hess told him ; 『Raphael, keep what you heard for at least thirty years after this war ceased.』 , so he kept silence till the Christmas time in 1975.]
Akemi	[Then, how will the future be going?]

While they were talking that way, warm soup dishes were brought about to their table. After they finished the soup, Akemi and Maria shared a dish of sautéed trout, and next to the trout,

Akemi took a canard domestique (=duck meat) dish. Season of the best quality fatty duck did not come yet at that time, but Akemi thought it was an idea to have duck as the majority of dishes popular in the midcontinent were four-legged meat. All through this dinner, they talked about Robert's grandfather and what he did.

Robert   [According to what Hess told, that Germany would lost the war but after Germany was defeated, there would come out once again a political power of ethnic radical faction which was symbolized by the color Black would lead the Europe. Then, after the era when America and Soviet led the world's politics, Soviet would be split into plural number of countries. And moreover, Heinrich Himmer, too, had deciphered accordingly.]

Akemi   [But that did not happen.]

Robert   [Though the order is wrong, it is a fact that in the part of the Italian ruling party there had already come such an era when the former name of the political party was National Fascist Party.]

Akemi   [Then are you saying what Hess had told your grandfather turned out to be real?]

Robert   [Yes, Part of it came true.]

Akemi   [So you mean the rest did not come true.]

Robert   [No, not necessarily. How to sequence the whole happenings is the difficult point. Psalms are not written in the chronological order. They are shuffled. And this is why it is difficult to sequence them. Even at this modern era, quatrain psalms written by Nostradamus cannot fully be deciphered even by French people..or more correctly, Nostradamus carefully chose such words that were too difficult to be understood. People who try to understand the psams are spending difficult time sometimes trying to supplement the missing meanings or removing the misleading lines or replacing the words.]

Akemi　[And what will the further future go ahead ?]

Robert　[Raphael let me make a promise not to tell that to those who do not have a power to see through the future.]

Akemi　[That means you scarcely told us any important part.]

Robert　[Show must be trying to read it, I guess?]

Akemi　[Reading what?]

Robert　[Prophecy of the future, in other words 「Les Centuries.」 You can get enough information from him by just asking him.]

Akemi　[Can Show Taro see the future?]

Maria　[It will be possible for him to descipher it. But to see through the future is not an easy thing.]

Then Akemi took blue cheese on her plate and ate it with honey so much as dripping off the cheese. Honey with the citras scent softened rather salty flavor of cheese. And the sweetness of the Hungarian Tokaji Wine was super delicious.

Akemi　[Bob, This dinner is a feast. I hope you will not be complained by your superior when he checks your expense account.]

Robert　　　[No worries.]

Akemi　　　[You shall meet Show again after a couple of days.]

Robert　　　[Will he truly be safe?]

Maria　　　[Will it be a case that at your insurance company some thing wrong keep happening on your co-staffs?]

Maria asked looking at Robert as if she were sure about every thing.

Robert　　　[No, Our situation is not that bad.]

Robert (Both this fox with nine tails and Ave Maria, those women really look suspicious about me⋯)

Akemi　　　[We have no reason to suspect the fact that you are engaged in insurance business, but⋯]

Robert　　　[But⋯what?]

Akemi　　　[We do not believe it at all.]

After dinner, Akemi and Maria returned to their room, but at that same night, Maria made a call to Kato.

Maria　　　[I wish you to make an investigation and put it on a list as this may relate to Robert's connection which was shown on Enigma.]

Kato　　　[What do you want me to list?]

Maria　　　[A list of those names of the buildings that are still used in Hague or Netherlands which were used by SS or Gestapo during WW2 and a list of the present users of those buildings, please.]

Kato　　　[By when do you need these?]

Maria　　　[The sooner the better.]

— 211 —

Kato   [Tomorrow in the morning I will ring and report to Heinrich or his staff, as I'm afraid he is no longer in Europe by now.]

So, as was written so far, at this hotel restaurant in Vienna, Akemi and Maria tried not only to bemuse Robert but also to uncover his true profession. Around the same time as when they were having dinner, Show Taro was flying with a business class ticket from the airport in Vienna to Tokyo. He was flying by the flight which had been reserved by Heinrich and Kato, but he was intending to spend only about a couple of days at most in Tokyo. Arriving at Narita, he returned to his office at Nihonbashi Muromachi. This action of his could be carried out as scheduled but Show Taro kept the fact that he was back in Tokyo itself in secret to Robert.

20. Antique Festival in Kyoto

On return to his office, he hurriedly located the Ippin-do business card from the card holder and made sure that the cell phone number was on it. He went outside to seek better radio wave connection and using the cell phone which had not been deposited with Robert called that cellphone number.

Show Taro [Hello, is that Mr. Yamashina of Ippindo? This is Hayashi of Palais Flora.]

Yamashina [Hey, you···What do you want? I didn't expect you to call me.]

Show Taro [Where are you now?]

Yamashina [I'm attending the Kyoto Antique Festival.]

Show Taro [Do you still keep it?]

Yamashina [How can I get what you mean by just 'it'!]

Show Taro [That crystal ball of Yosuke Matsuoka.]

Yamashina [Oh, yes, I'm still holding it, but I won't sell it to you as you are a fellow share trader. I wouldn't mind an exchange deal with you with some thing that has worthwhile story.]

Show Taro [I will be there to meet you tomorrow at 10 o'clock.]

Yamashina [I will be there without looking forward.]

At midnight on the previous day Show Taro rode on a long-distance night bus for Kyoto from Tokyo owning nothing except the clothes on his back and arrived early in the morning in Kyoto. He took a quick set breakfast at the coffee shop in front of the Kyoto Station and slided into the site of the Antique Festival.

— 213 —

Show Taro [Good morning, Old Man!]

Yamashina [Good Morning. Aren't you lively. Guess that's what the being young for.]

Show Taro [Souvenir.]

Yamashina [What's this?]

Show Taro [Tokaji wine. Sweet and the best one. And, this cheese, while you're waiting for buyers.]

Yamashina [Well, then, what do you offer for exchange?]

Show Taro [Will it do?]

Show Taro unstringed the parcel in a leisury manner and explained slowly.

Show Taro [This is of the 1st century marble patterned core molded glass and was unearthed out of the coffin of a princess of the 8th century. Here is the export permit of the unearthed goods and the other is the export permit issued by Austria.]

Just to add, Show Taro who knew that Heinrich could counterfeit any kind of necessary documents, he asked him to prepare such documents overnight.

Show Taro [As is written on this book, it has been exhibited at the special event held by the Vienna National History Museum and the owner at the unearthed time was Nazi Alois Brunner ex-Commander who is lost at this moment. Don't you find both the history and the background of the owner pretty eye-catching?]

Yamagata [I see, it may be of better value than that crystal ball with that worn-out note.]

Show Taro [Thank you.]

Yamashina [Won't you wrap it by yourself? Oh, Ya, you don't have
your booth today. I will wrap it for you.]

The old man humming a tune pushed the crystal ball and the
stand into the paulownia wood box and double-wrapped the box
with air packing material.

After he confirmed that the package does not rattle, he handed
the parcel to Show Taro.

Yamashina [Where are you taking it?]

Show Tari [Overseas. By the way, do you have any idea about
this bracelet?]

Yamashina [Several of my non-Japanese customers since old days
are coming from Kobe. They expect new items in
exchange of old ones. You, take care.]

Show Taro [Farewell.]

He bowed once to him and quickly left there. After a while, this
old man would start again telling the history of his merchandise in
his own ryithmic flow of words to his regular customers.

Yamashina [Hi, Mr. President. You know this bracelet was⋯it was
the one used by a princess of Syria⋯It digged out of
the grave of the 8th century⋯ who do you guess is
the person that digged it out? He was a commander of
SS Nazi Troops. He was uncatcheable⋯ even though
the Jewish Mossad chased him. I guess that was his
old wife who became hurt for money must send it out
for sale..Are you satisfied with this perfect explanation
of mine about it? Well, now I need water for
refreshing. He told me this is a tokaji(=meaning urban
in Japanese) wine. I wonder which tokaji area?]

— 215 —

Talking this way to himself, he took the cork stopper of the wine bottle off and poured the wine into a paper cup for about half of the cup and put the stopper back to the bottle placing the bottle besides him, then, just at that time, his regular customer who was a monomaniac lover of antieques came into his booth.

That was Simon Zamir who was running the wholesale business of diamonds in Kobe. He was living in Japan for a long time so his Japanese was fluent. He, too, was a feverishly enthusiastic seeker of lucky finds. Reason why he was dealing antieques was due to the fact that he disliked superstition and did not believe that such things as spirits would exist. Therefore, he did not rely on intuition and therefore was rather relying on his own close inspection and consequent findings of the goods including the belongings to the goods.

And that was the very reason why he could have a long association with that indecent and speculator-look Old Man.

Simon   [Old Man, So you got this bracelet. It is of the 1st century⋯By the way, how come are you taking Tokaji?]

Yamashina [Oh, hi, Mr. Simon as usual. Just now my acquaintance brough this bracelet to me and in addition gave me this wine saying it was an awesome wine which was produced in whatever town and country I don't remember the name of. Isn't this wine becoming to such a city boy as me ?]

Simon   [Are these two permit licenses and the book inclusive

— 216 —

of the bracelet?]

Yamashina [Yes, you're right.]

Simon [Tell me the price.]

Yamashina [1.5 million!]

Simon [···Say 1 million?]

Yamashina [No way, no way. I understand this is an artifact excavated by SS Nazi Troops.]

Simon [Are you sure?...By the way, is the person who brought it to you the one that gave you this Tokaji as a souvenir?]

Yamashina [Is that any problem to you?]

Simon's eyes had caught SS in the runic letter and the skull design emblem on the label pasted on the tokaji wine bottle. One mistery about the label was it did not carry the name of Chateau. This observation of his was about to convince him that the bracelet might truly come from the Nazi-relations.

And, as is, there were thirty seconds of silence.

Simon [What about 1.2 million in cash?]

Yamashina [It needs a special service, but, Okay.]

Simon [One condition. Won't you tell me who brought this to you?]

Yamashina [That is···against the rules in this business field.]

Simn [I accept it. Then what about another hundred thousand on top of 1.2 million as an information fee for which you don't have to issue a receipt as I will not process that account. Do you accept this condition?]

Yamashina [You're pretty flexible. Okay, very well.]

Simon [Can you tell me his contact details?]

Yamashina [I can give you his cell phone number, as he called me yesterday.]

Kanji Yamashina of Ippindo showed the incoming call history on his cell phone.

Simon [That number, I see.]

Yamashina [But I'm not sure if this number can be connected as he was saying he was flying back overseas by the first flight this morning.]

As Ippindo was afraid, Simon tried that number only in vain. As a matter of course, Show Taro at that time was shifting to Tokyo by bullet train and was refraining from receiving or making all incoming and outgoing calls for the purpose of a complete shutout of wiring connections. As Maria is afraid, there is a possibility of Robert to totally refuse payment of any expenses other than what came up in Europe insisting on his right in accordance to the European law to apply any business contracted in Europe alone and to refuse all others that were conducted other than in Europe. As a normal employee of an insurance company, it is unusual that he could travel at his will from London or Hague to freely travel to Switzerland or Austria. Much caution does no harm. Simon left a message on Show Taro's phone but it could not have a chance to be checked till he comes back to Japan on the next occasion.

Coming home Simon checked on his home computer the resime of the Nazi SS related excavater of the bracelet by the name f Alois Brunner. Information he could gather on PC told him that Mossad, the Israelean intelligence agency was chasing this man around, but he seemed to be under the protection of the Sylian Government and was hiding himself somewhere in Damascus. Of the Mossad

— 218 —

pursuing team, many spies were sent but none of them made a safe return. Simon gathered Alois Brunner's last military rank served at the army seemed to be a commander but no news about whether he was dead or alive since then and the only footprint he left was that bracelet.

That such armed insurgents as Palestine Armed Organization saluted the Nazi salutation rather than Roman salutation was evidencing the possibility that their military instructors used to be the Nazi SS officers. The name Palestina came from the name of a state which was established after the conquerence of ancient Rome, so it seems that name Palestina was started to be used after the name Israel had been fixed. This may have been the reason why their salutation style was to open palms facing to the earth and to extend the right arm forward.

For those people who know world's history well, the Roman style satulation has much older history than the one which is widely practiced in the armies all over the world coming from the knights touching the visor of the helmet or the large coller of bonnets. It was Mussorini who intended revival of that salutation style of the Roman territory at the Mediterranean coast. Taking this salutation style in and instead of the restoration of Rome intended by Mussorini, Hitler and Nazi schemed revival of the territory of Holly Rome Empire and tried to achieve reinessance of it.

What the history shows is the Nazi · Germany ranked the first for the Holly Rome Empire, the second of the Geman Empire which rose by Prussia, and that the Third Reich(=Empire) which in German words means what was coming in the future was propaganded by Nazi German. And SS (Nazi Troops) was established in the Third Reich as an Empire in the Shadow.

What SS aimed at was a revovery of a German Knight group of the Saint Roman Empire as shown by that the enlistment ceremony of the knight group copying the administration of an oath by knights. In other words, what SS aimed at was to grow another self-governing organization in the Third Reich. In addition, they came to understand that the Saint Rome Emperor was admitting the German Knight Group their right to conquer Russia. There may have been some connection between the fact that Nazi armed SS took a major role at the Operation Barbarossa and the right of concurrence of Russia.

Simon, finished his investigation so far, sent an e-mail to his cousin in New York.

21. Operation Rosalia

Nicola Zamir who is the cousin of Simon received the e-mail Saimon sent to him and he was excited reading Simon's message. Nicola's group was consisting of the liaisons of Mossad. His public face was a large-sized wholesaler of diamonds and for that reason he was in a position of collecting information of the wealthy people all over the world. On usual days, he is buying and selling jewelries at a lane called Diamond Row in Manhattan, but originally, using his established concessions, he was importing stolen paintings that Italian Mafia handled and wholesaling those to galleries in Manhattan. But in 1996, this illegal route was destroyed so he and the successor of the Mafia's Don called Bernard Gambino were in the midst of working out remedial measures. For some time from the past, he and Bernard had been cooperation for destroyal of the Neo.Fascist routing.

At that time, the extreme end of the organization which Bernard was chasing was a world where Mafia could not reach, being governed by Neo Nazi. That in this world the shadow of Alois Brunner appeared was an important news so the news was sent to Jerusalem right away.

Nicola Zamir was not dressed in the typical Jewish clothes because it was needed when he was secretly buying stolen paintings and transporting these. Though he was wearing black hair, his height was 170cm which was not too conspicuous and was used to mix well with common businessmen in New York. He was consciously trying to melt into the residents there which was what

— 221 —

his deceased father had lessened him, telling him that the grandfather had gone lost in the troops where Alois Brunner belonged to. In this regard, Simon in Kobe was in the same situation. One hour or so elapsed and there came an instruction from the Mossad staff department in Jerusalem.

TO Nichola Zamir

FM Headquarter Staff Department

This is to appoint you as the commander of Operation Rosalia. Rosalia is an operation for kidnapping Alois Brunner.

For the activation of Rosalia, cooperation of Europole is under request.

Show Taro Hayashi is also an agent of Europole but to him it has been understood in the form of the contract concluded between the insurance company and himself.

Codename of Hayashi is set as Tom Boe, but his appearance is not Nordic (popular Scandinavian blonde hair) but of Asian look.

Basically, he is a free lance antique dealer. At the moment he is investigating the fake manufacturing route in line with the route of stolen paintings. Also, retriving stolen paintings. Looks like a spender, but seem to be getting information from a woman by the code name of nine tails. Watch a woman by the code name of Madonna while whether she is a friend or a foe is unknown. These two women are both of Asian descent.

Need to have Saimon attached to him and make negotiations as Saimon is fluent in Japanese.

May God's justice be fulfilled.

Late at that night, Nicola who transferred the mail called Simon.

Saimon seemed to have just waked up and sounded sleepy. There are a forteen hour time difference between New York and Kobe.

Nicola   [Did you read the transferred mail?]

Simon   [Have just opened the mail.]

Nicola   「Rosalia is expected to be invoked.」

Simon   [So does it mean I am supposed to pair with Mafia?]

Nicola   [This is to take revenge for your old man. I do understand you dislike Mafia so you were not put in charge of New York.

Simon   [What do you expect me to do?]

Nicola   [Contact Robert who has been lent out to Europole from U.K. If Alois Brunner, take precedence over the confirmation of his bodily characteristics.]

Simon   [Teach me if there is any specific method?]

Nicola   [If he is an SS, there must be a tattoo under the arm. We also need to confirm his face feasures though he may have more wrinkles now. Please send his photo.]

Simon   [Any other information useful for me?]

Nicola   [Leader of the abduction implementation unit in Italy is Bernard Gambino, husband of my wife's cousin.]

Simon   [I think I somewhat remember that name.]

Nicola   [He is Don of Mafia.]

Simon   [Disgusting partner if Alois is not involved.]

Hearing his words, Nicola tried to talk in the most casual way so as to keep Simon be willing to participate this program.

Nicola   [Won't you be patient till Alois is successfully escorted to Jelsalem. We plan to take him into a party that is going to be held at the yacht of Bernard and cruise

— 223 —

offshore in the night time. We will put a sleeping drug in his champaigne glass and will come across with an Islaeli cargo vessel to which he is to be transferred. If all this can be done smoothly, Simon, you will be a hero.]

Simon   [And the medal is to be decorated on your chest, right? Incidentaly, have the Italian authorities admitted this case, Haven't they.]

Nicola   [You must know in recent years, number of cooperators of Mafia in the Italian Police are drastically decreasing. This plan is maneuvers to infringe on the sovereignty of the Italian Government. It cannot be helped that some risk may be fraught with it, Comrade.]

What he said sounded unbelievable to Simon's ears, but Simon over again tried to make questions.

Simon   [What sort of possibility of the enemy secretly passing through the Italian authorities?]

Nicola   [Fascists' influence is getting stronger as they go to the north, therefore, if possible we should start this maneuvers while in the south. As they won't come up to Sicily, please try to organize this operation to be centered in Napoles.]

Simon   [If it is denied even in Napoles, what do you suggest to do?]

Nicola   [At worst, Rome shall be the place for Rosalia to be activated, though I am reluctant to see that happen.]

Simon   [Got it.]

For Simon who dislikes to work with Mafia, this mission will pose him an uncomfortable situation. It was a mission that could be unpleasant to him.

In this world, there exist two kinds of humans. One is consisting of such humans that are mastered by the logics and the faith of the organization they belong to under the name of the assigned duty or the authority of that organization, while the other is of such humans that are mastered by love for being humans and for caressing their families. Both has pros and cons and both of such kinds respectively exist in any race or nation.

In the Arabic world, there are businessmen who believe they can live together with Israel and in Israel, too, there exist businessmen who believe it is far better to share the same life style with Palestinians than to hate each other.

In the vast universe, the earth is nothing but a small fragment of soil. Especially in view of the fact that the human race already has come to hold neuclear weapons that can destroy the whole human race for several tens of times.

22. Inspection of Rock Crystal Ball

Show Taro, who just finished a quick round trip to Japan, returned to Vienna and on the following morning he visited Kato at Euro Midori Manji taking Akemi and Maria. From there, they changed to a helicopter as previous and flew to the castle of Heinrich Hizinger, and there Show Taro showed Heinrich his souvenir from Japan, the crystal ball.

Heinrich [Why did you come to realize this rock crystal ball is what we need?]

Show Taro [This allonge tells that this rock crystal ball was what Hitler gazed for a continuous few minutes. Hitler at the time when the Triple Alliance of Japan, Germany and Italy was formed must no doubt be full of fighting spirit.]

Heinrich [Essential condition is whether Maria can prove it or not. If this point is clarified, I will certainly hand you over the promised painting.]

Maria [Very well, I will take a good look at it.]

Maria went into the next room taking the paulownia wood box which contained the crystal ball. That room was a demarcated sacred space and in the center of the room Solomon's seal was written. This Solomon's seal was necessary to seal the spirits that were released out of the crystal ball so as not to allow the spirits to leave the ball till the spirits again need the ball. Also, if the evils around there possess the ball that will arise a troublesome situation, so it was needed to set the barrier against the invasion of wicked

— 226 —

souls from outside.

She chanted a spell and made a symbolic sign with her fingers, then gradually spirits were floating out vaguely in the crystal ball which had been transparent in the first place. In this way, what began to be showing was the Nazi high-class officials who related to the Triple Alliance of Japan, Germany and Italy. Besides Hitler, Goebbels and Hess were also looking into the ball.

Goebbels was the propaganda minister of Nazi Germany who oftentimes quoted from the prophecy called Les Centuries by Michel Nostradamus in his own scheme broadcasting. When he came to learn the self suicide of Hitler, he let his child take hydrogen cyanide and he with his wife committed self suicide. He was following Hitler like his shadow, but at speeches he was a talented speaker and often made speeches in place of Hitler. At the end of WW2, he tried to have Hitler survive till his destiny turned to be better, by making a lot of unscientific speeches.

Talking about Hess, he was following Hitler all the time guarding him till May 10th ,1941 before Barbarossa, the German blitz tactics against Soviet, was actuated, on which day he launched in U.K. alone by himself and made overtunes of peace for unknown reasons.

Hess was supposed to have no relation with the German war crimes, however, strangely enough the U.K. Government did not release Hess from the prison although other German war criminals were getting old and were released from the prison, so Hess died in the prison at his age of 93.

Of those spirits, what Heinrich needed was only the spirit of Hitler so the souls of the rest of the two needed to be kept sealed. At this spirit in the aggressive state, Maria could call the soul.

— 227 —

When she finished seeing that far, she returned the spirit-filled crystal ball back to the box.

Then, she returned to the room of Heinrich and reported.

Maria [I have surely ascertained in this rockcrystal ball the spirit which makes me feel the Hitler's aggressive fighting spirit so that it is possible for you to utilize this ball for your plans. However, as regards how to use the other two spirits is not what I am supposed to decide.]

Heinrich [What you mean is in here in this rockcrystal ball there are two other spirits contained?]

Maria [You're right. In Addition to that of Hitler, spirits of Goebbels and Hess are also contained.]

Heinrich [What you suggest is that I am to think about the usage of the other two spirits other than that of Hitler?]

Maria [Whether you can use them, or otherwise, you wish to keep these into the ball is left to your consideration.]

Heinrich [Very well, I will give you, Show Taro, the 『The Man with the Golden Helmet』 as promised. Are you planning to take it directly to Japan by yourself.]

Show Taro [As I need to receive it in Japan, I am hoping Maria will take it to Tokyo and pass it to me there.]

Akemi [Why, why she? I will take it.]

Akemi felt vexed to learn Show Taro appointed Maria as a bearer.

Show Taro [No way, your luggages will surely be marked.]

Akemi [You wish to meet her, is that why?]

— 228 —

Show Taro [No, you are wrong. Suppose you take the painting, it will be seized at the air port baggage check counter. Robert will sure be marking you at least.]

Heinrich [Alright, I will keep it and when I sent her by my private jet I will let her carry it.]

Show Taro [I am waiting for you in Tokyo.]

Maria [I will contact you on arrival in Tokyo.]

Heinrich [When you return this painting will you take the work as our art consellor, Show Taro?]

Show Taro [As long as the contents of the work you offer me are not illegal, I am willing to take your offer, depending on the conditions.]

Heinrich looked to be satisfied with this reply of Show Taro's. They spent the balance of that day for making a U-turn to Vienna by helicopter. Akemi was feeling a bit uneasy to meet Maria again in Japan. Her instinct was telling her something that would disturb peace might be coming.

That night, on their arrival back at the hotel, there was a visit of Robert.

Robert [What on earth, were you out of my reach for the last few days? Where in the world have you been, Tom?]

Show Taro [I went to a certain place to get the clue of this work. On my return to Tokyo and when I can get the original painting of 「The Man with the Golden Helmet」 I will certainly contact you so be patient and just wait.]

Robert [So the painting was in Japan…]

— 229 —

Show Taro [Just about you're right.]

Robert [Is some one like Mafia organization holding it?]

Show Taro [Not really. As I came to learn one different person owned it. By the way, I am willing to do the additional tracing investigation as a supplemental task if only you will guarantee payment to me of the fight money.]

Robert [You mean that is a trade secret.]

Show Taro [Suppose the thing I am talking about is authentic, reward I am demanding is very reasonable, isn't it.]

Robert [Well, I don't disagee to that point···]

Show Taro [As soon as you ascertain it is authentic, I expect you to issue a checque right away.]

Robert [Needless to say.]

That night, with blue cheese and Tokaji wine delivered to the hotel room, Show Taro together with Robert and Akemi toasted while making a promise to meet again back in Japan.

Show Taro [According to what I gathered from Akemi, was your grandfather Raphael counselling the Nazi high class officials?]

Robert [He used to be engaged in the military work but in that case he was almost compulsorily forced to perform that assignment. However, the subject of that counselling was not all the Nazi high rank officials, namely not the normal officers of German Defence Army, but the prime purpose of that investigation was aimed at some people among the Nazi party members and those who were ranked above SS generals who had the possibility of holding the information which might be happening in the future.]

Show Taro [The first object was Rudolf・Hess. He must have been quite surprised?]

Robert [Firstly Raphael was taken to the castle, so he thought some one in the royal family might have been annoyed with such mental trauma as war phobia.]

Show Taro [And he found he was wrong.]

Robert [Whom he met at the castle owner's office was Rudolf Hess. And just before his meeting him, he had been told Hess may be insane so check him up…]

Show Taro [Was Hess insame even a bit?]

Robert [According to Raphael's diagnosis, Hess' brain was working more than clear-cut.]

Show Taro [What was Hess' demand other than superficial ones… ?]

Robert [The hidden demand of Hess' was…he had already read through all the books written by Nostradamus which had been stored in French Archieves, including, of course, 「Les Centuries」 (The Hundred Psalms) and also other related literatures. On top of these which he had aready read through, he demanded another copy of 「Les Centuries」 which existed in U.K. Responding to his request, the Prime Minister Charchill send him the copy in London in exchange of his knowledge about the fortune of U.K. Reason of this arrangement to show the Paris copy and U.K.copy is by so doing the the part which is missing several pages is different to each so by viewing both the missing parts could be

— 231 —

supplemented. At that time, these two are the only ones as the first edition of this book.]

Show Taro [So the recovered missing parts taught him some new prophery?]

Robert 『Les Centuries』 2-68

First line   Extremely struggling with the north wind

Second Line   The sailing is to be freed away on the sea

Third Line   Administration over the islands will be restored

Forth Line   The shaking citizens of London will sight the enemy and set the sails

This means that if people endeavored on the Arctic Ocean, they will come to be able to sail on that ocean so that the administration of U.K. will be restored and the citizen of London will become capable to fight against the enemy.]

Show Taro [That sounds containing an adverse meaning for Nazi・Germany. That is teaching how the destruction of trading by U-boat will be transiting.]

Robert [Hess was given the copy on the condition that he ought to tell U.K., matters relating to U.K. that will be happening in future.]

Show Taro [What actually was the aim of the U.K. Government that they wished to obtain by giving the copy to Hess?]

Robert [Amongst the high class Nazi officials, U.K. is to utilize the one that knows the future of the world. U.K. also seemed to learn how to combat with the threat of communism. In other words, what U.K. wanted to find out was the power relationships of the world after the

— 232 —

corrupsion of the power of Nazi. Charchill seemed to participate that Germany could never win the war but on the other hand he had a concern about the violence that communism could produce.]

Show Taro [Didn't U.K. Government wish to analize what other Nazi high-class officials knew about?]

Robert [Yes, indeed. Therefore, Raphael was ordred to counsel all the captured Nazi generals to find out amongst them those who could foresee the future.]

Show Taro [But how?]

Robert [So that the search was carried on in the form of Nurenberg Trials. Namely, those could have quickly been executed by the style of military execution but U.K. chose to find out those Nazis high-class officials who might know about the future by interrogating them.]

Show Taro [Then, as a consequence of such interrogation did they find several of those who could tell the future?]

Robert [That Heinrich Himmler and Josef Goebbels had been studying the future respectively was already known. Other than them, there was a plural number of officials who had been nominated by Hitler to work as prophesists. Likewise, there seemed to have existed a plural number of officers who knew the full picture of Heinrich Himmler's SS Rehabilitation Plan. SS was belonging to the headquarters of armed SS to which shamans such as Asian-decent monk soldiers were joining. To begin with, in such multi-national troops,

— 233 —

whatever races were mixed they looked less represented.]

Show Taro [U.K. troops, too, are not totally consisting with Europeans only.]

Robert [There existed U.K. Colonial Army of which the major force was Indians. Therefore, SS which expanded in such an area where collision with that U.K. Colonial Army was expected was naturally in need of such human resources that can talk other languages than English.]

Show Taro [Consequently, were they able to foresee much of future?]

Robert [Correctly, it should be said that this task could not be performed well by people of the common level. Therefore, Raphael was sent to Tokyo as well and tried to investigate the Japanese high-class officers. However, there he met with a check by the American troops. Raphael, being a U.K. millitary doctor, was refused to have an interview with the 731 Unit related personnel. Such personnel should have been exchanging information with SS concentration camp related people but such information was not made known to Raphael. Likewise, Stalin refused to have his hostages being interviewed. Talking about China, they acted that extremity as putting Japanese army power into their troops to deal with the domestic warfare which outburst immediately after WW2.]

Akemi [So that means he could not meet any high rank

— 234 —

officials of Japanese Troops though there did exist such that could tell the future.]

Robert [Such being what was happening, what I have heard of was they programmed to eliminate under the name of banishment of militalists such people in the government that knew future.]

Akemi [If basing on that fact, that the American troops made an investment in the 731 Unit related people must be double dealing.]

Robert [The American Army released all people that were concerned with the research of seeing through the future off the list of the war criminals, so the U.K. side had no way to touch this matter. That tactics seemed to be used against Soviet as well.]

Akemi [It looks to me that people are all gone insane on obtaining the power.]

Show Taro [Authority is a more powerful demon than women.]

Akemi [Why can you say 'more than women'?]

Show Taro 「Even those kings or ministers who do have their own heirs could be dazzled by power. In China till the era of Qing Dynasty, a group of the castrated government bureaucrats had existed in the inner palace and those bureaucrats changed the history.」

Akemi [If you are talking about Sei Taigu (West Empress Dowager, Xi Taihou)T, I know the story about her.]

Show Taro [She clinged onto power even after all of her children died.]

Akemi [That means authority has more masical power than

— 235 —

women.]

Robert [But there was a king who threw away the crown in U.K. in the past.]

Akemi [Well, then women might still have more magical power than authority, might they not.]

Show Taro [That time of U.K. had already entered the era of 'the British sovereign reigns but does not rule'].

Akemi [⋯.]

None of the three was aware that the situation might be changing the complexion of it as converced at the time of the dinner.

23. Painting Transference and Next Order

A few days after Show Taro's return to Japan, there came a phone call from Maria. She then brought 『The Man with the Golden Helmet』 with her to the Palais Flora office. She opened the door of the office and handed the painting over to Show Taro in his office where no one but Show Taro was there. While Show Taro unpacked the painting and acknowledged the painting, she was waiting in silence sinking herself in the sofa.

Show Taro [I duly confirm I received the authentic painting here. Do you need a receipt or the like?]

Maria [No receipt is needed. Only, Mr. Heinrich and Mr. Kato wish you to undertake the job which they will need to be done into the future.]

Show Taro [I can accept that offer, but what about the content of the work?]

Maria [Please continue to work for the Robert's insurance company. And keep reporting to Midori Manji as to the details of the investigation you do at request of Robert. If you can promise that you will do this, we will transfer one million yen per month to your account. Duration of this contract is to be one year per time. Here is the contract document. Contact to Midori Manji will have to go through me. You must keep this deal in secret to other company staffs of Midori Manji.]

Show Taro [I will not tell any others so tell me why you are showing interest in the contract period with Robert's

— 237 —

| | company which is less than ten months now.]

Maria   [Talking about the office building where Robert is working, I could see what was called Solomon's Seal on the people working in that building. I therefore listed up the buildings which are exisiting at this moment in Netherlands in the area with Hague in the center, where the branch of SS or Gestapo had been placed during WW2. In my investigation, it has been made clear that the ex-Gestapo branch office is the present Europole, in other words, the building which the European Police Organization is now using.

In view of this findings, Robert can be considered as a police-related person. In addition, the sir name Boe that can be considered in Enigma, Boe which is a name of Nordic origin means you in the circumstantial evidence.]

Talking about the word Enigma, it is a code used by Nazi Germany, with the meaning of puzzle in Greek. Hearing the talk of Maria, Show Taro now came to understand that the Robert's identity was then open and that the police related information was leaking out. Show Taro thought secretly in his mind that he might be going to be involved in some problematical matters and situations.

Show Taro [Then, what am I supposed to be expected to do?]

Maria   「What we need to learn is only what he was going to order. We do cooperate with you for your continuing the work Robert will assign on you. But one thing we wish is the place where the paintings are handed over is here.」

Show Taro [I understand. What you mean is that you do not want to be traced back.]

Maria [As Robert, too, is lying about his identity, I believe you will not get any mental burden, will you?]

Show Taro [It is a rather thrilling experience to be able to receive the reward of my work from both sides.]

Maria [Will you take this offer?]

Show Taro [Yes, I will.]

Maria [Now that you accepted our offer, both Mr. Heinrich and Mr. Kato will be able to rest their mind as they now can make their prediction seeing through the future.]

Show Taro [But I do not have such power to see through the future.]

Maria [To me, the future of the person who is in front of my eyes can only been seen on that person. What I can decipher from there are only the individual's future or past. Talking about the future of an organization, I must see the fate of a plural number of the higher rank people in that organization.]

Show Taro [But what I can only say is that even the fate of an individual cannot be deciphered by me.]

Maria [On 「Les Centuries (the Hundred Psalms)」 fate of an organization as a whole or nations are written and the power to deciper the meaning of it is bestowed. This

you must know before any one else. According to the
talks of Luc Gauric whom you met before, or should I
say, Maestro Luka Gaurico, when his grandfather was
working as a librarian at the national archieves in
Paris, the grandfather deciphered that just a part of
the Nazi high-class officials could live a long life such
as Rudolph Hess.]

Show Taro [Did he talk about this to anybody?]

Maria [I understand he taught something to Rudolf Hess who
used to commute to the archieves every day.]

Show Taro [I guess his grandfather could meet Hermann Georing
or Heinrich Himmler?]

Maria [It seemed to be Hess only that came to the archieves.
But I also heard that Himmler had sent a request of
copies of all pages of Les Centuries.]

Show Taro [Is there any relation between that and the happenings
at this time?]

Maria [According to Gaurico, Nostradamus seems to have
established a lock per psalm. There seems to be locks
that can open only during a few years before the time
comes or also such keys that can be used only by a
specified people ⋯one thing that can be said is the
person who stands at the peak of the power is fated to
be never able to open even with the key⋯Therefore,
in case of NS, or Nazi, the first person that could take
notice of Hitler was Rudolf Hess, then followed by
Himmler or Goebbels so they altogether lifted Hitler
up . But as they went up and up to the peak of the

— 240 —

power, the key came not to work to open.]

Show Taro [Mr. Gaurico could see the fate of each of them, right?]

Maria [Yes, So that it was made clear that the lives of the high-class officials would not last more than ten years. I gathered Hess had been very surprised hearing that.]

Show Taro [I'm not surprised to hear that. Was the fate of NS, or Nazi deciphered then?]

Maria [With the conclusion first, yes. About the final destination of WW2, I understand 80% of it was deciphered by then.]

Show Taro handed the contract sheet over to Maria and wrote a mail to Robert while Maria was watching him. Needless to say, what he wrote was to urge Robert to come to Japan taking with him a check of 50,000 pounds as the authentic 「The Man with the Golden Helmet 」 was in his hands then. Maria browsed the content of the e-mail and went out in a satisfied look. As the organization that is backing Maria is also not a mere normal organization so it goes without saying that he could not refuse their offer, therefore the whole flow of what happened with Maria just then was a matter in due course. Maria herself being provided with the capability of spiritual vision, it is clear that he could not run away from them in a safe way.

Two weeks after Show Taro received the painting, Robert came to Japan. Needless to say, Show Taro asked Robert to show the check before he showed the painting to Robert.

Show Taro [This is the painting in question. Please examine it.]

Robert took photos out from his bag and firstly he checked the photo that is showing the back side of the painting and carefully compared the position of the knots shown on the photo and on the back of the painting. Finishing this work after taking a few minutes, then he for the first time gazed at the painting comparing with the photo checking the touch of the brush on both for another couple of minutes. After that, he checked inside of the cardboard box, and finding a paper napkin he took it out of the box. There on the napkin the familiar word Passo Romano was shown and the mark A as well. He reconfirmed the napkin is marked A which is to prove that painting was the authentic painting.

Robert   [As promised, here is the check. The next assignment is a personal background investigation. I trust you will cooperate with us. This time, on condition that you take a photo of the person in question we will pay you an incentive of 5 million yen and full travelling expenses. As you are still in the contracted period of this deal of the paintings, the monthly payment will be made by British pounds as same as before.]

Show Taro [By the way, is there any particular reason why so much success fee as £50,000 is accessed on this deal?]

Robert   [This painting was the one that was in the castle of a noble who was said to be related to Raphael, too. This portlait is said that one of this noble's ancesters went out of his way to request Rembrandt to draw.]

Show Taro [So that this painting was owned by a castle load of several generations back in the past.]

Robert   [It will be that way. As the painting that was making the front entrance look gourgeous being placed at the side of the front stairs was gone, the owner was

— 242 —

	extremely disappointed.]
Show Taro	[Is that the whole reason why this request was made?]
Robert	[I was profested by a certain astrologist in London that such fortune as I was going to fly about outside of U.K. had come, so I am specially assigned to do this searching work.]
Show Taro	[But, how long will that period of fortune last?]
Robert	[I may have several more years.]
Show Taro	[So, has this case been chosen as your first task during the period that was fortune-told by that astrologist?]
Robert	[Even if it may not be in the perfect condition, if the painting can be returned to the owner without any serious damage so that the castle can restore the appearance in the past, that will make me relieved.]
Show Taro	[Regarding the next task of personal enquiries, to this case, too, your organization seems to be ready to pay a good sum of expenses.]
Robert	[That particular person has been very difficult to be located⋯I felt you as a Japanese might have a better chance to trace him.]
Show Taro	[Is he a European?]
Robert	[Yes.]
Show Taro	[And also an art lover?]
Robert	[Exactly. And moreover, it seems he may have some association with you.]
Show Taro	[Some one with whom I have conversed before⋯who can he be?]
Robert	[You can guess who without much wondering.]

He sounded somewhat putting on airs.

Show Taro [Is what you want something like probity check?]

Robert [From now, I am taking you to a certain person. Do you mind meeting him?]

Show Taro [Okay.]

Then the two went outside and took a taxicab to meet that man in question in the lobby of a hotel in Tokyo. The man to whom Robert introduced Show Taro named himself as Simon Zamir. Simon rounded his black jacket and was puting it at his side. He looks to have been working in an office where is well airconditioned so he did not have any sunburn in that hot summer.

In addition, the dress shirt he was wearing was a color of somewhat bluish white and unlike other Japanese businessmen, it was not a short-sleeved shirt in that hot weather. Judging from this fact alone, his task is not much like an outside job. He was slightly plump of a height of approximately 175 cm. He was wearing darkish hair and the whole appearance was not too conspicuous among Japanese businessmen. He looked like a coffee lover as he ordered Columbia produced coffee and was taking it straight. He looked like in his middle fifties and talked in a subdued voice checking out his surroundings. He looked to be bewaring not to be heard by others.

Simon [My request this time is a research about a person who is connected to some matter. If you will be cooperative with me and will succeed in taking several photos, I will reward you with 5 million yen.]

Show Taro [Well, please understand our company is in the antique dealing business. Can I be of help to you?]

Simon   [As a matter of fact, I obtained this at a certain place in Kyoto. I wish to have a photo of the person who unearthed this bracelet.]

So saying, what Simon took out of his bag was no doubt the bracelet which Alois Brunner unearthed as his hobby from the tomb of the former royalty of Syria and was the one that was with Heinrich. Show Taro unmistakenly confirmed it was what he brought into Japan. He turned it back and checked the feature of the pattern basing on his memory. Then he slowly opened his mouth.

Show Taro [Mr Alois Brunner is alive. Why do you need his photo?]

Simon   [When I sculp it, if it is accompanied with a photo, it will make the sale easier.]

Show Taro did not miss that eyes of Simon shined. Show Taro may be able to lift the amount of rewards a little up.

Show Taro [Do you say that such photo has a value of 5 million yen?]

Simon   [Yes, the photo has that much value. Such a person who was an ex-SS commander and is still alive has a historical value.]

Show Taro [If you put another million on the allowance to get myself up, and if you pay that million yen in cash, I will agree to this contract.]

Simon   [···Okay, I will pay you today.]

Show Taro [Do you, Mr. Simon, wish to meet Mr. Alois Brunner?]

Simon   [During WW2, my grandfather was taken a good care by him, so when next a party in Naples is held on the yacht owned by a relative of my cousin, if his health allows him to come, we are talking about inviting him there.]

Show Taro [Does what you mean your cousin wishes to meet him there?]

Simon [You're right.]

Show Taro [So, what you want is that I tell him so?]

Simon [I hope you will do so, in addition to photo-taking.]

Show Taro [Okay, I will try to do so. By the way, what nationality is that cousin of yours?]

Simon [He is an Italian.]

Show Taro [Incidentally, Robert, how does this work relate to your insurance business?]

Robert [Mr. Simon's clan is the owner of my company. Didn't I tell this to you before?]

Show Taro [So, what you mean is there whould be no problem for me to accept this deal.]

Simon [Absolutely no problem.]

Show Taro [In any case, that you own an insurance company would mean you are of a wealthy family.]

Simon [I have only a few percent of the shares, but that [a few percent] is good enough to exercise my veto so that the insurance company gives me due respect.]

Show Taro [Bob, is your meeting with Mr. Simon also according to your superior's instruction?]

Robert [Right, of course. This is the first time for me to meet Mr. Simon. I was suddenly called by my boss and asked if I am familiar with art products and as this case happened to be one going on in Japan I was chosen to deal with it, though there are a few who can speak Japanese other than me···well, as well as my schedule was matching the timing.]

Both Robert and Simon seemed to have never expected to be asked by Show Taro about the inside information of the insurance company, so they were taking pains to adjust their stories.

Show Taro [The waves of internetization are surging in the insurance business field in Japan, so those eldery personnel of insurance agencies seem to be having a difficult time. Is this also happening in the western countries?]

Simon [As I am a mere share holder, only what I can say is that the settled account report of every three months is now being shown on the internet which is quite handy for me to review.]

Robert [I, too, am writing my business report and sending photos via my personal computer, but I am apt to be accused when I cannot contact my superiors at the scheduled timing. They accume me that I am neglecting my reporting work. This is annoying, indeed.]

Show Taro [In my case, an onslaught of incoming mail that is nothing to do with my business such as offers of loans or investments are so disturbing. In addition, sales of some kind of weary drugs are often coming in through the net.]

Simon [I heared that my acquaintance bought an enery

enhancer called Bio Glow which unexpectedly sent from Hong Kong so he could not trust it and he threw it away after all.]

Show Taro [Such drug as Bio Glow and Hagenu are so popular that even the hostesses in Ginza do have them for their customers' use. One advice is this kind of products are so popularly sold that lots of iminations are mixed on sale, therefore, you had better watch yourself not to get such imitations.]

Simon [Yes, as I am scared to get such wrong thing, I cannot but buy them at a drug store in my neighborhood.]

Lightly padding the top part of his head, Robert joined the conversation smiling.

Robret [Me, too, am trying Hagenu Kureuz of the Midori Manji product. That hair restorer is quite effective but the CF which I saw on TV in Japan has no possibility to be broadcast in Europe. That CF was a real astonishment to me. The word Hakencreuz itself is voiolating the broadcasting code, but the high point is the scene where a row of skin-headed men marched through the shower were getting the hair growing all of the sudden. Among those men on some of the skin-heads hair started growing in the shape of Manji. Such is something that could well be sued as showing the subliminal effect of Nazi. This may not be able to be broadcast in America, either. But honestly as a hair restoring agent this product is of a very good effect···I am not surprised to hear if this kind of invension

— 248 —

would be worth Nobel Prize.]

Show Taro [Haven't heard that Nobel Prize idea. By the way, are there many of such imitation phermaceuticals around in Europe, too?]

Robert [That problem is being taken up for the sales on the internet. Too much immitations are around on the internet.]

Show Taro [Hagenu Kroiz is not a medicine that is taken orally, so it may not pose much problem, I guess?]an apart

Simon [My cousin in New York was crossed saying he got more bolded by taking such medicine orally.]

In this way, Show Taro received the moving allowance from Simon, he went on to see Maria at her fortune-telling parlor located at the side of the Ginza street, only to find that place was already closed. He rang her on his cell phone and was told she was living in a condominium nearby so he was invited to come to the apartment. Such movement of Show Taro had been followed from Ginza by one shadowy person.

— 249 —

24. Identification of Maria

Show Taro arrived at the address that was given by Maria and found a condominium which was equipped with a fully automated locking system. He pushed her room number and Maria responded and opened the door for him. He went up to her room on the top floor. He found the door of her residence without the doorplate showing her family name and also found her room with such an atmosphere as an extension of the fortune-telling parlor rather than to be called as a room where a woman was living. Maria who is travelling all over the world told him she was studying astrology and divination lore besides the way of Yin and Yang. Maria was listening to Show Taro who was telling her that the offer of the work which Robert brought about to Show Taro as an offer from his insurance company is to take a photo of Alois Brunner who is a survivor of Nazi SS. Robert said for Show Taro's expectable help to get the photo of Alois Brunner, the Italian cousin of Simon was offering a reward as a return present to Show Taro. Hearing that much from Show Taro, she abruptly asked.

Maria   [Can you obtain the name and the profession of that Italian?]

Show Taro [I will ask.]

Maria   [By the way, won't you have some meal with me here tonight? Take my offer as a return courtesy of the feast you bought me at the hotel in Vienna⋯will you please take my offer?]

— 250 —

Show Taro [If it is not too much trouble to you⋯ I am pleased to take your offer.]

Maria smiled and ordered two servings of Sushi by home delivery. Waiting for the delivery of the Sushi, the two talked about this and that from which talk Show Taro gathered that because the Tsuchimikados objected the introduction of Gregorian Calendar in the Meiji era they were made to sink and especially like Maria for those who had set up a branch family, a long difficult period of days seemed to have continued.

Fortunately, in Maria's case, she was taken up on magazines and consequently she could gain relatively young business women as her customers so at time of her developing more number of fortune telling parlors or change of living quarters of apartments, she can use the fortune-teller hearing fee which comes into her hand on monthly basis as consulting fee from each company Maria is related to, but a bigger amount of money is being earned by the love advice for those business women who are dreaming a happy married life despite the busyness of their daily business work.

The jewelries she is currently wearing on or Mercedes she is driving around are presents from such business women who have been able to safely gain a baby or two so Maria says these are unearned income and not her working income. Maria's grandfather did not have a talent as a fortune teller or the like, so he seems to have led a difficult life but what happened was a club in the Ginza area was hiring and using such widows of old families who did not have enough means to procure foods during the time of confusion after WW2 among whom one of the women was also working as a Geisha at the Shinbashi area. She is the mother of Akemi and there

Kato of Midori Manji was frequently commuting. Mother of Maria was suffering from tuberculosis and did not live too long but the right of the club which owned by her mother was left to Maria though it was a small club. She was talking about herself in that way when the Sushi arrived.

After the Sushi dinner, Show Taro was shown Maria's collection of masical goods. The crystal ball was said to be owned and used by a fortune teller after the war who was popular and called as Mother of somewhere and the spirits in this rock crystal ball has a power to mirror the future of the person who sits against the ball, is what Maria told Show Taro. Naturally she interprets what those spirits mean into words, but when she fails to express the meaning fully, her telling is said to be a miss or a disappointment. In fact, the ball itself was a real crystal ball but the polishing must be done in Kofu probably around the era of Taisho. He however felt a certain old woman of a foreign country in the ball so he told her about his feeling on which Maria opened her mouth and said as follows:

Maria   [Well said. This rock crystal ball itself was transferred from a visiting European when a fortune teller was doing his job at a club in Ginza. What I wish to say is, some person who related to this European may have been using this rock crystal ball as a fortune teller.]

Show Taro, who was observing the ball both from the vertical and horizontal angles, felt something was pulsating inside the ball and said:

Show Taro [This is a crystal ball from which spirits have not been extracted.]

Maria   [No, That's not really the case. As the the ball and I go well together, I am just continuing to use it. If I cannot use the spirits in the ball, the situation will get into hot water. This means that the fortune tellers who are said to tell the fortune correctly are always using powerful spirits. Otherwise, future shall not be getting clear to the fortune tellers.]

There is a story which is quite similar to what Maria commented. There is a female fortune teller called Jean Dickson in America who was summoned to the White House by a plural number of the presidents. In her case, she was handed over a crystal ball by an old woman who visited her without any prenotice. That old woman said to Jean that that crystal ball would become more useful to Jean than to the old woman and left to nowhere.

Those whose profession is called as medium may be trying to find out their successors being led by something like souls or spirits. Jean, after obtaining that crystal ball from the old woman one day came to witness a horrible incident. It goes without saying that that incident was projected on the crystal ball as an image. And that was that historical accident of assassination of John F. Kennedy. This happening rocketed her name up to the stardom. Many of similar stories to this exist in the world of antiques. It is that a thing draws and gathers another thing. The writer will write about this mysterious phenomenon later on.

Show Taro [But I can rightfully guess this rock crystal ball cannot be the power stone which drew you into this mysterious world.]

Maria   [As you seem to understand much, I will show you one more thing.]

She went into her bedroom, whorshipped the gods on the household Shinto altar and took one black lacquer box down. Out of that lacquer box another box made of cedar wood came out. She opened it quietly and there in the box was a necklace made of red and white banded agate with a comma-shaped Magatama made of jade attached at the end of the necklace. Looking at it carefully the jade is a big one of almost as large as one Sushi size. It was not alike the popularly worn nice shape Magatama which sort came out only in a later era. Such as Komochimagatama came on stage at very last.

Show Taro [I see it is keeping the ancient style.]

Maria   [The koma-shaped bead (Magatama) called Yasakani-no-Magatama is also said that it must have been a Magatama with a red and white banded agate stringed to it. Anyhow, I'm a little surprised to learn you know so well about these matters.]

Show Taro [Regarding Yasakani-no-Magatama, a theoretical explanation could be made to take Yasaka (Eight-Saka) as length which might simply be meant as large, and 'ni' could be a large size agate. However, if Yasaka is taken as length, that should mean the length of the bead string which stands for Ni, namely red color agate. In other words, this unit of length and the size of agate may be construed as two different things. All what I know is there exist such two different semantic interpretations.]

Maria   [Those unearthed goods out of ancient tombs range in wide variety. Taking this reality into consideration, if the meaning of those words is construed in this Land of Kotodama (Land of Spirits), which do you presume would be applied?]

Show Taro [Provided it has a meaning, it will be unit of length. When talking about the size of a crow which lives in the sun, when the size of it is spoken about, it is a size of it when it spreads the wings.]

In Japan, three treasures which are said to be in connection to the inheritance of the emperers position and it is also said the existance of those three treasures and the crowned emperor's position are said to be matched. These are called Three Sacred Treasures. Explaining about the 'Three', in the shapes of tools, there are a sword, a mirror and a Magatama. Of these three, the mirror is treated as that which shows the God of the Sun, which is the incarnation of the goddess, Amaterasu Ohmikami. Usually, it is placed as an object of worship housed in the inner Ise Shrine. The length of circumference measures 18x18=144cm and the diameter; 144 ÷ 3.14=approx..45.9cm. Such size is not only unsuitable for practical use and quite difficult to produce. If those who do not possess high technological strength cast it in a mold, it will end up to be a solid burrow and it is also needed to finish the surface of the mirror flat at time of producing the metal mold. But, just to add, this mirror is for being warshipped in the inner Ise Shrine and is not supposed to be exposed to the public people.

Magatama has been where spirits gather ever since the ancient time and it is understood that Magatama cannot be left uncovered at any time. If the measurement of eight shaku of the Yasakani-no-Magatama is simply taken as a large Magatama, such Magatama will be understood as a red color Magatama stringed by agate beads. When the scene of the shrine maidens in the ancient era dancing wearing this Yasakani-no-Magatama with a red color Magatama attached, it can be taken that the color of Magatama they were wearing was meant for the color of the string that was holding Magatama. In this case, it can be considered that the Magatama they were wearing was a necklace made of glass beads or agate with a Magatama attached to it. As a fact, since the era of Edo, there exists no Magatama inspection record left so what we can do is just to make a guess.

If talking about Solar deity, it can be considered that the color red may have some relation, but as all Japanese soccer fans know, in the sun there live three-foot crows where such crows are in black color. In this way of thinking, in addition to onyx, there comes a possibility that obsidian may have been used.

However, on the heavenly crown that the principal image of the Sangatsu-do at Todaiji Temple wearing jade taken from River Itoigawa is used and a document that shows the record of discontinuation of mining of jade by the public people after the jade was used for the crown. What does this mean? Naturally it is considered that that was a measure to prevent common people from getting jade from that river. With regards agate, unfortunately the writer has no knowledge of a similar prohibition being applied or not.

Having been considering this way, the idea of a necklace consisting of the eight-Shaku length string constructed by red color beads with a red color ruby attached in the center of the string comes up. Talking about the other two kinds of the sacred treasures, the mirror is made in the form suited to the human's use and not as the material state of copper or nickel. This is the same with Kusanagi-no-Tsurugi, the sacred sword. It is not a mere clump of copper or iron but fnished in the shape which humans can use in their life. Considering these facts, it would come rather unnatural to expect that Magatama only could exist just for being worshipped.

In addition, of the three sacred treasures, the mirror is meant as a symbol of technology in addition that of wisdom, and the sword a symbol of courage and also that of military strength, and lastly, the precious gem as a symbol of humanity, in other words, to be benevolent to the people as well as the symbol of the treasures that are presented or the symbol of the economical power. In this way of consideration, as a symbol of those treasures that are presented from various local places, rather than taking up one big precious gem as a symbol, a red necklace with five-color big gems attached could be more easily accepted. It may not be the writer alone who may think of a symbol that will be a suitable style to have ancient imperial princesses or shrine maidens use it at time of some ritual or else for them to present their dancing.

Needless to say, as long as the Imperial Palace will not expose the three sacred treasures to cameras, whatever the writer writes here cannot exceed the level of just a guess work. But as it is not wise to express what the writer thinks merely by writing only, the writer has no other choice but to seek the truth on the backside of the facts. The writer then keeps considering the relation of what he is pursuing with other similar cases and facts and reasons the use of the most mysterious treasure that is Magatama. So, the result of his reasoning is as stated above.

Then, all of the sudden the chime at the entrance rang. Maria looked puzzled talking to herself it was too late a time to expect the circular community bulletin board coming. She answered the knocking and Akemi showed up.

Akemi   [I know Show Taro is here.]

Maria   [Yes···but how do you..]

Akemi   [You told my fortune with him, but you said it will not go smoothly.]

Maria   [Yes, that is what the holoscope told me.]

Suddenly, Akemi strengthened her voice.

Akemi   [Truth is, aren't you trying to take him over from me?]

Maria   [He is not here to talk about such a purpose.]

Akemi   [Then, can I join you here alright?]

Maria   [You're welcome.]

When the two came into the room from the entrance, Show Taro was peeping into a loupe to examine the Magatama. When he lifted his face, he saw the two who had come in without his knowledge, so he was somewhat surprised but started to talk to both.

Show Taro [Hi, Good evening. This Magatama is polished with powdered jade. Such as diamond paste is not used.]

Akemi   [Will you let me see, too.]

Akemi quickly took a seat next to Show Taro and checked and confirmed that the sofa she sat down did not have any warmth. Then she goggled her eyes and borrowing the loupe started looking at the Magatama. Looking at it, Maria thought 'My God, How troublesome she is!' but made tea for her, too.

Show Taro [If it were polished using modern adrasives such as diamond paste, the surface would become slipperily smooth, but this is not, you see?]

Akemi [You're right.]

Show Taro [How long has this one been with the Tsuchimikados?]

Maria [It may have already been with us in the era of Muromaci. Or it could have been since when the Name Abe came out before that era.]

Show Taro [I can appraise the paint on the outside box was added in the middle of Muromachi era, while the inside box is older and has an ancestral appearance.]

Akemi [How can you say you can make such a guess as it is of the mid Muromachi era.]

Show Taro [Look at the surface of the box carefully.]

Akemi [I notice fine cracks.]

Show Taro [That is so-to-called 'Danmon'.]

Akemi [What can be known by these cracks?]

Show Taro [the way of cracks differs to the quality of lacquer.]

Akemi [Is what you mean difference of the lacquer producing area can be identified?]

Show Taro [Difference of Japanese or Chinese lacquars can be determined.]

Akemi [And, besides that, do you mean the era when the lacquer was produced can be determined by the number of the cracks?]

Show Taro [Yes, that is the case. Besides those, the characteristic of the era (time spirit) or the area where the creater lived can be instruded by examining the way of the gold coating, so the careful observation enables the observer to obtain various crues from one lacquer ware.]

Akemi   [Pshaw, that's incredible.]

Maria, who was watching them and their conversation opened her month.

Maria   [So you can also appraise those other than western antiques.]

Show Taro [My research as a hobby is Eastern antiques. But you know hobby cannot be used as one's main business.]

Akemi   [Is here any other treasure you are possessing?]

Maria   [What I have inherited are those only. Apart from these, I have a manuscript, but it is worm-eaten and covered by mold. Those which are displayed here is my collection which was gathered after my job as an astrologist came on a right track.]

Akemi   [Is that, too?]

Maria   [That is a mask of an African shaman.]

Akemi   [What is the one next to it?]

Maria   [Teddy Bear for sacrifice.]

Akemi   [Does it have a name?]

Maria   [Grace is the name. In America, on the doll that is to be used as a talisman to protect the owner from evil spirits, they often put the middle name of their child on such doll.]

Show Taro [But it is not wearing a personalized jacket with its

— 260 —

	name on. I guess this is not what you bought as an antique item.]
Maria	[My father who was killed by accident in America leaving my mother and me, had sent it as a Christmas present to me.]
Show Taro	[So, were you born in America?]
Maria	[But I have dark color eyes.]
Akemi	[If blue, that would have posed another problem. Aren't they both Japanese? I mean your parents.]
Maria	[He was a pressman and was writing the articles concerning Mafia. As he had been receiving many kinds of threats, my mother and I were sent back to Japan leaving my father in America. That's all what I know.]

There, Maria dared not to touch the subject of whether her parents were both Japanese or not.

Show Taro	[What sort of the age was it of your story about your family?]
Maria	[Around 1975.]
Show Taro	[As it was around 1969 when Mafia started to resell the Sicilian stolen goods, your father as a pressman may be related to that period of time. As the strong buyer of art items are usually Americans.]
Maria	[How do you know it was 1969?]
Show Taro	[In November, 1996, on the witness stand of the trial of corruption of Giulio Andreotti, the ex-prime minister of Italy, Francesco Marino Mannoia revealed the fact that Mafia sold during 1969 to 1996 in the Palermo

— 261 —

District goods which they had stolen.]

Maria [How does it relate to America that Mafia increases their power?]

Show Taro [Among those immigrants to America from Italy that was suffering from poverty, the group which turned to be gangs are Mafias. At the time of WW2, in an endeavor to acquire cooperation from Italy, the American Government released Italian Mafias from the jail and used them for the wartime obstructionism. At that time, they were sent to Sicily or the southern part of Italy by submarine for instance. After the war was over, instead of parging fascists, the common criminal offences were released, who stood in with people of influence and controlled Italy was the Mafias.

This group of Mafias created a system to smuggle pastas mixed with heroin into America and that people who order pizza delivery drugs were delivered instead. The financial support of this scheme was filled by Anti-Nazi funds so it is considered that Jews became the sellers of the goods stolen by Mafias.]

Maria [I see. Now I understand why and how Mafias increased their power in Italy. They were taken to Italy from America by submarine, that's outrageous.]

Show Taro [To add to what I told you, this had also been predicted in Les Centuries.]

Maria [In what way?]

Show Taro took out from his pocket a pocket notebook and turned the pages.

— 262 —

Show Taro [Here it is⋯2-5.

First Line When weapons and documents are taken into the fish, namely, a submarine

Second Line Following those goods, people to fight a war will be coming out

Third Line The people of that classe, namely Mafias, travel on the sea to far away

Forth Line And reappear in the land of Latin, namely near Italy.

Here, if I translate the classe on the third line as class, the translation will become as above.]

Maria [You have very well studied the psalm. You are comparable as Mr Luc Goeric whom we met at Mr. Heinrich's place.]

Show Taro [As there are many researchers of Nostradamum here.]

Akemi [Though the 20th century is almost finished?]

Maria [Those that cannot be concluded as finished could be coming hereafter.]

Akemi [Is there any further chance that catastrophe may visit us?]

Show Taro [Yes, in comparably near future.]

Maria [Provided the present time matches the age stated in Apocalypse.]

Maria's compartment was where no sign of the opposite sex was being shown or felt, but for the meaning of a research of a shaman, Show Taro understood the place was filled with unique ambience.

Show Taro [By the way, have you, Maria, chosen to keep yourself isolated?]

Maria　　[Pardon?]

Show Taro　[Those among fortune tellers who hit their tellings are one of the three, namely, alone, or dubious, or poor. God will never let them see the future unless for exchange of any of those three.]

Maria　　[You may well be right.]

Show Taro　[Please excuse us now for today. Will you advise Mr. Kato about the work assigned to me of Alois Brunner.]

Maria　　[Yes, I will. Please come again.]

On their way back from the Maria's apartment, Akemi said she was to procure some taxi tickets before coming back to the hotel so he was to escort her there.

Akemi rolling her eyes showed she was thinking about something and then spoke up to him.

Akemi　　[What sort of person is Maria?]

Show Taro　[She is a person who is collecting things and goods which are filled with spirits. I think she obtained the power to see the future in exchange with solitude. She is already the third person who came to possess that crystal ball⋯what can be said is that place of hers is filled with variety of something. Didn't you feel that?]

Akemi　　[Do spirits dwell there?]

Show Taro　[She is using spirits. They may not be seen by ordinary people but I do feel them. Only the tree of mediums can summon and use spirits.]

Akemi　　[Is she making spirits her servants?]

Show Taro　[You're just about right. And for that reason she will

	not get married.]
Akemi	[Why won't she?]
Show Taro	[It is a prerequisite not to publicize own real name in order to use spirits or evils.]
Akemi	[Is her real name different from her present name?]
Show Taro	[Taken it for granted that her Japanese sir name is Tsuchimikado, that she was born in America means she has quite a few different real names.]
Akemi	[Like the teddybear acting as her proxy?]
Show Taro	[You may be right. Possibly, she may have some more, like Christian name and should her parents be non-Japanese, she may have far more names than I imagine.]
Akemi	[She is like a detective novel.]
Show Taro	[Antique dealing as a job is always like a detective novel. Budget the customer is setting, goods he wants, and the timing for him to accept my offer, all of these need to find each other's real intentions between the customer and the antique dealer. Customers will not teach dealers their economical situation. Depending on customers, some know well about how much they can afford to pay and what sort of character such fund is that they hold to spend and for what kind of antique merchandise they are prepared to spend that fund but they won't tell any such info to the dealer. Also, similar to masters of tea ceremony's Mitate, such a case can often take place as to be away from the original way of usage of the thing and to be satisfied with a

— 265 —

substitutional thing using it in place of the original in the same way as to use the original.]

Akemi   [Mitate···for instance?]

Show Taro [Well···for instance, flower container was originally a Chinese copper vase. Also, a celadon vase which copied the shape of bronze bowl was used as a vase till the middle part of Muromachi era but during the process of it being changed to Japanese baked bowl the name was changed to flower container. In the beginning of this change, under the guidance of masters of tea ceremony, such vase with different pattern and color on each side of the two sides began to be produced in Shigaraki, Iga and Bizen. More accurately, baked ceramics in Japan tended to make an unexpectable change in the baking kiln influenced by the flame movement that changes from time to time. This change of the color and pattern due to the condition of the flames in the kiln was esteemed by masters of tea ceremony as 'kiln-made variation'. And those tea ceremony masters choose which side to face the front according to the kind of flowers they use or to the environmental condition in which such vase was placed. For example, if they use red color flowers the vase was placed to show the side which was not in red color and was showing the black-burnt more stripy side of the vase, and in case of using white flowers, they used red flowers as well so that red and white flowers were to stand out on festive occasions, or, for

— 266 —

small flowers, they put the side of sober color of the vase to come to the front. By using such technique, this type vase trys flower arrangers' ability to be utilized in a frexible way. If it is in a good harvesting time or a sowing time, seed containers are used as vases. Talking more about this, when at Buddist's memorial service, lid of the unearthed sutra-containing cylinder was used as a vase putting the lid of the cylinder besides the body of cylinder which was being used as a vase.]

Akemi   [So, Mitate means to use something different as a substute. Thanks to Show's explanation, I feel I may have understood why at the first look such plain earthenware vases are valued as flower containers. As you say, flowers vary from big to small and dense to scarce. The flower arrangers' ability to make the flowers look in the best possible way is tried when they arrange flowers.]

Show Taro [A buddism word which is frequently used at the tea celemony is 'an once-in-a-lifetime encounter'. This means what happened at that place at that time will never happen again, therefore, at such time you have to meet the counterpart with utmost sincerity, and if you don't, then the meeting itself becomes false.

This word is a truth not only between you and your counterpart but also the encounter of this flower container and these flowers. This is also applicable to the cuisine and the tea which is called Cha-Kaiseki (dishes served before tea ceremony). As Rosanjin, the giant of cuisine, said in the long past, there was an encounter between cuisine and the plate which contained the cuisine. The plate can for the first time be complete when it comes with the cuisine on it, so he tortured himself to create such plates to his satisfaction and put them on sale. However, his plates were copied in quantity and such fakes were abundantly on the market so that to distinguish the authentic pieces from fakes has become a very time-taking and difficult work.]

There, what concerned Akemi all the same is whether Maria would be her opposing forces or not.

Akemi [Incidentally, Is Maria not going to get married?]

Show Taro [If she decides to get married, she will have to return to a common person or to become dubious or poor in exchange of solitary, otherwise, her fortune telling will not come to hit any longer.]

Akemi [How come can you see that will happen?]

Show Taro [If you will carefully read the life history of fortune tellers whose tellings hit well, you will find none of them could lead a normal happy life. They would die alone, or would not believe anybody whatever they say, or would get involved in crime. That is what is called a turn of Fortune's wheel.]

Akemi [hmmm.]

Around when their taxi arrived at the condominium, Akemi had fallen asleep perhaps having got calmed down at Show Taro's talk,

so Show Taro had to face a heavy labor to carry her up to the
room.

25. Guessing each other's intentions

Two weeks afterwards, Show Taro was contacted by Maria. He was scheduled to meet Heinrich again via Kato's arrangement and this time he was to meet Heinrich in Japan. It seemed to be without doubt that Heinrich was flying about all over the world. The special room where Heinrich was staying was not very broad but at this meeting after a long while, Heinrich looked to be in good mood.

Heinrich [Long time after last we met, Show.]

Show Taro [You look busy as usual. As I have already told Maria, An export-import businessman called Simon was saying his cousin was wishing to meet Mr. Alois Brunner.]

Heinrich [Have you gathered the name of that Simon's cousin?]

Show Taro [The name is said to be Bernard Gambino.]

Heinrich [So Bernard is hoping to hold a party on his yacht. Is it correct?]

Show Taro [That's what I heard.]

Heinrich [Before then, he wishes to have a photo of Alois Brunner, is it also correct?]

Show Taro [Yes.]

Heinrich [He should be taking a swim at the pool so I will show you to him. Please take your camera with you.]

What he suggested is to let Show Taro meet Alois Brunner at the pool side and rightfully he was introduced to an old man wearing sunglasses. Then complying to Heinrich's suggestion, a

— 270 —

photo-taking was done of the old man lying on a beachbed relaxing with his hands inserted in the back of his head while having Show Taro standing besides the old man who is lying on the bed. In Japan, too, there are quite a few city hotels which equip a pool on rooftop. If amenity service is poor, hotels cannot get successful businessmen and such businessmen are always busy flying about all over the world constantly treating their business contacts of various kinds. City hotels are targeting at such customers offering them place right in the urban cities for them to take a rest without going far to the countryside to pursue restful places.

At half past ten in the morning, temperature has risen enough high for a swim, but on week days there were few Japanese hotel stayers at the roof pool.

Heinrich   [Can I just press this button of the camera?]

Show Taro [Yes, and this button is for zooming up.]

Heinrich   [How can I handle this camera when we don't wish the place and the date and time to be recorded on the photo?]

Show Taro [In that case, you do this way⋯to cancel the recording of the day and the time.]

Heinrich   [I guess we should not take much background view in.]

Saying so, he carefully observed the whole area of the pool side. Finishing his observation, he proposed one particular angle with which he wishes to have the photo taken.

There was one other man with sunglasses lying on another beachbed on a beachtowel spreaded beneath him.

Heinrich   [Josef, cross your hands at the back of your head.]

Josef   [This way?]

Heinrich   [Good, good.]

Show Taro   [What am I supposed to do?]

Heinrich   [Will you stand besides Josef.]

Show Taro   [Is this position okay?]

Heinrich   [Yes, with smiles.]

Show Taro   [….]

Heinrich   [I think I did it alright.]

Show Taro   [Do you also like a keep-safe photo of you in the scene?]

Heinrich   [Not for this time, thanks.]

He finished the photographing having taken a few cuts and one more cut which was zoomed out fairly largely.

Heinrich   [These photos will be good enough to satisfy Simon and Bernard.]

Show Taro   [Tell me one thing. Why this pose, and who is this person?]

Heinrich   [The SS related personnel were putting on a tatoo in order to get blood transfusion on a priority basis. I asked him to make a posture that exposes the tatoo. He is Josef Brunner, the son of Alois whom they are chasing. Old man in his 90th and another old man in his 70th look not much different to each other, and to begin with they have features that look quite alike.]

Show Taro   [What is your intention to do all this?]

Heinrich   [You will know it quite soon. You must at least have investigated what Simon is handling as a trader.]

Show Taro   [Yes, I understand he is engaged in wholesaling business of sundrygoods mainly from New York.]

Heinrich [I wish to find out Bernard Gambino's true face other than that as a business man. Instead of the party in Naples, as it is difficult for him to squeeze time to join it and due to his chronic condition, he would rather like to have a meeting in Rome, will you seek their acceptance of this offer, please.]

Show Taro [I will try to ask. What about the place to meet?]

Heinrich [Our plan is to borrow the basement floor of Café Sfolza.]

Show Taro [When is convenient to you?]

Heinrich [Will you and Mr. Simon participate this meeting from Japan. We are willing to match our schedule with theirs, but while their identity is unknown, we could not meet them on their stage, so this answer. In addition, Robert, too, is not the member of an insurance company, according to our investigation.]

Show Taro [Can I tell them about that you wish to meet them at Passo Romano?]

Heinrich [Please don't tell them till both of them are ready in Rome, as we may change the meeting place to the yatcht of Romano or their family castle.]

Show Taro [Sounds like the situation is complicated.]

Heinrich [You must know that after the WW2, that Mafia took back the political power backed up by America or Jewish capitals and the remnant of the Fascista Party's effort to recover from the setback, the dommestic situation of Italy is in a total chaeos. Mafia

— 273 —

in these day keep failing to penetrate into the foundation of government and therefore they are engazed in secret maneuvers to reinstate their position. In Japan, too, the case of a ruling party politician' s blacky association with Japanese Mafia (Yakuza) is being taken up on the newspaper. In Italy, it can and is happening that all cabinet minisers and bankers are the members of Mafia.]

Show Taro [I don't think Japan is that much infected by Mafia⋯]

Heinrich [We need to use industrialists of Naples to check the actual condition of the movement of Mafia in Italy. We also ought to know what is the real purpose of theirs.]

Show Taro [Do you mean you believe it is a trap.]

Heinrich [What specifically are you talking about?]

Show Taro [Do you feel a need to investigate Mr. Simon?]

Heinrich [He is the window person at their side. All what I need is that he listens to their assertion and pass what he heard over to me in all details. To them, we will send only the information that we choose to send. Any more difficult part of the talk is nothing to do with you as a Japanese person.]

Show Taro [As regards my side, as long as your request is conforming to the contents described on the contract, also as long as it does not conflict with laws, I see no problem and I will keep off the glass any further.]

Heinrich [Good choice.]

Show Taro [Not really. I am just simply business like.]

Heinrich [Will you contact Mr. Simon? As I am listening to your conversation with him by you.]

Show Taro [Yes, I will try to call him.]

Show Taro quickly picked Simon's business card out and called up his mobile.

Show Taro [Hello, Simon. I contacted the other party and gathered that due to his chronic desease, he could still be able to meet you but not in Naples but in Rome.]

Simon [What about Mr. Alois' convenience?]

Show Taro [As he is a retired old soldier, he said he would go matching the convenience of Mr. Bernard and Mr. Simon.]

Simon [Were you able to take a photo of Mr Alois?]

Show Taro [Yes, shall I send it as enclosure of a mail?]

Simon [Did you use a desital camera, and at what number of pixels?]

Show Taro [16 million pixels and it is a high-mode shooting.]

Simon [Okay, then please send it. Address on my card will do.]

Show Taro [I will send it perhaps tonight.]

Listening to this conversation, Kato made his thumb stand up and winked to Heinrich.

Kato [Now, we could escape from their trap and could also earn time.]

Show Taro [They will also see what we will do next. One thing important is, have you finished confirming how much information of this side has already leaked to them?]

Heinrich [So far I have heard is the enigma has not been solved by them as yet.]

— 275 —

Show Taro [But there may be other type of decryption programs, I wonder?]

Kato [There is MM98 of Midori Manji, but this decryption is for an exclusive use for our company's new drag development.]

Show Taro [Is that frequently exchanged?]

Kato [With overseas a few times per day.]

Show Taro [You had better watch those as well.]

Heinrich [Two more weeks, then we expect the antecedents of Bernard and the framework of Simon's organization can be clarified so that we wish to ask you to keep the delaying tactics as much as possible.]

Show Taro [As a matter of course. As it is business.]

That day, Heinrich and others left Show Taro in order for them to meet some people in Japan. Most probably, they might be meeting Yamagata Defence Minister or such line of persons.

A few days afterwards, a contact from Simon came in. Bernard, the cousin, also contacted Show Taro telling Show Taro that he had received the photo. Bernard continued that as he would not mind Alois being accompanied by his doctor so Alois would be welcome to visit Bernard's yatcht which is parked in the port of Naples, or otherwise, Berbard continued, what about cruising together with Bernard by his yatcht to Venice, say, after a month later. What is meant is that by all means Bernard wishes to meet Alois even for one time at least.

This message was supposed to have been passed to Kato via Maria, but as Kato was cautious not to have the code cracked so he would not dare to communicate with Europe by MM98. All what he said via MM98 was that he would need to adjust the timing. Doubtlessly, the side of Simon must have enlarged the photo of Josef Brunner and have confirmed the tattoo on his under-the-arm position. Simon and his group must have understood that as they had time, the Nazi SS members marked their skin with tattoo to show each blood type to enable to get a blood transfusion on a priority basis. However, this tattoo became the conclusive factor to find SS members who were mixed in the war prisoners captured by the German defence army.

If Alois Brunner is proven to be genuine Alois Brunner, who is the person that wishes to meet him the most? And for what purpose does that person wishes to meet him that earnestly? To solve these questions, it may be a good idea to visit Simon and get the crue of the answer of those questions. Show Taro then decided to go and visit Simon's company in Kobe taking the chance of his scheduled visit to Kyoto. He traveled by Shinkansen to Kyoto and finishing his work there, then he headed to Kobe and arrived in Kobe in the afternoon of the same day. As Show Taro's face has been recognized, he asked Maria to be with him, and they kept this fact as secret to jearous Akemi.

According to Maria, as long as the Simon's business card shows, what Simon is handling seems mostly American sundrygoods, but he owns one other company in the neighborhood and there he seems to be personally managing that second company as well. Items this second company handles are mainly diamonds being imported from New York. Having found out these facts, Show Taro placed a call to Simon's cell phone and said to him that he was in

Kobe then and asked if he could meet him somewhere like at a beerhall or so.

Simon's reply was that he could meet Show Taro for just one-beer time. He persistenty asked Alois Brunner's availability to him, so Show Taro tried to keep it just telling him that at this time, it is medically unknown whether he could get a consent from the doctor.

Simon [Long time no see.]

Show Taro [Likewise.]

Simon [After we met before, were you able to obtain some middle eastern unearthed goods to add to your collection?]

Show Taro [No, My speciality originally is not for Middle East but my main interest is middle to modern Italian antiques.]

Simon [From Italy, what sort of antiques are deemed as bargains?]

Show Taro [Those people who are trying to develop such as sightseeing business utilizing their palazzo or the small size palace called palazette are selling part of their furnitures.]

Simon [I see⋯then among those furnitures they are selling antiques of which era seize the majority of those?]

Show Taro [Those of 17th to 18th century are so-so mixed.]

Simon [Any thing older?]

Show Taro [It's not unavailable, but those which are not accompanied by export permit can no way be bought.]

Simon [After procurement of such antiques is finished, how long do these take till you receive these?]

Show Taro [You will have to wait after you place orders, four

	months at the shortest, to half a year.]
Simon	[That is a very time taking business.]
Show Taro	[From Italy, this duration is deemed as pretty speedy.]
Simon	[Selling those things, what then do they intend to do?]
Show Taro	[Then, removing those things, if some reasonable space in the palazzo can come to be available for use of other purposes, the owner remodels the space into a form of a hotel, or, if the location of such palazzo is in the center of the Florence, it comes to be feasible that the owner leases such space for a boutique of a brand business.]
Simon	[So in such ways they utilize their assets that they inherited from their ancesters, don't they.]
Show Taro	[I am so jealous in a sense. By the way, do you, Mr. Simon, have any collection of rare things?]
Simon	[As nearly thirty years passed since I came to Japan,So I did collect many kinds of odds and ends.]
Show Taro	[Are those folkloric items?]
Simon	[Some of those which may attract the interested people can be said forkloric. For instance, according to what I have heard, of such items as the Three Sacred Treasures of Japan, the monumental inscription on the mirror is curved in Hebrew with the phrase reading [I am that I am] which is the phrase of Book of Exodus of the old testament 3-14. I am looking forward to a chance which will enable me to see and read it with my own eyes.]
Show Taro	[That mirror is the enshrined object in Ise Shrine so

even we Japanese have no chance to sight it. For sure, that mirror is huge in comparison to Chinese mirrors so I wonder if it was cast in Japan for the supplication festival use. Such possibility of the sealing of something or a story relating to mythology cannot be denied of course.]

Simon [In Japan there should further exist mysterious things.]

Show Taro [Of what kind?]

Simon [Those which were used as talisman or lucky charm at the old Daimyo families or old families. Of Japanese products, probably crystal balls have been exported to all over the world. Most of the crystal balls which astrologiests in Europe used were the ones that Netherlands had imported into Europe. However, talisman, which may be an equivalent of Magatama, which ranges from Jade to Agate and Crystal and used in Japan has not been exported to Europe.]

Show Taro [Magatama has been a talisman started to be used in the era of the ancient tomb to the era of Nara. When merchants' vessels of Spain or Netherlands started to come around to Japan, Magatama was off the mainstream to be used as talisman.]

Simon [I see⋯As Japanese stays in Japan, for that reason there may exist many things of which Japanese may not realize the mystery those things contained in them.]

Show Taro [I agree to the point you just raised. By the way, do you, Mr. Simon, possess some talisman yourself?]

— 280 —

Simon   [I am possessing a large rough diamond which my
           grandfather left to me.]
Show Taro [May I take a look at it?]
Simon   [No problem.]

Saying so, he took out of his pocket a small plastic case in which there was a thing that looks like octahedron glass in the mass which is so big as called sawable.

Simon   [When I made my decision to go to Japan, my
           grandfather living in New York gave it to me.]
Show Taro [Is there in this stone lessons are crushed in?]
Simon   [Yes, indeed. I guess he must have given it to me for
           me to become able to ascertain the good quality
           diamond. If this is polished, it cannot be more than one
           and half karat brilliant cut diamond, but I believe more
           than one and half karat is the minimum size unit with
           which one can keep the asset value over the border
           line of any country.]
Show Taro [This rough stone is not perfectly transparent. It
           shows slightly bluey color.]
Simon   [This has a slight fluorescent which makes bluey color
           tint which can be felt by the observer of it. In usual
           cases, the less expensive price goes, the more
           yellowish color is to follow.]
Show Taro [And this is what you make your standard to
           distinguish the quality of diamond.]
Simon   [Yes, I think your interpretation is correct. Nobles in
           Europe possess far older rubies.]

Show Taro [But most of those they possess are Barlas rubies which in today's mineralogy are spinnels. In addition, in most cases the cut is Cabochon.]

Simon [You're quite knowledgeable.]

Show Taro [Talking about other instances, do you know that those talismans that were possessed by the group of people who were prosperious during the Age of Discovery were mostly Spanish emeralds?]

Simon [Well, those are called in Europe as Spanish emerald but in realty, these are emeralds sourced in Columbia in South America. Talking about those in the old ages, those are of cabochon cut. Do you know in the handle of dagger used by Saltan of the Osman era three emeralds of each of 50 karat or so are inlaid?]

Show Taro [Several years ago when there was an exhibition in Japan, I went to view the exhibition. Those of the old era have a good old style.]

Simon [Those old ones did not use the polish such as diamond paste so the surface is not too excessively shiny. Perhaps emerald powder or the like must be used for polishment. And that a little blunt shine appearance is the difference between the genuine old thing and fake one copying the old appearance.]

Show Taro [Do you no doubt do your observation by a loupe of ten magnifications?]

Simon [Yes, that's nothing unusual. Only constant observation makes it possible to get such power of observation.

While he was taking beer, he took cheese or peanuts as finger food but never touched the served diced Kobe beef steak in spite of the fact he lived in Kobe, nor sausages of Berkshere pig. Spending time with Show Taro for about one hour, he went away leaving his words such as 'This beer is on me, so please take whatever you like without reservation'.

Show Taro then went to the hotel lounge where he had made reservation, and asked Maria there.

Show Taro [Were you able to see something on Mr. Simon?]

Maria [Though he is hiding it, he should be jewish.]

Show Taro [Did you see Solomon's seal, namely, Star of David on him?]

Maria [He seems to believe in it still now.]

Show Taro [Is your judgement from the food, after all?]

Maria [He never touched pork. This has been pointed out by Kato so I purposely offered it to him.]

Show Taro [Is that how you arrived this conclusion?]

Maria [I think probably he is passing information to the Jewish special service agency.]

Show Taro [So, is Bernard Jewish related, too?]

Maria [According to Mr. Kato, he doesn't seem so.]

Show Taro [Did Mr. Kato gather that information from Heinrich?]

Maria [I understand this is according to the information from Romano Sfolza. Bernard is from a family of industrialists and is engaged in export business of pasta or pizza or such food materials mainly to America, while his other face is Mafia. In other words, with high possibility he might have been helping business to smuggle the stolen paintings in Sicily into America from 1969 to 1996.]

Show Taro [But if that is the case, for what reason did he need to lie as the owner family of the Robert's insurance company?]

Maria [Robert is hiding his status of being engaged in Europole, isn't he? And here, This Simon may possibly belong to Jewish special service agency. And moreover, Bernard coming out this time is a Mafia involved in smuggling of paintings.]

Show Taro [I am at a loss. Look, the assignment posed on Robert is to collect stolen paintings. And the job role of Bernard is sale of stolen paintings. This is what is said in Japanese 'match pump' which means they play their own work.]

Maria [Can you take this as such? Simon incites Bernard to destroy Romano's stolen painting business. Therefore, Robert is conniving their actions.]

Show Taro [Simon himself is not talking about such plan to invite Romano to the party.]

Maria [But, he does understand that Alois is not going to their yatcht, doesn't he? There must be a pitfall somewhere.]

Having said so, Maria sacked Margarita which was left in the glass by a straw.

On the following day, on Maria's proposal, Alois Brunner came to agree to meet them if in Rome, Show Taro was asked to make

— 284 —

readjustment of appointment so he transmitted this condition to Simon. One week afterwards, Simon replied that he would meet Alois on one day after about a couple of months and the week and place were fixed as somewhere in the city of Rome.

26. Talk with Josef Brunner

On the promised day, Show Taro shown by Maria arrived at Café Sfolza about half an hour earlier than the appointment and was spending time doing man watching. Jazz Piano by Romano Sfolza was sounding in the air.

Then, there appeared Simon though he was also too early by about 15 minutes and sat at the same table with his back at the counter and ordered American coffee. Usually Italians arrive 30 minutes later than the appointed time.

Simon [How is Mr. Alois' health condition?]

Maria [As he is already in his 90th, it depends on doctor's judgement. He will come if his doctor does not say No.]

Show Taro [Does Mr. Simon meet him?]

Simon [If I could, I wish to shake hands with him and have some commemorative photograph taken.]

Show Taro [Is Mr. Bernard usually punctual?]

Simon [As he is a busy guy so I can't say yes.]

Maria [As he is an Italian, a 30 minute delay is quite possible.]

Simon [Incidentally, does Mr. Romano Sfolza come, too?]

Show Taro [He seems to have the door kept open, so the melody that can faintly be heard here must be his playing.]

Maria [Oh, Yes, I can hear it.]

Show Taro [Smoke gets in your eyes. Flames of love rise up, and the smoke makes your eyes blind..and the second part of the song says when the flames of love are gone, your eyes again get blinded with tears of sorrow···

— 286 —

such song is that.]

Maria   [But, why your? Hasn't that to be my?]

Show Taro [As God is seeing it, the writer of that song is seeing. That's why.]

Hearing the words of Show Taro, Simon spoke out in a subtle nuance.

Simon   [It means that each and every thing is thoroughly foreseen. The bad deeds in one's life will come to the time to pay the piper.]

All of sudden, a tall old man came in from the front street and was about to pass by the counter.

Maria   [Mr. Alois. Welcome.]

Josef   [Hi, Miss Maria, Long while no see, Let me meet Romano first.]

Maria called Josef acting the stand-in of Alois, who was passing by the backside of Simon. Simon, who heard this conversation with his body leaned half way back, saw him at his back off to see Romano, told Show Taro and Maria that he would go outside to make a call by his cell phone. Coming out of the café, he looked around and started to use his cell phone speaking in a small voice.

Simon   [Pizza and tart are ready. Please have gelato served now.]

Just about five minutes passed and then Bernard Gambino showed up. He knocked Simon's shoulder familiarly and then they hugged each other and Bernard asked Simon where Mr. Alois is. Simon replied to him that Alois was in the room inside the building, so Bernard went into that room with three guardmen following him. Simon was about to follow them, too, so Show Taro stopped him for more chatting together with him.

At the bottom room, postures of carabinieri (military police) were glanced, then Simon dashed out to the street. Simon jumped into a delivery car which had been parked at the other side of the car of Bernard, and jump-started the car and is gone away, but following his car right away, the car of carabinieri started to chase him. Both Show Taro and Maria were at a loss being unable to understand what was happening. That such two persons, who were totally divorced from such world, somehow got involved was what happened then.

All people concerned were gone and there were only Show Taro and Maria left at the table.

Show Taro [Do you, Maria, dream some mysterious dreams?]

Maria [What kind of dreams do you often dream?]

Show Taro [Such dreams of mine have several patterns. When you come to this place, Rome, do you notice obelisks here and there?]

Maria [You mean by obelisk the square pillar standing in the places which are located here and there of this city.]

Show Taro [One of my dreams is a dream in which I am in Giza in the era of Pharaoh called Raneb.]

Maria [Giza···Is it the place where Pyramid of Egypt is located?]

Show Taro [In the era when I was living, that earth was the sacred place for solar monitering observation where sphinx was being built. I was there making plans to build sphinx, which was also meant for serving for the festival ritual to the sun.]

Maria [You were serving as a flamen oracle.]

Show Taro [That could well be. However, pyramid was not yet been seen.]

Maria [Why not?]

Show Taro [Pyramid was built in the forth dynasty of Egypt. The era of Raneb was the second dynasty. Considering the then government finances, the very limit of the largest pyramid was that size.]

Maria [You know that much.]

Show Taro [Do you know about the story of the epitaph called sphynx stella of Thutmose IV at the later era?]

Maria [Thutmose IV at the later era was taking a nap in the shade of sphinx when sphinx came into his dream. Contents of that dream was if Thutmose would dig the sphinx out from the sand, it would promise to make Thutmose a pharaoh.]

Show Taro [And, that sphinx was not sphinx.]

Maria [Plural number of names as God existed, which were Horemakeht Khepery Ra Atum. Horemakeht was the name of the sinking sun, Khepery of the rising sun, Ra of the daytime sun and Atum of night-time sun and all of those four names were meant for the time zone of each God of the Sun.]

Show Taro [Just as I thought your research work is excellent. My memory tells me that pronounciations close to those

— 289 —

names you mentioned were quite alike the names at time when those pyramids were constructed. All of the names, Horemakeht Khepery Ra Atum, have relation with the operation of the God of Sun. And for the reason which is unclear, the earth of Giza was made the secred place where is related to the operation of the sun. There at the secred place a huge lion which had a human head was created to be gazing at the rising sun. It was a proxy of the flamen oracle and into this flamen oracle the God of sun entered.]

Maria   [Then there what did those sphynxes?]

Show Taro [They were observing the rising sun.]

Maria   [Observing what of the rising sun?]

Show Taro [Observing stars and zodiac signs before the sun started rising. By observing those, the flamen oracle check and find the summer solstice, vernal equinox, the autumnal equinox and the winter solstice by judging the direction of shadow.

Maria   [They were making calendars.]

Show Taro [That may have been the case. But what must be noted was, regarding the name Raneb, Ra is meant for being the God, but the construction of this huge Lion was not quickly completed. The date when it was finally completed and when the festival ritual was executed was the first datum point of Sirius Solar Calendar setting July 19, BC2781. That the sun travels the airy region had already known. It is certain that

— 290 —

Sirius, which shines more brightly than other stars even in the air region where was hidden at the other side of the sun, was showing up before the sun rise, was being observed.]

Maria [But what for does it need to be observed?]

Show Taro [During one-year time period, from then the time of the rise of rivers was to start. By this time of the year, harvest was over, and because the cultivating fields were covered by water, no agricultural work could be done. So that at that time, people sent their gratitude to the God together with the harvest festival. There also was a need to hold the festival ritual to enable the God of the sun to operate orderly. The huge figure called in the present age Sphinx was finished up and the first festival ritual was held, and the day when the opening celemony was held became the first new year's day of AD of Sirius Solar Calendar (Sothis Heliacal Rising Calendar).]

Maria [How come do you know such a history?]

Show Taro [When the mouth and eye opening of Horemakeht Kaepery Ra Atum was performed, I was Pontifex Maximus, though I was then quite old already.]

Maria [Your dream is quite queer.]

Show Taro [And in Egypt I was once again re-born in Egypt. When I was born, the new holy shrine which was located in Luxor near Karnak Temple was under the second time of the expansion work and there a huge Obelisk was built. This Obelisk construction was

— 291 —

meant for an access of Gods and for that that Obelisk is Gods' shrine where foods for Gods are prepared.]

Maria [Were you then in Luxor?]

Show Taro [As the branch shrine of Karnak was Luxor, the correct way to describe my position will be that I was sent to Luxor from the great holy shrine Karnak. There the dwelling place was with stone pillars different from the era of Sphinx. In the era of Sphinx people slept in a big tent so the living fashion between the two were quite different. But as I recall it, the height of the bed was 15 cm at most, but it gave me fresh feeling when the night wind blew through beneath my back.]

Maria [Are foods pretty different from the present age's?]

Show Taro [Meat dishes were mainly grilled dried meat in that era, but when Karnak was in its prosperity, various kinds of other living creatures could be obtained without using the method of hunting. It means procurement of such foods changed to stock raising from hunting. However, as regards Gods' foods, in addition to fresh fruits, dried meat was mostly served. Drinks for Gods which stayed same from the old times was limited to the blood of sacrifice only. When the time came to this era a fair amount of wine came to be supplied.]

Maria [So wine was being taken starting that era?]

Show Taro [As a rule, one cup only at time of celemony was made, even for Gods.]

Maria	[You dream such every-day life.]
Show Taro	[I do dream dreams other than those every-day life dreams.]
Maria	[Are those dreams all about Egypt?]
Show Taro	[Of the dreams I dreamed at Obelisk there were ones about the happening in the ancient Rome. In that dream I was visiting province of Rome as Imperator (imperium holding general) of Republic Rome where the pharaoh of that province proposed he was willing to present anything I wished as a symbol of friendship. Therefore, taking his offer I had Obelisk hauled to Rome using our horses and theirs. Roman Forum was still not broken and at both streets in the middle of which we marched hauling Oberisk, and crowds were shouting for joy. This dream means I was presenting Obelisk to the senate as a trophy.]
Maria	[It really is a mysterious dream.]
Show Taro	[But when I got aged, I became Pontifex Mamimus.]
Maria	[So, this time, too, will you be a hieratic?]
Show Taro	[But I can only become fairly irresponsible hieratic so when my friend begs for my help saying he cannot pay the interest which he is supposed to pay per year and may go broke, my humanity won't allow me to refuse him.]
Maria	[Then, did you do anything?]
Show Taro	[I abruptly declared and publicized to insert inercalary month into the calendar.]
Maria	[That was a fould-up means⋯didn't you receive

— 293 —

complaints?]

Show Taro [I feel to remember that I brazened it out for at least a few years.]

Maria [Are those all of your dreams in the era of Rome?]

Show Taro [Another dream is that I was going to Egypt taken by Augustus.]

It seemed that this dream of his was attracting her interests so her tone of voice came up.

Maria [That is incredible! Did you really meet Cleopatra VII?]

Show Taro [I do remember the magnificient palace and the thin silk shroud, but I did not meet Cleopatra in person.]

Maria [You don't know what you are missing. You should have met Cleopatra as Caeser.]

Show Taro [Dreams can never go as you wish it to be.]

Maria [As you were in the column of Augustus, you could easily get that chance? Don't you have such memory of what you saw in your dreams?]

Show Taro [We marched through the sacred palace of Egypt and the Egyptian streets but fortunately, I was not marching on a horse. But here again as the same as⋯]

Maria [You were hauling Obelisk, right?]

Show Taro [You're right. I was at all times hauling one Obelisk. I had a big raft made, though the woods used for the raft were later sold, and hauled the Obelisk by horse power to the riverside of Nile River and from there putting the Obelisk on the raft sinking ourselves by half of the bodies to Alexandria and from there by galley. The labor to pull out the Obelisk is highly demanding, but to carry it by the raft and the boat was also a highly pain-taking work.]

Maria [But those were not all the works needed, I guess.]

Show Taro [Those which are not that bulky and heavy are brought back carrying them. I bought some of articles from the merchants who thieved these from tombs.]

Maria [For what purpose?]

Show Taro [To sell, needless to say.]

Maria [What kind of goods did you take out from Egypt?]

Show Taro [Not only the jewelries incuding gold and silver, we peeled off the thin silk used for the shroud at the palace. Also, papilus and woods that could be used for construction material, Baroque pearls, emeralds, and medicines could make a good money though these were not bulky booty. There also were glass products which were not yet mass produced at that time.]

Maria [Did you arrest slaves or the like?]

Show Taro [The General who did not surrender to the last moment was hostaged and taken to Rome where he was made marching in Rome.]

Maria [Was that all what happened?]

Show Taro, [No way, Maria, Talking about ancient Rome, Colosseum comes out. Such general is to be disposed to the related group of people for gladiators' match.]

Maria [There are the words as Bread and Circus…]

Show Taro [In the morning section, a matching game with a human versus a beast. Next at the noon time the public execution of offenders are displayed in the

— 295 —

	presence of the whole company.]
Maria	[Such a situation is totally unthinkable in the modern world.]
Show Taro	[In that era, it was worldwidely a popular and well accepted practice that those commonly existed criminal offenders were executed in public based on the rule of 'what goes around comes around' and in order to keep the maintenance of public order.]
Maria	[And in the afternoon section, then came the fight between the graduators. Is it correct?]
Show Taro	[In ancient Rome, the war hostages were to flight as gradiaters and if some won over ten opposite gradiators, they were given by the Emperor swords made of wood and were freed. Those war hostages were originally no criminals so if they prove themselves as brave worriers, they could be forgiven. They were originally nobles or the like so by being drawn around in Rome their shame was thoroughly exposed to the public. In other countries most of hostages were executed, but in Rome strong warriers were given a chance to recover their fame by winning ten matches at the colosseum. One of the secrets with which Rome could continue their power for a thousand years may be such as this.]
Maria	[I now understand that Show has been aware of your past to some extent.]
Show Taro	[Even if I see my past in my dreams, that shall not directly relate to my present life.]

About ten minues afterwards, Bernard and others went outside taken by the group of Cavalieris, and after them Josef and Romano came out.

In the brains of Show Taro, who was seeing those scenes, memories of matters that happened during the past few months were coming back swelling. It must have been only about thirty seconds but during those thirty seconds he was completely absent minded from what was happening then around him. When he came back to himself, there has been exchanged conversation going between Romano and Josef.

Romano   [Thanks indeed for your cooperation.]

Josef   [You have done it very well. He couldn't recognize the difference between you and your father.]

Maria   [As you are really alike.]

Show Taro   [Yes, indeed. Two peas in a pod is the word for you both.]

Romano   [As the tables will be cleaned up in no minute, why don't you listen to my piano at Passo Romano?]

Both Show Taro and Maria instantly stood up.

Show Taro   [Wow! That's great! Is that okay with you?]

Romano   [What's your request?]

Show Taro   [C'est si bon.]

Josef   [Lili Marleen.]

Show Taro   [That is the piano which Josef Goebbels prohibited.]

Josef   [That piano is my father's favourite. War companions will never forget those whom they left at the war place.]

Maria   [Please play that piano which you were playing then,

— 297 —

Smoke gets in your eyes.]

Romano   [All of those are also my favourites. Each of those pianos has each human drama.]

Romano looked happy as his organization was kept protected, so he was playing piano in a good mood. Today's his piano sounded uneasy before Bernard was arrested and after that turned to be quite rhythmical. The finger snacks he had brought to the table was Calpaccio of bluefin tuna which was caught in the Meditirranean and grilled scampis. In front of Josef, well-smoked salami and blue cheese were placed.

Show Taro [Tell me one thing. What did Bernard do?]

Josef   [Holdup. He tried to point a pistol.]

Show Taro [Did he try to kill some one?]

Josef   [No, just kidnapping.]

Show Taro [What is the purpose of that kidnapping?]

Josef   [To put the kidnapped on a cargo ship off from some port to send him to Israel.]

Show Taro [Why?]

Josef   [Simon is a cooperator of the Israelian Special Service Agency called Mosado. They are still chasing the SS Nazi remnants.]

Show Taro [Are they continuing that chasing even now?]

Josef   [My father Alois Brunner is still on top of the wanted list.]

Show Taro [His grade at the army was a commander, wasn' it. He must be nothing to do with that case.]

Josef   [They are in need of scapegoats. In addition, do you know what is happening in Palestine?]

Show Taro [They are still killing each other.]

Josef [They have no logical reasons. They are killing each other simply because they hate each other on a biological level.]

He took one sip of wine and continued.

Josef [Palestina is the name of a state of the ancient Rome, but Israel is a much older geographical name. This claim is admittedly accepted at that place only. If Germany speaks out that it will revive Holy Roman Empire or if Italy declares they will rebirth the Mediterrenian territory of Ancient Roma, they will be accused under the name of the act of aggression. So, this claim is somewhat out of forcus. Don't you think so?]

Show Taro [Therefore, the idea of these two peacefully becoming one unit as EU would be an answer which is sufficient enough to solve such dispute. Don't you think now is about time that such situation where people are bound by the past so that door to the future cannot be open has to be treated as a past story.]

While they were unaware of it, Romano seemed to finish his piano and came around to them. He looked like a sweet-tooth so he put plentiful honey on blue cheese and had a bite of it without caring the dropping honey, then he started to talk.

Romano [The border line between the countries is getting to be a past regulation now.]

Josef [And that's why Heinrich is reflourishing SS.]

Show Taro [What do you mean by that?]

Josef [SS are using a skull badge, do you know that?]

Show Taro [Yes.]

Josef [Reason why the badge is of skull is because Heinrich Himmler established his bodyguards as a successor model of the teutonic knights. In other words, Holy Roman Empire was all through the time followed by the German knights like a shadow. That situation was carried over till Germany came to be called The Third Reich via Prussian German Empire, when SS as a chivalric order is to start to expand into borderless Knights not staying as national German knights. As they are no nation, territory and the people are not necessary factors so only sovereighty exists. That is the reason why the majority of the army force that counted 900,000 soldiers is non-German.

If this way of thinking is extended, the revived SS with Heinrich Hitswinger as a leader collapse Soviet with its anti-communism policy and also keep funding the political power in South America. As Hitswinger knows well that political leader is bound by the border, he will not publicly grasp the political power.]

Romano [In that regard, Barbara, my daughter, is taking the conservatives and continuing her political actions in Italy only forcusing elimination of the Mafia economy, which is completely different from what Hitswinger is doing.]

Show Taro [Bernard, this time, was cooperating with Mafia, is this true?]

Bernard   [Do you think that it was necessary to kidnap Nazi SS at my café?]

Show Taro [Is that to start a bad rumor?]

Romano   [The purpose of it is to take back to the hand of Mafia the business route which ceased to work since 1996.]

Show Taro [What will happen if you refuse to cooperate with them?]

Romano   [I guess you may have heard from Antonio, but I say that the lost packages of art are due to their action behind the scenes. Putting it in other words, in Italy, those who refuse to pay money will have to bond together. In Japan, police causes the crackdown of Yakuza, doesn't it? In Italy, police is unreliable due to frequent leak of information that can draw out more dangerous Mafia movement.]

Josef   [Politics are carried out in a limited region by the nation and the politicians. What Heinrich's Neo SS insists is now is the time when sobereignty alone separately exists which does not have any nation or territory surpassing the boundary of nation.]

Show Taro [In Nostradamus 「Les Centuries (100 psalms)」 There is a paragraph stating Hitler dominates the Donau watershed.]

Noticing Show Taro taking out a pocket notebook from the inner pocket of his jacket, Josef opened his mouth.

Josef   [You, too, are studying that, aren't you.]

Making a gesture to show he has finally found it, Show Taro replied.

Show Taro [Here it is···6-49. These are not very good figures.]

Josef showed an attitude that he, too, was studying it and raised a question to Show Taro.

Josef [The first line of 'De la partie de Mammer grande Pontife'···How do you expound this line?]

Show Taro [Mammer is alike Mammon but is also alike Mameluk. Mameluk meaning the bodyguards, this part could be translated as a party of the bodyguards led by the great bishop.]

Josef [What about the part below that?]

Show Taro [Second Line They will conquer the rivershed of Danube

Third Line They proceed chasing the iron cross that is the symbol of the plunder and the weapons···and this part is partly uninterpretable···

Forth Line They will get hostages and more than 100,000 pieces of treasures

I make a rule to skip to read the uninterpretable part, so this is what I understand.]

Josef [You have an interesting ability. I didn't think you are good at skip-reading !]

Show Taro [When Champollion deciphered Hierograph, he noticed that number of words is more of Hierograph than those of Greek. At the present time, it is understood that the number of words comes to be more because of the additional words that are meant to be used as signs. Therefore, in order to make the statement unable to be deciphered, such words in the equivalence of signs are mixed, so that if we stick to these Even if we skip-read those words meaning of which are difficult to understand, I believe we can still grasp what is meant. In the first place, Les Centuries are predominantly short of verbs, and the ordering of the words varies like Latin so ways of deciphering comes to vary, too. This is the reason French people cannot easily decipher Les Centuries.]

Josef   [Your way of deciphering is quite unique.]

Show Taro   [The statement of Les Centuries has not been completed as yet, so in futue, such happening that this undeciphered part of Les Centuries may happen.]

Josef   [Many people are saying statements in Les Centuries did not hit as they had thought. What do you think about this?]

Show Taro   [Reading the preface which was addressed to his son, Cesar Nostradamus, generally speaking, the period has not yet been completed. There, before big flood and big water invation of the over the world size takes place, those literary people make a big propaganda. Till that point, Nostradamus has completed his performance to make such come true. Before and after that big disaster, there will come terrible drought when fire or flaming stones will fall down from the sky which will burn out the earth, and then, the last part of this big disaster will come. Around that time, the Great Plague as well as War and Famine which are caused by Three Men will arise. This is the part which has not yet come to happen.]

Romano [That is an interesting semantic interpretation.]

Maria [By the way, what do you intend to do to Bernard?]

Romano [you can see it better than I can, I guess?]

Josef [You will know it if you wait and read the newspaper after several months ahead.]

Romano, fighting with his hands which became sticky, changed the subject before Maria replied to him.

Romano [Honey is the best companion with any food we take. Also, it is a long-life food.]

Josef [Is the best-before-date of honey so long time ahead?]

Romano [Do you know of the story of an American excavation team in the past licked honey that was unearthed from the ruins?]

Josef [Was the honey packed in a glass container or the like?]

Romano ⌜When the ruins of BC1300 or thereabouts was unearthed, honey in a jar was digged out. The American archaeology doctor committed such embezzlement and injury of an important cultural property.⌟

Josef [So, did he secretly sell it?]

Romano [Here is that important property. It was replaced into a jar of my exclusive use and see? it comes out this way]

Josef [Really?]

Noting even Josef was surprised, Romano continued.

— 304 —

Romano　[That doctor read the hieloglyph and cut the seal of the jar and put his index finger into the fruid that was contained in the jar and licked the fruid and said 「Oh, good」].

Josef　[Well, so…Do you mind if I lick some?]

With a smile, Romano offered Josef the honey jar. At this word, Josef scooped a bit of honey and timidly put the spoon into his mouth.

Josef　[……]

Romano　[Do you like it? Ottimo (best taste), isn't it?]

Josef　[As you say it, sure‼]

Romano　[The best honey of Italian produce!]

Josef　[Why Italian?]

Romano　[This story of the contents in this jar is my big joke.]

Romano was in a triumphant air.

27. Request of Simon

In the mid night time of the same day when Bernard was arrested at Passo Romano in Rome, Robert came and visit Show Taro at his suite. He was continuing to play the role of a member of an insurance company but Show Taro had no intention to touch that point as Robert now is his important customer who is promising a good reward to him. Robert looked to be feeling a little low, but trying not to make Show Taro aware of it he spoke out in a very calm way.

Robert [What happened today at Passo Romano?]

Show Taro [Manhunt, it was. Bernard, cousin of Simon, was arrested by Carabinieres.]

Robert [Is he going to be killed?]

Show Taro [As they said I will know it by newspaper report after a few months, I feel they have no intention to kill him.]

Robert [I see, That may mean they will treat him with a direct and fair attack. Haven't you heard anything else?]

Show Taro [Romano Sfolza was saying that Bernard seemed helping Mafia activities.]

Robert [That you helped Simon is as you had known that arrest drama to happen?]

Show Taro [No, I just wanted to talk more which we did not talk about when he bought me beer in Kobe.]

Robert [Well, I will believe you, though not aggressively.]

Show Taro [Is Simon keeping safe?]

— 306 —

Robert [Yes, he is safe. Did you hear anything else?]

Show Taro [If Simon has any additional contract relating to Simon to be signed, won't you let me talk to him?]

Robert [He seems to have no connecting route to Carabinieres, so he looks to be seeking information.]

Robert rang Simon by his cell phone and when the mobile was connected he handed the phone over to Show Taro.

Show Taro [This is Show.]

Simon [Thanks for today. Thanks to you, I could escape from getting involved.]

Show Taro [Romano was saying Bernard is a member of Mafia. Is that true?]

Simon [I didn't know that. Honestly. By the way, isn't there any way for you to hush this case up to save his life?]

Show Taro [For how much incentive?]

Simon [What about 10,000 Euro in cash?]

Show Taro [As your request carries considerable risk, I may consider it for 30,000 Euro to be paid to me in advance.]

Simon [⋯Okay, done.]

Show Taro [Subject to your bringing the money to my hotel during the morning of tomorrow, I will talk to Romano.]

Simon [Understood. You have my word.]

The conversation was over and receiving the cell phone, Robert told Simon.

Robert [Tomorrow, see Tom by yourself alone. Bye.]

That day, Robert said nothing else and left there. He comes and

— 307 —

goes very unexpectedly which is unlike a mere investigator of an insurance company.

Reviewing the past, that he started saying he wished to call Show Taro Tom Boe which by itself was a strange request. Also, it was a matter of course that Show Taro was to undertake the work on request during the contracted period even if Robert is related to EuropolF as Maria told him. Before anything, there was no such statement on the contract sheet to prohibit Show Taro from concluding advisory contract other than Robert. To add more, in the original place the contract was nothing else but a contract for recovery of stolen artworks.

Before 10 o'clock on the following morning, Simon came to the hotel so Show Taro made and served tea to him.

Simon put in an offhand way an envelope which was thick with the contents on the table.

Simon　　　[Roll of 30,000 Euro notes with wrapper tape. Those are all used notes for your convenience.]

Show Taro　[I acknowledge the receipt. Then, this money is for the safety of Bernard, in other words, for him not to be killed, right?]

Simon　　　[Yes. After all, he is my cousin. But I did not know he was working for Mafia. As Carabinieres look like having not publicized this arrest of Bernard, won't you find out what's going on with him with Carabinieres from Mr. Romano?]

Show Taro　[May I e-mail the result of my finding directly to you? For me it is easier to do so as you can read e-mails written in Japanese.]

— 308 —

Simon   [I will explain to Robert accordingly.]

Taking a sip of tea, he continued.

Simon   [Incidentally, didn't you really know about that arrest at all?]

Show Taro [Yes, Unless I reach them through Maria, I cannot contact them.]

Simon   [But you did hold me back.]

Show Taro [As I had a question to ask.]

Simon   [What is your question?]

Show Taro [I understand other than sundrygoods you are doing wholesale business of diamond under a company of a different name. If you are wholesaling in the Tokyo area, won't you let me join in your trading group and offer me a special price?]

Simon was aware spying is not the Show Taro's primary role.

Simon   [My pleasure. Don't you have some other request, too?]

Show Taro [As Maria is a medium, she seemed to wish to see what is obsessing you.]

Simon   [That sounds pretty unscientific.]

Show Taro [If you say her unscientific, to feel beautiful looking at beautiful things will also become unscientific.]

Simon   [You're quite right.]

Show Taro [As I am scheduled to meet Maria at noon, do you wish to join me and see her?]

Simon   [I think rather not. As she makes me feel a bit weird.]

Show Taro met Maria in the early afternoon of the same day

when she made an arrangement for him to meet Romano Sfolza. Not to mention, Romano's side looked like wishing to learn how the Simon side will move.

28. Interrogation of Bernard Gambino

Strangely, Bernard Gambino and the three guardmen who were altogether arrested were not taken to the headquarters of Carabinieres. They were taken by a truck to a castle in the surburbs. The four guards seemed to be imprisoned right away. When the truck was parked inside the gate, they went into the underground prison surrounded by several Carabinieres. However, Bernard alone was taken upstairs in the state of being handcuffed.

This old castle was standing on a hill with a nice view for as long as several centuries and kept viewing the changing history. In the past it was facing the military road of ancient Rome controlling the important turning points of that road, but with the introduction of highway, the streets which contained this castle came to be loosing popularity. In contrast with this quiet rural embironment, there the inside of the castle was filled with a tense atmosphere. The owner of this castle was Francesco Borgia who is a general and a top of Carabinieres.

The wall of the castle was originally constructed in the 12th century and at each of the four corners, a cylinder shape tower was built. At a later time, to make it suited for war fighting, loopholes were equipped on the chest walls which was renovated into a roof covered by salt-mixed overglazed roof tiles in red color in the Renaissance period.

Since when it was built, this castle had a construction near that of fortress presenting inpenetrative appearance but the castle gate on the hill was still iron rivetted, nevertheless it was getting slightly

— 311 —

decayed, somewhat showing economical difficulties of the owner. But the castle was still maintaining its obdurability, so it was difficult to perceive the state of the inside. Family of the owner was said to have led culture of the Reneissance period.

In the chair of Franchesco's study, Bernard who was still cuffed was made sit down. Besides Bernard, a doctor of about his age of 40 was standing and injecting Bernard solution from a brown color ampul.

He was a French origin doctor. Out of his family tree, astrologists came out per several generations and those who became astrologists were often called their names in Latin. Their true names were totally unknown.

Bernard [Call a solicitor···for what the hell do I have to be shot?]

Borgia [Maestro Gaurico···No, Dr. Gauric, About how many minutes will take till the effect comes out?]

Gauric [This is the most effective truth drug so effect must be coming out within about 20 minutes.]

Borgia [But, I was not aware there exists a company using Nazi trading mark···I have seen such for the first time.]

Gauric [Please take a good look at it. This mark is the other way round. This Manji is in the reverse shape. It is a product of a Japanese company by the name of Midori Manji.]

Alois [This solution made by this company was on the stage of being developed during WW2 with exchange of information between Dr. Mengele and 731 Unit related

— 312 —

personnel of Japanese Army.]

Borgia   [Well, I am looking forward to learn how it works.]

Bernard   [Isn't it an illegal measure?]

Borgia   [Isn't the phrase of 'matters illegal are all forgotten' Mafia's monopoly patent?]

Bernard   [Sicilian men won't sell their companions.]

Borgia   [But you won't care to sell drugs over the sea in New York.]

Bernard   [Whatever happens to Americans is not my business!]

General Borgia, while taking a side glance that Bernard was shot the fluid, continued talking.

Borgia   [I wouln't mind showing my respect to the long lasting Sicilian history. But here, I think you ought to raise your hat to the height of our cultural level.]

Bernard   [For what reason do I have to take my hat to the Borgias. No way!]

Gauric   [I gave him an injection using the latest medical technic which also serves to restore his mental balance.]

Borgia   [Good job. Your ancestors have been maintaining strong relationship with our family ever since the era of Reneissance. Let me make a personal inspection of the effectiveness of these current medical supplies.]

Gauric   [I understand we the Gaurics used to commute to your head family quite frequently in the era of Reneissance.]

Alois   [And after that time, your family played at a tag of war with Catherine for many times.]

Borgia   [Catherine de Medicis, Queen of King of France, Henri

— 313 —

II.]

Bernard [Was she the instrument of King of France?]

Gauric [What you said cannot be allowed to pass. The Queen came as a bride from Casa de Medici.]

Borgia [Bernard, what did you learn at school?]

Bernard [School is a place to grow up relationship with friends.]

Borgia [Well, I'm impressed at your Mafia's cohesiveness···if with that cohesiveness you should have made efforts on some other matters, I guess you wouldn't have been to commit crimes.]

Bernard [If not crimes, you the Borgias are the shame of Italy!]

Borgia [You know you can't argue about the fact that Reneissance is the pride of Italy. And that Reneissance is nothing but the biggest heritage that the Borgia left on the world history and for that heritage, today's numerous Italians can get fed. Don't you know that.]

Bernard [Sicilians are originally mixture of Greeks and Phoenicians. That such people that belong to the peninsula butting in is wrong to start with.]

Borgia [Ancient Rome dispatched her troops on request from the Greece related cities. Expedition by Rome was not done due to our arbitrary request. Don't you know such an explicit matter?]

Bernard [It must be a plot that was framed ever since ancient Rome to have left Sicily in the state of poberty.]

Borgia [Plot? You seem not to know the scripture of God helps those who help themselves.]

Bernard [Paolo is reading Bible every day.]

Borgia	[So you mean Mafia when he becomes Big Boss makes it a rule to convert to Christianity?]
Bernard	[In Ancient Rome, when St. Peter came out, he convered to Christianity.]
Borgia	[Our family tree introduced the Pope of Rome out to the world.]
Bernard	[After all that position, too, must have been bought by money.]
Borgia	[Monies gathered by themselves by justifiable means.]
Bernard	[How can you say that while selling such a lot of indulgences?]
Borgia	[Where indulgences are really needed is against your lifestyle itself. Isn't it correct? Prostitution, murder, sale of narcotic drugs, do you dare to say any of those could be God's permitted deed?]
Bernard	[History of prostitution is older than that of ancient Rome. And older than church, of course. Those that came later have absolutely no right to criticize those historical facts.]
Borgia	[But murder ought to be deemed as an evil deed before the age of ancient Rome.]
Bernard	[But drugs were used by shamans in primitive society.]
Borgia	[Sharmans are mostly doctors. That doctors use drugs under their management is not illegal in the modern world, too.]
Bernard	[Well, it may be the case···]

Then at that moment, for some unclear reason Luic Gauric cut into their conversation.

Gaurice	[After all, what bad is the Borgias doing?]
Bernard	[What a surprise! Don't you know such widely known facts···The cardinals making mistresses and committing incest···How can you say such people can make themselves good examples for the public people?]
Goeric	[In the modern world, as it has long been bespoken, sexual love has become out of order. The modern people have no right to condemn the Borgeas as sexually deteriorated.
Bernard	[I never know such prognostication···Who the hell is bespeaking the modern world is more in disorder than the past?]
Gauric	[Don' t you know the name MaestroNostradamus?]
Bernard	[Are you talking about the book titled Les Centuries (The Hundred Psalms) that is impossible to be deciphered?]
Gauric	[What was materialized can be deciphered.]
Bernard	[And how does that book decipher the modern society?]
Borgia	[I wish to learn that, too.]
Gauric	[To start wth, 4-25 The age when Woman's body of acme of beauty can be viewed limitlessly And that makes rationality clouded Sense of brains is getting lost captured by the

— 316 —

woman's body and features.

In that age chances to offer up a sacred prayer shall decrease

This psalm if verbes are supplemented, is doubtlessly meaning such as you Mafias are flooding Internet with pornographic films and as a result people in the world are getting deluded by attractive women's bodies and feasures and consequently come to lose their religious devotion.

In this psalm, there is no definitition of the age when this happens, but what can be said is that the first part of it cannot be meaning the era of Belle Epoch. It is true that in the time of Bell Epoch, like in Paris high class courtesane offer all the techinics of sexual love plays and even the common people could view such attractive women's bodies at Moulin Rouge, however, the psalm does not mean that that age would continue for ever. In addition, in this modern world such can be spead by Internet system. Development of the Internet system means at any time, even children could have a chance to get to the adult information.]

Bernard [Okay, but how can you explain the latter part of the psalm?]

Gauric [People nowadays, even including all the actors or actresses over the world have obtained trainded bodies or breasts like melons. More than that is, they get plastic surgery or shots of mastle enhancer. That

— 317 —

kind of happenings are nothing less than blasphemy against God.

And, in addition, many of Christians are no longer visiting churches. Not only the world of Christianity, Buddhists in the orient world are now modernized and take meat and have lost feeling to respect the universe and even Muslims are coming to Paris or New York to get drawn in alchohol drinks.]

Bernard [May be you can read the modern world that way, but that does not come to conclude that people in the world will get deteriorated like the Borgias.]

Gauric [If you say that far, I will teach you. Next in 8-14,

First Line The age in which plentiful gold or platinum credit cards are ready for use in a large scale

Second Line Honor is overwhelmed by sexual desire

Third Line The sin of adultery knocked honor down

Forth Line Age when people disgrace themselves to no end will come

That part of the psalm can be taken 'credit' as credit card and 'argent' as not the color silver but as a pratinum credit card, meaning it is no doubt Nostradamus was deciphering what is happening in the present age. He is saying this age shall become an age when such men and women will increase as a result that sexual desire was over-stimulated, and those people give and are given outrageously expensive tributes for committing adultery.

Open your eyes and look at Demon of Disease of the

present society···you can obtain even a queen of a country only if you are able to make a tribute using huge amount of money and financial power. Those extra busy renouned professional sports players are breaking children's dream of that their success was and could be earned by their own efforts, and are obtaining expensive women at night clubs for their names. What's worse is in this age of flooding information such misconducts were publicized in detail to all over the world.

In the era of Reneissance, suppose a cardinal had a manshion of hetaeras built next to his villa, such shameful deed of his had no chance to be reported over to Japan or China which are located on the reverse side of the globe. If leaders of world's powerful countries committed some unethical deed in his office, that such facts should be reported to the whole world could never even be imagined. If The Great Suleyman the Magnificent had mistresses surrounded him, such was never reported as scandal. Based on the past criteria of Value, leaders of the world's most powerful countries were nothing to do with adaltery.

The first part of this psalm is meaning that in the age which is flooded with gold or platinum credit cards, all the value standard changes completely. Nostradamus is telling an age which has largely different sense of values from when kings or cardinals were storing mistresses.

— 319 —

It can also be considered that the United States of America where such situation took place would not be able to escape from the binding of the prophecy of Nostradamus. The huge production construction of America will be spreading all over the world which in the consequence will also spread the sense of value of monogamy but later this sense of value will go collapsing. Such society which at the first glance looks like opulent consumption society is in fact demoralizing humans to no end.]

Bernard   [But the cause of such consumption society is not attributed to our fault.]

Gauric   [Don't you forget that Mafias are operating nightclubs everywhere. You are trying demoralizing people using all means available.]

Bernard   [A man travelling needs staving off boredom. Before anything, travelling itself is what can be done by a man who has money to spend. It's only natural he extends his hand to a drink or two.]

Gauric   [And, next to alcohol, what do you offer to such a man?]

Bernard   [Roulette or card games and the like. To spend a merry night, there are many of those means available. Do you think it so very bad to fill the human desire in such ways?]

Gauric   [It may make him happier to have him spend all his money playing such games.]

Bernard   [You may be right. If he has too much money, he may be lured to flirt with bar garls, and then if the bar girl suggests him to take drugs, he may be able to spend a happier time.]

Gauric   [Finally, everyone rush into the bad.]

Bernard   [Man's greed is limitless.]

Gauric   [Therefore, that's God who exerts divine judgement.]

Bernard   [What you mean is the age of Apocalypse?]

Gauric   [It is Mafia who opened the door of it.]

Bernard   [You could say so⋯but such system like credit card which makes it feasible to make payment of what you buy without taking cash with you is not our creation.]

General Borgia [Putting aside whoever is right, Maestro is predicting that we are living in the age of Apocalypse. Is it correct?]

Gauric   [Yes⋯Regretfully.]

Bernard   [What can be said at least is that we are not doing such business because we have too much surplus of money.]

Gauric   [People have freedom to choose their professions so they are not bound by the place they are living. In that sense, Mafias may be aggressively choosing to be Mafias.]

Bernard   [Outsiders who do not understand agony of Sicilians and regulations assessed on people living in that place are always say such a thing and never try to understand the reality which is going on there.]

A few minutes later, cars stormed into Borgia's castle breaking the gate. Without allowing time for the sentries to pull out their guns, mass shooting of submachine gun brought them into honeycomb forms. Four men coming out of two cars were armed by submachine guns. They came downstairs to the basement compartment and invaded into the section again bringing a couple of Carabinieres into honeycomb forms who were confronted them in front of where they thought their fellows had been imprisoned. A man who seemed to be the ringleader stayed at the outside of the prison with the key of the prison in his hand. Rest of the three men given the key from the ringleader open the lock of the prison and helped out their companions from inside the prison, then at the next moment those hunted changed to the hunt. The ringleader seemingly, standing at the entrance, was shot to death and the whole basement compartment was intercepted.

At the same time, from upstairs several men in Nazi SS uniform came down together with Carabinieres. Those uniformed men are members of troops directly reporting to Alois Brunner. They came from outside for a support, hearing the sound of the battles of Mafias taking their fellows back.

Around the same time zone during when Bernard was arrested, Europole was arresting in unison the three painters who was painting fakes in Switzerland and this information had already been transmitted to Nazi SS. In Nazi SS, there was Alois Brunner in the uniform of a General. He was maintaining Heinrich's confidence as the eldest fighter who survived WW2 and was kept being promoted.

Alois Brunner made a question to the Carabiniere who was assuming responsibility for shutting this district out .

Alois   [How broard is the inside size of the basement?]

— 322 —

Carabiniere [Six single cells, but they are altogether in one cell which is located at the bottom of the left side of the corridor.]

Alois [Is Bernard Gambino being investigated upstairs?]

Carabiniere [Yes, the General is enquiring him.]

Alois [What about the loss of each side?]

Carabiniere [Three dead at our side and the seven Mafias are still alive.]

Alois [Seven enemies in the basement, I see. Is that cell the one an air vent of which is facing the courtyard?]

Carabiniere [Yes.]

Finishing the talk, the Carabinieres left the place. Alois Brunner called his subordinate near to him. She was also in SS major's uniform but with blue eyes wearing blond hair and looked like a native Austrian noble. Her name was Luise Dietrich. She was looking around with slightly cool-looking eyes.

Alois [Louise, Inject carbon dioxide! Bring bodies to the chicken house where dead chickens due to bird flu which were disposed earlier today were piled. We will make up a story that such Mafias died by accident in the district which was to be disposed together with the chicken house. Carbon Dioxide is much safer than hydrogen cyanide gas, but you must be alert to danger anyway. Sieg Heil!]

To finish sending this order out, Alois showed the style of Nazi Salute to her and she simultaneously responded to him with the same salute. Then she made a sign by her hands and called several SS members near her.

Louise   [Send the truck to the courtyard. Inject through the air vent.]

SS members [Yes, Sir.]

Alois   [By the way, about those two we made die by traffic accident in Zurich, did you check and confirm their identity cards?]

Louise   [As there were public people around, we did not have a chance to check their identities.]

Alois   [They seem to have been Europols. Today, police raided in Switzerland and three painters producing fakes were arrested. Mafia came to have connection with police since the world war. We must be careful.]

There into the courtyard, a truck was entering backing. Next, about 20 cylinders of carbon dioxide was started to be taken down in an efficient way. In the basement, the seven Mafias were getting ready with their breath pressed for the invasion of SS.

Louise   [Start injection. Twenty minutes afterward, we will confirm the process after exchanging the air.]

SS Members [Yes.]

The Cylinders were released. That was the situation against which Mafia even though they were heavily armed could do absolutely nothing to protect themselves. Alois processed this problem efficiently with a practiced hand. To Alois this killing series of Mafias meant just a process and not murder.

Twenty minutes afterward, the outside air was injected. Then a surgeant carrying a cage of a canary came downstairs and confirmed bodies which had fallen down on top of each other and several SS members carried out those bodies by stretchers. Alois and Louise, after viewing those bodies exchanged conversation.

Alois [The Broiling specialist, Himmler, devised a very effective means indeed. For me to use this on an actual battle is after quite a while. For you, the members of SS, it must be a good experience.]

Louise [Thank you for your guidance. This is the first experience to me to use these tactics at an actual battle.]

Alois [Your grandmother marked her name in the history by peeling skin off bodies which had tatoos and have the skin made into a lamp shade. But this issue of today was done for the purpose of destructing the evidence, so just forget it.]

Louise [Understood. Load the bodies on the truck as they are! Because they died accidentally, don't draw the bodies.]

SS members [Yes.]

The seven bodies which were still leaving some warmness were loaded in good order and the truck soon departed to a chicken house nearby. Tomorrow in the afternoon, this will be on the news that Mafias who chased by the military police escaped into a chicken house which was treated by carbon dioxide gas in the bird flue infected chicken house and died accidentally due to the gas.

And next, Alois went to the office of the General's and had an Italian Carabiniere report in a loud voice so as to have cuffed Bernard hear it.

Carabiniere [I report as follows. Just now we had an attack by Mafias but death of all of them was identified. Loss at

— 325 —

our side resulted in a total of three members. Also, right prior to their death, they testimonied that together with Bernard they had killed in 1982 Mr. Giacomo Rosetti, chairman of The Commercial and Industrial Bank.」

Hearing this, Bernard firstly turned pale but at the next moment he was infuriated and spoke out. Because of the shot, he was in an uncontrolleable condition.

Bernard   [I was just made to help drive the car and nothing more!]

In comparison to Bernard who became frantic, the General just grinned, while Alois was observing that scene extremely insensibly. His behaviors were such as that he was trying to discriminate which of Bernard or the past partisans are more guts holders. Or, more correctly, he was trying to confirm the effectiveness of the drug produced by Midori Manji.

Borgia   [Who was the principal offender?]

Bernard   [That was Pinocchio.]

Borgia   [Is that Paolo Geppetto, the big boss of Mafia?]

Bernard   [La Cosa Nostra. He is no Mafia.]

Like Japanese Yakuzas prefer to call themselves as Ninkyo (Chivalry), Mafias tend to avoid to call themselves Mafias.

Borgia   [The naming Mafia is more pupular in the public. Whatever the name is, this case may take time till it gets to a right commentary.]

Bernard   [Geppetto got furious when he found that the donation he made to the deceased cardinal was cut of the profits by Rosetti, so Geppetto choked his neck too hard on his gut feeling. True story, you must believe it!]

Borgia [Try remember the names of those related to this incident. From here it will belong to the job category of the prosecutor. Good thing I had decided to use this castle for this rough-and-tumble just for the record. I can assure you no more recapture of your fellows will happen, Bernard.]

Having said so, the General took out from the bookcase a bottle and four glasses and started to walk towards Alois and Louise.

Borgia [Thanks for all troubles you took. Grazie. Let's shift to the next room.]

After General Borgia and the doctor left, the prosecutor who till then had been keeping silence spoke up to Bernard.

Prosecutor [So, finally you are ready to talk about what happened honestly.]

The serious conversation between the prosecutor and Bernard was to start from that point.

Observing that scene, Gauric, too, stood up and opened the door. The saloon adjoining this study looked to have at least double size of th study.

From the middle part of the plastered ceiling of as wide as 3.5m which is painted in blue where angels were flying about, a Venetian glass chandelier was hanging, showing the lingering memory of the prosperious Borgias in the past.

A rock-made fireplace was built in front of the other front side and in the middle there, a white clock of a hight of about 30cm was swinging the pendurum and ticking down. On the both sides of the fireplace a pair of one meter high Imari-made agalloch bottles was placed symbolizing that the Borgia family was a prosperious family till 400 years ago.

On the carpet designing the big ancient Roman Major Scipio fighting against Hannibal, a set of ottoman sofa of deep blue color was placed. Borgia shifting to the one-man sofa which was placed near the side where Borgia was standing, suggested Alois and Louse to take seats on the three-seat sofa which was the largest sofa there. When they sat down, Gaurice sat on a two-seat love chair 13 seconds later than them, and the General, having seen them sitting down altogether, carefully poured the amber color fruid into glasses.

Borgia [Today has become a very good day. We could open the road to arrest Mafia's big boss, Paolo Geppetto.]

As the General took his glass up, the other three responded to his action and took their glasses up, too.

Alois [But, I am a bit surprised that Bernard so easily broke Omerta (The Rule of Silence). It seems that that drug is quite effective.]

Gauric [It is regretful that is not sold in Europe as yet.]

Alois [Is it sold in America?]

Gauric [Midori Manji is said to be given a permit to deliver that drug only to the governmental related facilities of Japan and America.]

Alois   [I'm surprised you could get it.]

Gauric   [As I have some connection through my acquaintance.]

Borgia   [Don't be concerned so much about the drug.]

All of them toasted and took the glasses to their mouths.

29. Palazzo of Romano Sfolza

Show Taro went to the palazzo owned by Romano Sfolza together with Maria by a car sent from Romano. The palazzo had an appearance of a temporary abode in the town and had a look of nothing special. The entrance did not really look gourgeous but rather it looked a little massive than it could be described as refined, facing the street. To Show Taro who knew their subordinates are saluting Roman style salutation of the ancient Roman Troops, that building looked like Roman styled quite obviously.

It seems the building was watched by a monitoring camera. As soon as the car was parked alongside the entrance, the entrance door was opened and two butlers came out to welcome them. After saluting to them in a polite way, the butlers showed them to the office of Romano. Stepping up by a slope made of marble steps, there was a big door and the both side of the door ancient Roman warriors were standing.

They were wearing red hair planted helmets and glittering silver color armors, and around the waist leather strips split in several strings were winded but their gladiuses were stored in each sheath.

They must have admitted Show Taro and Maria as special guests, so they received the two with Salute Romano.

Roman warriors [Ave Senetous!]

Show Taro, too, Stood still and copied the Salute Romano greetings back to them. Then the large door which could measure

— 330 —

almost 3.5 m in height was opened heavily squeeking. And there stood an eldery man wearing a scarlet color clothes, and lightly bowed.

Marx   [Welcome to Senatus. I am Marx, the butler.]

From there, Marx played the role of guide for them. They proceeded on a scarlet color carpet and came out to a long corridor facing toward courtyard. On the wall of the corridor, several pieces of tapestries with the design of ancient Rome myths were hunging. And in front of the tapestries, white marble made bust herms of ancient Roman politicians or cultural men were placed.

Marx   [That statue you have seen is Scipio Afiricanus Major
                  and here is Caeser. And this is Cato Major and there
                  is Seneca, the philosopher. And there over Cato Major
                  is Marcus Aurelius.]

He added such supplementary explanation without being asked. Hearing his explanation, they turned at the next corner and there were more Roman warriors dressed as same as those they met before but at that time those warriors were not wearing helmets. That may have meant that from that corner onwards Show Taro and Maria arrived inside the boule. Beyond the door, the melody of 「O sole mio」 cheerfully played in habanera rhythm by Romano was being overheard. The warriors Roman-saluted and opened the door in silence for Show Taro and Maria with much care not to disturb Romano's play inside the room.

They entered through the door which the butler held open and saw a Venetian glass chandelier hanging from the high ceiling which is very Italian like, Romano being an Italian. And on the rosy color marble stone fireplace, a clock which was placed in the center was swinging the pendulum and the both side of the clock each of a pair of Aquilaria Aloe wood jars was placed. The grand piano was a custom-ordered piano adorned by fine inlays which was showing Romano's earnestness to the piano. Those ivory keyboards that were frequently touched by his fingers were getting slightly yellowish which seemed to be representing his attachment to the piano with which he had been spending his life of musical activities at good and hard times together.

Romano on that day was wearing a toga dyed in the ancient purple and lined Manjis were embroidered with gold thread.

That toga was giving an impression of a little bit disturbing for playing piano, but it must have been the formal wear when he received his guests.

Marx [Ave Senatus!]

At the sudden voice of Marx, Romano stopped playing piano and looked towards the direction where Show Taro was standing.

Show Taro 「Giorno ! You are in a good mood.」

Romano [Welcome.]

So saying, Romano embraced Show Taro's shoulder and greeted. Then he gestured for them to sit down on the sofa. When the three sat down, Romano started talking.

Romano [Regarding the arrest of Bernard the other day, Has Simon tendered any demand?]

Show Taro [Yes, He just asked not to kill him.]

Romano [Bernard is the member of Mafia and since 1996 his selling route has been completely destroyed and we know the truck which picked Simon up ran into

Israelian Embassy. Judging from this, Simon was a Mosad after all.]

Show Taro [Was Bernard arrested on suspicion of attempted kidnapping?]

Romano [Don't be silly. Talking about suspicion of attempted kidnapping, I shall also be suspected as relating to the remnants of Nazi SS. We are taking him to task for suspicion of another case which has been under investigation since quite some time ago.]

Show Taro [Is that the reason why you will not chase Simon?]

Romano [If we cause problems with Mosad, our relation with Neo Nazi may be revealed as retaliation. So, we will not make any ship inspection of the cargo vessel staying offshore of Israeli nationality.]

Show Taro [Then, how do you intend to process this problem?]

Romano [Do you know the case that in London in June, 1982, Giacomo Rossetti, the chairman of Commercial Bank was murdered being disguised as suicide?]

Show Taro [That is the case of him hanged from the bridge with a brick weight in his pocket to make his death extra sure.]

Romano [His family was talking he seemed to have been threatened by Mafia, but so far who did it is not officially clarified. I received a report stating quite soon the interrogation record will be completed.]

Show Taro [Then what sort of contents will the interrogation record state?]

Romano [It has now become a matter of time that Geppetto by

— 333 —

the nickname of Pinocchio who is the big boss of Mafia will be arrested as the true curplit.]

Show Taro, being rather surprised at hearing the name of such fairly huge deal, continued to try to get his reply.

Show Taro [Will Mafias keep quiet if Pinocchio is arrested?]

Romano [As the cardinal to whom Mafias kept contributin deceased, their mastery of the air has been lost now.]

Show Taro [So they intend to take advantage of this chance and arrest him.]

Romano [By this means, that Bernard can be proven as no principal offender even though he may be assumed as accomplice in that murder case but not the principal offender so as a matter of course he shall not be killed. Please tell Simon he does not have to worry about this point. This time, due to the Mosads who were poor actors we could eliminate a few Mosads that tried to approach the Heinrich's organization and at the same time could eliminate the Mosads who were trying to destroy Passo Romano of the selling route of the art products.

But it is a problem that the three or so fake painters were arrested. They were professional fake painters. Now, we will have to scout art students who may have nothing to live on. Branches of art-stealers and fake-painters are two intensively exhausting branches. Well, Show, please don't tell this comment of mine to Simon.]

Maria [Are we supposed not to tell this to Kato as well?]

Romano   [No, no need to hide this comment of mine from Mr. Kato, as he is in the same position as Heinrich as regards he has to keep hiding even his trade mark of Midori Manji in Europe.]

Show Taro [By the way, what is Heinrich aiming at?]

Romano   [To line up his members amongst politicians in every country in the world and create on them a Shadow Empire.]

Show Taro [And under his influence there must be a fair number of politicians.]

Romano   [Correct. Of whom, you already know Yamagata of Japanese conservatives. In addition, besides Fujimura of South America, there are a fair number of anti-American politicians.]

Show Taro [So you mean the majority of such politicians exists in South America.]

Romano   [Neo Nazis in the occupation zone of former Third Reich are all under the influence of Heinrich. Also, of those leaders of radical groups in the area from Syria to Middle East, there are those under the influence of Heinrich.]

Show Taro [In Italy, too?]

Romano   [I would very much like to say that Italy is in the sphere of influence of our Neo Fascism, but in reality, there exist Mafias who are connected by Jewish power and their interefence as offerers of assistance cannot be declined. And that is the very Achilles Tendon in the Italian Political circles.]

— 335 —

Show Taro [How long do we have to wait till Mafias are swept away from Italy?]

Romano [Mussorini once captured them all at once. Nevertheless, due to political machinations of America, they did extend their power right into the center of political power.]

During the time when Romano kept talking, the butler prepared cappuccino while they didn't notice it. Show Taro and Maria were taking the cup of cappuccino, and Romano started talking about business.

Romano [Incidentally, I understand you two are acting as advisors to Mr. Kato, but can you sometimes spare your time to take my work request?]

Maria [In addition to advisory fee, I am receiving fortune telling fee as well.]

Romano [I have heard about your ability from Mr. Kato and Heinrich.]

Maria [If you will accept the same amount as I am getting from Mr. Kato, I will accept your offer.]

Romano [Very well. I will pay you as much as Mr. Kato does. By the way, will you, Show, take my offer, too?]

Show Taro [If you can accept the same condition as that of Maria, I am willing to accept your offer.]

Romano [I reckon there will be a case when I wish you to find out what I need. If the searching area is limited to the western world, I may not need your help, but these days logistics have been spreading all over the world.]

Show Taro [What specifically do you want me to find out?]

Romano   [Not yet decided. I just want to forward buy your talent as I understand you two have a peculiar ability to be able to find out without me pointing out what I am in need.]

And there was a knock at the door and the butler opening it, and General Franchesco Borgia came in together with his subordinate.

Seeing that, Romano stood up and walked toward them. Both met in the middle of the room and the two people faced Romano and clicked their heels and stood straight tendering a Roman salute.

Both   [Ave Roma!]

Then General looked like reporting to Romano in Italian in low voice. Romano also seemed to make several questions to General and they kept exchanging words in that way. Then, lightly knocking the shoulder of General Borgia with both of his arms, Romano with his face beaming with smiles turned to Show Taro and Maria and walked towards them.

Romano   [Bernard did sign the record of interrogation. Now, Pinnoccio shall finally be arrested. Let's toast tonight.]

Show Taro   [Aren't you in an excellent mood.]

He came forward to shake hands with Show Taro.

Romano   [Thank you. We owe you much for this.]

Show Taro   [May I ask you, incidentally, that the clothes you are wearing today is dyed using purple shellfish?]

Romano   [In the era of the Roman Republic, all of the senators used to wear the ancient purple clothes, but in this modern time, only available way to get this color is synthetic dye, due to economy.]

Romano turned around and waved his hand to the two people to

— 337 —

leave, who were still standing there. They turned to right and went out with Passo Romano (the goose steps). Sound of their military shoes seemed to imply the tension of arresting scene of Mafias which was about to take place.

THE END OF I PASSO ROMANO

Published List

SS 影の帝国（正典 No.1）日本語版　PASSO　ROMANO
ISBN 978-4-7876-0071-4　　　　　April 2011
SS 影の帝国（正典 No.2）日本語版　ABALON
ISBN 978-4-7876-0072-1　　　　　June 2011
SS 影の帝国（外典 No.1）日本語版　Queen's Books
ISBN 978-4-7876-0097-4　　　　　September 2016
SS SHADOW EMPIRE English Edition

　Canon 1　Passo Romano
　ISBN 978-4-7876-0108-7　　　December 2019
　Canon 2　Abalon
　ISBN 978-4-7876-0109-4　　　December 2019
　Apocrypha 1　Queen's Books
　ISBN 978-4-7876-0110-0　　　December 2019

ISBN978-4-7876-0108-7

**SS SHADOW EMPIRE Canon Ⅰ
English Edition
SS影の帝国　正典Ⅰ　英語版**

令和元年12月7日　第1刷発行
Dec/7/2019　1st edition issued
著　者　author　　Tycoon SAITO
翻　訳　translator　Yoshie HIYAMA
発行者　publisher　Yasushi ITO　伊藤泰士
発行所　株式会社創樹社美術出版

（乱丁・落丁はお取り替えいたします）
©Tycoon SAITO 2019 Printed in Japan